DARK CARNIVAL

BY JOANNA PARYPINSKI

ISBN: 978-88-31959-38-4

COPYRIGHT (EDITION) ©2019 INDEPENDENT LEGIONS PUBLISHING

COPYRIGHT (TEXT) ©2019 JOANNA PARYPINSKI

JUNE 2019

COPYEDITING: MICHAEL BAILEY

COVER ART: WENDY SABER CORE

SPECIALTY PRESS AWARD RECIPIENT

SUMMARY

JOANNA PARYPINSKI

DARK CARNIVAL

CHAPTER 1

What happened with the coyote was an accident.

This is what Dax Howard told himself, hands clenched on the steering wheel, sweating with the shock of hitting and killing an animal only trying to cross the lonesome highway. The sick part was that he saw it first. The coyote darted out in front of his car, turned its alien eyes toward him as if it knew its fate. He told himself it was the cruel April sunlight glaring against the windshield, or the benumbed mental distraction of a long car ride, but he didn't even react, didn't flinch, until he felt the sickening telltale crunch of roadkill beneath the tires. Hitting an animal like that, you feel it in your bones. Only then did he swerve and skid onto the gravelly shoulder, where a tire popped and the car tilted drunkenly.

He stepped out into the settling dust and followed an ominous smear of red to the tire-crushed carcass twenty feet behind. At least it wasn't a deer, or a cow. A big animal would have disfigured the resilient old Bronco, but the coyote barely left a dent in the fender. Small comfort.

Dax was in the habit of rejecting small comforts, as one does when ensconced in his own grief. When it's there, it's all you feel, and small comforts seem cruel, deceitful tricks to be scorned. Irrational though it may be, he would have none of it.

So he wandered down the road toward the corpse to look upon the damage he had wrought. Prairie grass shivered in a breeze still stinking of hot rubber and exhaust. The burnt smell reminded him, unpleasantly, of the slaughterhouse in nearby Bannon, a place forever saturated with the stink of incinerating meat.

He crouched over the corpse and looked down at this stupid animal who might have waited only three more seconds to run across the road and lived.

Well, it was only an accident. That was what he told himself. And his dad's death, that was an accident, too.

7

That was the accident that was bringing him back to Conjunction for the first time in years. It wasn't as if he wanted to go back, either. Conjunction was a mean little town planted stubbornly in a neglected part of northwest Nebraska, its people bored and bitter and starving for morsels of happiness.

At least, that was the way he remembered it. He didn't want to go back because he had already spent eighteen years of his life there—and he'd told himself, when he left for school almost four years ago, that he had put his hometown behind him for good. He hadn't been prepared to wake one morning to his phone ringing and Phil Sawyer's voice on the line telling him *come home, your dad's dead.*

Now he saw death everywhere he looked: in crumbling billboards, half-rotted buildings, and the alien arms of slowly rotating turbines; in the husks of empty silos that stood metal and naked in the open air; in the broken chicken wire fence that lined the edge of a field in a crumpled mess like untwining strands of DNA; in a tractor enshrined in a thicket of weeds, orange with rust, its wheels partially decayed, vines tangled up in its exposed innards.

Decay was as part of the natural landscape here as life, existing in a symbiotic relationship with vegetation and man's ruined machinery.

"Sorry, friend," he murmured to the coyote, whose ribcage had caved in on one side, with a broken bone piercing through the skin and bloody fur.

He stood and went back to assess the damage. The Bronco's front right tire sagged around a nail puncturing its flesh like the coyote's bone. After finding the spare tire and securing the jack, he knelt in the knee-biting gravel and removed the hubcap to start loosening the nuts.

His father had taught him how to change a tire when he was about twelve. He remembered sitting cross-legged beside the Jeep while his dad worked the jack, watching, and then trying it himself. It was autumn; his father was sober, or at least sober enough to have a decent conversation, and Dax was happy.

When he paused to lean back and wipe sweat from his forehead, he happened to look back along that red streak on the road, and he dropped the lug wrench with a clang.

The coyote was gone.

Though it had been fourteen years since he'd heard it in person, his mother's long-ago voice rang in his head: *That coyote was dead, kiddo. Killed by its own carelessness.* The ghost-voice was right, of course. The coyote *had* been dead. Killed by Dax's carelessness, more like, but dead all the same, and what, had it been taken by the roadkill fairies? He became acutely aware of a kind of dread inside him, like the uneasy electricity that fills the air before a storm.

He looked ahead, thinking he might see its mangled corpse limping up the highway, on its way to the incinerators in Bannon, but there was the familiar black billboard that declared in tall white letters, HELL IS REAL.

Or maybe, came his mother's voice, or a sibilant approximation of it, *maybe it was a trickster.*

The unsettling red smear ended in a thin, tacky pool of drying blood.

A shrub shuddered nearby, and he flinched.

All right, so now he was spooked by the wind. But had he felt any? He held out his arms and waited maddeningly to feel for a breeze, and when he didn't he went to the bush and started pulling apart the snarled branches, peering into the darkness for signs of the undead creature.

He was on his knees, half his body tangled in bristly scrub, when a car approached and pulled over behind him. Yanking himself free, he tried to shake the bits of foliage from his hair and clothes as he stood. A police cruiser had parked on the shoulder, a man in uniform stepping out.

Lord, save us from unnecessary encounters with small-town police, is what he thought with some amount of blasphemous irony when he saw who it was.

Sheriff Anderson looked older than Dax remembered: gray hair peeked out from beneath his hat, lines carved grooves around his mouth, and a bulging paunch strained his buttoned shirt. Hitching two thumbs into his belt loops, he appraised Dax through dark sunglasses.

"Dax Howard?" he said. "Well, what in the hell?" He took stock of Dax's rumpled, bristle-snagged clothing, at the dirt stains on his jeans, at the bloody streak on the road. "All right. You want to tell me what's going on here?"

"There was a coyote. It ran out in front of me. I couldn't avoid it." They both looked again at the empty spot where the red line ended. "I guess it was still alive."

The sheriff frowned at him, bent down to look more closely at the blood, as if it might reveal itself as human, as if he fancied himself a detective in a police procedural on television. Maybe he thought there was a dead body in the trunk. At least he didn't go so far as to ask Dax to open it. He did, however, stand slowly, like he was considering it.

"Coyote, huh?" he said at last, sounding skeptical. "All that blood, poor bastard can't be long for this world."

Dax imagined the animal in the bushes somewhere, wheezing its last breaths, having lived just long enough to die somewhere else. He hoped it was dying or dead. The alternative prickled the hairs on the back of his neck.

"What were you doing in the bushes?"

Dax shrugged.

The sheriff didn't seem to like this answer. Still frowning, he went to the bushes and poked around inside. What did he expect to find? A severed head? He kept at it for a little longer than seemed strictly necessary, and when he was satisfied there was nothing in there, the sheriff grudgingly turned and gave him a look that said he would love to book Dax on something for this strange, suspicious meeting, but there was nothing he could do.

He eyed the jack and the spare and said, "Need any help?" with the kind of flippant tone that suggested it was a courtesy statement, not an offer.

"No thanks. I'm just about done."

The sheriff nodded but didn't move away. He stared at Dax, inscrutable behind those dark lenses. "What's it been now? Couple years?"

Dax didn't feel a reply was necessary, and the sheriff didn't wait for one.

"I expect I won't see any more trouble out of you while you're in town, will I?" he said, as if striking the coyote had been some punishable offense for which he was letting Dax off with a warning.

"I'm just here to bury my dad."

"That's right," the sheriff said. "My condolences."

Dax wondered how satisfying a crunch the sheriff would make under his tires.

The sheriff tilted his head toward the Bronco and said, "Well, make sure you get her up and running soon."

Dax watched him saunter back to his car and pull away. He turned to face Dax as he drove past, his dark glasses catching the sun, and then he was gone, the cruiser rumbling away into the flat distance.

Once Dax finally got the car back on the road, he drove carefully, both hands gripping the wheel, on the lookout for more suicidal creatures. All he saw, however, about a hundred yards down the highway, was a pair of sickly yellow eyes peering out at him from the bushes.

Conjunction was the kind of place you glanced at from the corner of your eye and promptly forgot, like a shape at the edge of your vision that turned out to be nothing at all. It was a forgettable and forgotten place, full of people wanting only to forget.

His mother had told him a joke, or a riddle, when he was a kid that he hadn't quite understood at first: *What's the one thing connecting where you're coming from and where you're going?*

He'd deliberated over his answer a good while. Eventually, he thought he'd found the right one—he'd thought the answer must be *oneself,* since *you* are the only thing that connects where you're coming from and where you're going. But his mother gleefully told him he was wrong. When he begged her for the answer, she'd said *Conjunction.*

It didn't make sense to him at first. Then, when he learned about parts of speech at school, he got the literal part of the joke. The other meaning came to him later, even though his mother had said time and again there was a wide world out there, and to most people places like Conjunction were only a stopover.

Coming back to the place now, after being away, he found it hard to believe anyone would even stop there, however briefly.

Sparse and lonely gambrel-roofed houses dotted the roadside, their scarred wooden panels splintered by nails. Ahead lay a wasteland of dead fields and rolling sand hills. A rusting water tower loomed above, barricaded by a square of barbed wire fencing that had been erected after a drunk teen fell while pissing off the side and landed dead in a puddle of his own urine.

Dax turned on Cross Street, which ran through the center of town, and headed for the coroner's house instead of his own. He wanted to get it over with. He pulled up to the little white house and parked, but he sat in the car for a moment, steeling himself to see his father for the first time in almost four years—and for the last time.

The coroner, Eli Baumgartner, opened the door, looking serenely grave, with a facial expression Dax imagined he'd practiced in front of the mirror. He invited Dax inside, moving slowly from age or the spiritual weight of his business.

"I find most folks prefer to get right down to business," Eli said. "Does your father have a plot at the county cemetery?"

Dax shook his head, the floorboards creaking beneath him as he shifted his weight. A small wooden crucifix hung on the far wall, and he found himself both looking at it and not looking at it. He imagined his father in the ground, rotting slowly over the years, clinging with every last fiber to his form as a cruel reminder of what he once was.

"I've given it some thought, and I think he would have wanted to be cremated," Dax said. That was bull, of course. He had no idea what his father would have wanted, as the man had never shared such a thing with him, but it seemed simpler and he wasn't interested in making this more difficult than it was.

Eli's heavy brows dipped low over his eyes. "Your father was a Christian, I believe? I recommend a Christian burial. Cremation destroys the sanctity of the body in the eyes of the Lord."

"And does a Christian burial empty the pockets of the body, in the eyes of the Lord?"

"Oh no, we have very affordable casket options," Eli assured him.

"How affordable?"

As it turned out, not affordable enough. Dax chose cremation and asked to see his father's body.

Dreadful anticipation filled him as Eli led him down the stairs and into a cold room flooded with white light. A body lay beneath a white sheet on a metal table. The chill of the basement seeped into Dax's bones.

He approached the figure, the shape and semblance of his father made into a blank canvas. He stood close enough to touch it, to pull back the shroud himself, but he couldn't move. An irrational fear gripped him and didn't let go until Eli lifted the top of the sheet and folded it below his father's chin.

Eli gave him a few minutes alone, and Dax finally allowed himself to look.

Roy Howard's skin was dry and pale, and sagged around his closed eyes. His mouth stretched limply across his face. He did not look jaundiced, which Dax had sort of expected; he looked like clay. When Phil said his liver had given out, Dax wasn't surprised. You pour back a case or two of beer a night for ten years, and sooner or later your body won't take it anymore.

That it wasn't a surprise didn't mean Dax had been prepared for it. How can one prepare to see a parent's mortality laid bare upon a metal table? Would things have been different if he'd kept in touch? Would things have been different if his father hadn't started drinking? Would things have been different if his mother were still around? *Of course*, he thought. *Everything would have been different.* But she was gone.

His father was here, though, in front of him. Maybe there was a slight possibility of coming back from "gone," but there was no coming back from *dead*.

That was why he'd spent so many nights wishing his mother were dead. Then his father might not have lost himself chasing her ghost.

"All that time, I was here. I was right here," he said. "Why couldn't you just let her go?"

Standing with his father's body, he felt more alone than he could remember, and loneliness wasn't exactly new territory. He'd grown up with an absent mother and an emotionally absent father. He'd grown up lonely, had always been lonely, simply assumed loneliness was part of his genetic makeup.

His relationship with his father had been like all his relationships; in his immeasurable dissatisfaction, he slowly distanced himself from what he perceived as a source of trouble until he was as cold and remote as a star looking down and wondering how it could communicate in the language of that far-off planet.

Especially after the drinking started.

Roy hadn't started drinking until Renée's disappearance. It was just a little at first—a few drinks to get through those long, quiet nights. Roy had been a man with an unmatched work ethic once. A man who'd taught Dax how to run a tractor and milk a cow. Dax liked to think of that man, sometimes, and wonder what it would have been like if he'd been around during his teenage years. But the man who was around then was the kind who drank before lunch, who drank in the fields, who drank to fill the quiet moments. The kind who neglected the farm, leaving the chickens unfed and the crops unwatered until they withered and died. The kind whose main method of communication was gruffly asking whether Dax had finished his chores, and then a grunt of either approval or disapproval, usually directed into a bottle or can.

Perhaps the most bizarre thing about Roy-after-Renée was the obsession he had developed with old newspapers. He would order stacks of them to be sent to the house, and he'd sit for hours poring over them. Never read anything else. It had started with local papers, as far back as he could get them, and then he'd branched out to neighboring towns, then papers all across Nebraska, and finally papers from several states away. The only other reading material in the house had been his mother's old collection of books, which Dax had taken to slipping from their shelf from time to time, if only to fill his mind with a voice other than the grunts and growls into which his father's had devolved. Truthfully, though, it was never his father's voice he carried in his mind. Of all the fading, piecemeal memories he still had of his mother, he remembered her voice most of all. He was haunted by it.

The pain of losing his wife had been, perhaps, too much for Roy—Dax conceded the thought now that he was older and had some distance from the man. It wasn't that his father had ever been bad to him. It was just that, in the end, he was hardly a father after all.

The coroner came back in and pulled the sheet over Roy's face.

Eli showed him the crematorium—a brick oven stained black by flames with a semicircular chute for the body. Dax shivered in the basement's damp confines and wondered if Eli was only showing it to scare him. The burnt darkness inside the chute seemed to breathe the smoke of death. He couldn't get out of the house fast enough.

Once he was outside again, he realized there was only one place left to go.

He drove down Main Street and turned onto Wildacre Road, through a stretch of dilapidated houses. The road curved back out into farmland, where cows stood chewing on cud, and there against the horizon was his father's farm. The grain silo cut a sharp shadow against the sky behind the house with its peeling red paint. Behind it lay two hundred acres of neglected crops trying to poke their way through the dry soil.

His father's old Jeep sat out front, one of its tires flat.

Dax slung his duffel bag over his shoulder and trudged to the house. Insects buzzed and the wind whisked through the tall grass, and nothing else.

The front door creaked opened. Inside it was musty and dark; thin gray light filtered in through the dusty windows. Something about the air felt heavy, shut-up. Yet there, distinctly, was the smell of home, and he felt, immediately and joylessly, as if he had never left.

It unsettled him to be alone in the empty house, so when a knock came at the door, he went gladly to it, even though he couldn't imagine wanting to talk to anyone right now.

Phil Sawyer stood on the porch with quiet concern in his face. Everything about him seemed heavy, from his wild brows to the stoop of his shoulders. He was a mechanic, and his skin seemed always to emit a faint odor of grease and hot machinery. Dax got a whiff of it and felt enveloped by the old familiarity.

"You didn't come say hi," was Phil's way of greeting him.

"Hi."

"Heard from Eli you'd made it. It's good to see you, son. How're you holding up?"

Dax shrugged.

When he was a kid, he'd called them Uncle Phil and Aunt Helen—never Mr. and Mrs. Sawyer, even after he'd fallen out with Helen.

As Helen would say, God had never blessed her with children of her own, so she'd doted on Dax. He hadn't minded when he was young, but after his mother disappeared, Helen had exuded a fierce pride he later recognized as a concealed, monstrous joy. She wanted to possess Dax, but he had never accepted her as his surrogate mother. He'd always remained close to Phil, though, who had encouraged his interest in science, in going to college in the first place.

"Helen's asking about the funeral," Phil said. "She wants to plan something at the church, but I told her that's your business. You making any plans?"

"Not really."

"Well, she'll be disappointed, but don't let that worry you." Phil looked him over critically, as though making mental notes of how Dax had changed in the last four years. "She'll be glad you're back."

"I'm not staying. I mean, I've got to finish school," he said, knowing it was a lie. He was too far behind to graduate, and when the scholarship ran dry at the end of the semester, that would be it. He distracted himself from that thought by looking around at the house. "I was thinking of selling the place."

"That'll be a feat," Phil said, hands in his pockets. "Fixer-upper like this. Helen and me'll help you out, of course. We can spruce this place up. Meantime, you can stick around, stay with us. If you want."

"I don't know."

"Well, it's a thought. Free home-cooked meals. Free cable. You want to make some spare cash, Beau Montgomery's looking for extra help at the store."

"How come?"

"Your buddy, Wyatt, broke his arm fishing at the lake."

As if he had been floating, untethered in a surreal fog, Dax snapped back to the earth at the confirmation that Wyatt had never left town. After all his talk, he was still working at his family's store. The thought left a sour tang in the back of Dax's throat.

"How'd he break his arm fishing?"

Phil shrugged. "Must have been one helluva big fish."

He tried again to get Dax to stay with them, instead of here, all by himself, but Dax refused. Before he left, Phil hesitated on the porch and finally said, "I know I encouraged you to leave—but that doesn't mean I'm not happy to see you back. He never held it against you, for going your own way, not really. I thought you should know that, even if it didn't seem like it, with the way you left things."

While he chewed this over, Phil reached in and gave him a fierce, bone-crushing hug. Phil had always been uniquely empathetic; yet maybe because he was a certain kind of man in a certain kind of place, it usually came out as awkward sentimentality. He pulled back, nodding and looking away, and left with his words still hanging in the air.

But Dax was too busy thinking about Wyatt Montgomery.

Wyatt was the only real friend he'd had in Conjunction, maybe the only real friend he'd *ever* had, but he'd left him just the same and hadn't seen him since that last summer—that summer of high tempers and dead heat.

The summer before Dax took his full ride to the University of Minnesota and left town was the worst drought Crow County had seen in years. The swelter of midday stretched all the way from dawn to dusk. A permanent sheen of sweat had slicked Dax's body from June to August, which he mostly spent watching crops die. He and Wyatt had taken refuge at Sandpiper Lake, stripping down to their trunks in the cool, murky water.

Wyatt came from a breed of fair-haired, fair-skinned people who burned easily in the sun, so he'd peeled all that summer. He loved the cold, harsh winters that enveloped Nebraska from November to February each year. They seemed to suit him. He'd said he was going to become an Eskimo and move to Alaska, where snow and fur would protect him, and sled-dogs would pull him over vast fields of ice.

The summer Dax left, Wyatt was big on Iceland. He'd talked all the time about Nordic myths and glaciers and, not to mention, the hot blonde babes. Dax had barely paid attention, waiting so anxiously for the letter that would change his life. When it came, Wyatt said he had his own plans to bum his way to Iceland, maybe get work on a northbound cruise ship. While Dax was off getting more education, Wyatt would be journeying to the North Atlantic, home to a wide, cold ocean inhabited by the ghosts of Vikings. No more blistering, sun-drenched days. No more hot, sweaty nights—unless it was in an igloo with a sexy native Icelander, blue-eyed and honey-tongued and pale as ice.

It wasn't until Dax looked back on that summer that he recognized the artifice behind Wyatt's own boasting. Each time Dax mentioned school, Wyatt spoke over him. It had become so irritating that when Dax finally left, he didn't feel sorry at all. Wyatt had been wild about his own ridiculous plans, and they'd barely said goodbye.

But Wyatt was still here, working at his dad's store: the Montgomery legacy of bread, milk, and gasoline. Wyatt hadn't left, and had Dax really expected him to, anyway? At least he wasn't the only failure around here.

I'll have to go there, he realized. There wasn't much food in the house, and the Bronco's tank was almost empty. But who was Wyatt now? Who had he become in the last four years?

Dax closed the curtains against the intruding sunlight. The house creaked around him. He made his way down the narrow hall to the kitchen. The fridge was barren but for a half-empty ketchup bottle and something unidentifiable wrapped in tinfoil, which smelled vaguely of rotten eggs. He found a warm, forgotten six-pack hidden in the back of a lower cabinet and pulled a bottle free with shaking hands. The cap cut dazzling red streaks in his palms and sent him searching for a bottle opener. He found one in the silverware drawer. The warm beer left a stale taste in his mouth. Dax chugged half the bottle, then grabbed the pack and carried it with him. He stared down the long hallway. The drink blanketed him with a dull warmth.

He finished it off standing in the dark hall, staring at the one room he hadn't set foot in as he clutched the empty beer bottle and the formerly six-, now five-pack.

He felt like he was eight years old again, knowing his mother wasn't here and would never be again. She was gone, not a trace of her left except her things in the bedroom, still lying around because she'd planned to come back. Only she hadn't. Finally presumed dead, she wouldn't *ever* come back, and now here he was, fourteen years later, still standing in that hallway waiting for a parent's ghost to open the door and come back.

He drank the second beer, working up his courage. He was sure his father hadn't slept for weeks after his mother disappeared, always expecting her to come drifting back in the night. Dax didn't think he'd be able to sleep in that room at the end of the hall, either. His father had chosen to fill those lost hours with booze. Filled everything with booze, until there was no room left for anything else. Maybe it was a good strategy. Dax drank.

The second beer gone, he finally felt the urge to move. He left the empty bottles in the hallway. The door of his father's bedroom swung inward with a creak.

His mother's handmade floral quilt, now worn and dusty blue with age, still lay folded at the foot of the bed. Her mirrored armoire—never used by his father, still empty for sure—stood against the wall. The shades were drawn, the whole room tinted blue in the semi-darkness, dust particles floating on the air. Dax could see the rumpled place where his father had slept the night before he died—on one side of the bed, leaving the left empty for his wife's ghost.

Dax opened the third bottle with a pop.

Clothes lay strewn over the rocking chair in the corner, where his mother used to smoke as she told stories. Dax would lay rapt, belly-down, on the rug while the pungent miasma of marijuana pervaded the room. He remembered the crackle and red glow as she inhaled, the smoky smell, the empty Mason jar she'd use as an ash tray.

He found himself drawn to the rocking chair now, settling down on the floor in front of it with his beer. It was so quiet in here, he could hear the wind clawing its way through the cracks in the house. It sounded as if something were dying outside, and would if it didn't manage to get in before the sun set.

The floor was hard. He moved to the bed and settled gingerly on the spot his father had occupied. The beer was making his head fuzzy and his limbs numb. He closed his eyes against the swirling ceiling, felt weighed down and sluggish.

He thought of the carnival. The cold bite of the wind. Stars piercing the sky. Laughter and screaming as it echoed across the flat expanse of the surrounding fields. The huge, spoked wheel that slowly gyrated against the stars, the spinning rides, the house of mirrors Dax had been too frightened to enter. The smell of burnt popcorn and vomit. The tall crowd surrounding him on all sides, shutting him off from everything but the littered ground. The feel of his mother's fingers pulling away from his. Her face disappearing into the crowd. The ash that fell from smoldering cigarette butts. The ghostly echo of the crowd as it dispersed. The panic. The dreadlocked carnival woman staring through him with moonlike eyes, asking what was the matter. His father wrenching him away from her and hurrying them both into the night as they called out for his mother in the gathering darkness. The shadows that flitted in and out of his vision. *Renée, Renée? Renée! Mom!* The cornstalks swishing in the wind and the echoes of their cries. *Renée! Renée!* The sleepless night at home, phoning everyone they knew—no response, no explanation. The hollow look in his father's eyes, the stubble peppering his chin.

The next day, the carnival was gone, and so was his mother.

His father had been distant afterward, in his own world. Dax had grown moody and had taken to acting out, but he never got in trouble, just a slap on the wrist as the adults whispered about how his mother had gone missing, how they should take it easy on the poor boy. Dax hated the pity in their eyes. On his ninth birthday he had tried to run away, but he only made it as far as the outer edge of the cornfield before he'd sat down in the rustling stalks and waited for morning to usher him back home.

CHAPTER 2

Dax dozed in a half-drunk stupor on his father's bed and tried to etch his mother into existence using only his mind: green eyes, the color of summer algae filming over the surface of a lake. Light crow's feet made those eyes crinkle with delight between bouts of lethargy that made her look, instead, prematurely lined with a sad kind of wistfulness, as if she were never wholly present. Long brown hair pulled back impatiently under a bandana. Delicate fingers rolled joints at the kitchen table. Stories of her Lakota grandfather and the myths of his people.

In Dax's vision of her, a blurry memory, she placed one of those long, spidery fingers to her mouth. "Our secret?" she whispered as she tucked one joint behind her ear and hid another in the bottom of a junk drawer. "It'll be safe here. Nice and dark."

Twilight had fallen outside.

He thought of his mother's Mason jar and of his father, who, by tomorrow, would be reduced to ash.

Dax figured by now he was drunk enough to go to Montgomery's Gas and Grocery.

It felt wrong rooting around his father's room for cash, but he didn't have much choice. He was broke. He looked through the drawers and found folded flannel, stained shirts that'd been run through the wash too many times, and a few old pairs of jeans. He remembered these clothes, remembered them on his father. Grabbing a red flannel shirt, Dax brought it up to his face, breathing in the faint scent of cedar and laundry detergent. He pulled the flannel on over his T-shirt. It was too big. Then he dug through the pockets of the jeans, coming up with some bills. He found his dad's money clip in the next drawer and stuck it in his pocket.

He looked up at his mother's armoire on the other side of the room. What did his father keep in there? Her old clothing? Had his father even touched it in all these years?

Dax's skin itched.

He realized he was afraid to open his mother's armoire. What on earth was there to fear from a piece of furniture, but that its closed doors kept hidden its secret contents, its secret histories and artifacts of the dead? The mirrored doors reflected his image, gray and ghostly.

He sipped his beer and frowned at the closed double-doors and their brass handles, at the reflection of his dark eyes and mussed-up hair, disliking what he saw there. He set down the bottle and wrenched open the doors.

Floral shirts with ruffled sleeves hung within, faded and yellowish. Dax felt himself deflate as he took in the wardrobe, nothing but old clothes his father had kept for fourteen years. The inside of the armoire didn't smell as musty as he'd expected; Roy must have opened it up every so often.

He was about to close the doors when he caught sight of paper behind one of the shirts. He reached inside, brushing the dangling cloth, and plucked the paper from where it was stuck to the wooden back panel. When he pulled it free, a larger document fell, pages flapping.

A drawing, one of his mother's.

Whenever she'd told him stories, her grandfather's stories, she would supplement them with her own artistic flourishes, rendering the tales in colored pencil sketches. He had watched, over her shoulder, as mythological beings manifested from blank canvas. Heyoka, the sacred clown. Prairie Rose and the Wind Demon. The trickster Coyote. Whope, the falling star. Iktomi, the spider. Dax kept all the stories in his mind, gifts from his mother, though he had none of her drawings anymore—none save the one in his hand.

This drawing depicted the Lakota creation myth: a red flood overtook the bottom of the page, described in lurid swirls of blood and drowned bodies. A huge spotted eagle—his mother's voice whispered from beyond time, *Wanblee Galeshka*—saved a lone girl from the flood. She hung onto the eagle's feet while they soared away into the sky.

Setting down the drawing, Dax knelt to retrieve the fallen document. He opened its brittle pages, the paper fuzzy along the crease lines from too much folding and unfolding, and found an oversized map of the Midwestern United States. Here and there someone had circled places in black ink—small towns or sometimes what seemed like nothing at all. He refolded the map and put it down beside the drawing.

He stood and closed the armoire doors, then stumbled back when he saw the figure in the mirror. His heart leapt and he lost his footing. Sprawled on the floor, he gazed into nothing more than his own shocked reflection. He had forgotten he was wearing his father's shirt, and though his father had been stouter, and lighter in skin and hair, Dax thought he'd seen his ghost through the looking glass. His father was nowhere, though; it was only Dax, alone with his reflection.

He got to his feet, grabbed his keys, and hurried out of the room, out of the house.

Outside he found the deepness of the night sky above Conjunction. Stars spattered the darkness, and the sharp yellow smile of the moon calmed him as it always had. There was something unique about the country sky, something he couldn't put into words. It was nothing like the city. The Minneapolis sky he'd left behind was punctured by tall buildings, and at night, when Dax took his telescope to the roof of his apartment building, it was full of dull reddish light captured from the city. While he'd taken classes on stars, he could hardly even see them with the naked eye. He knew they were there, somewhere, if only he could find them again. He'd had them in his own backyard growing up. The country night was pitch black, and the stars cast out into that abyss cut clean through the rural air. They'd been his midnight companions, until he'd gone away and lost them.

He took a breath and got in the car.

While he never would have driven drunk in the city, the wide dirt roads beckoned him back into the lawless country of his youth, where teenagers could set off fireworks, shoot bottles, and trade drugs with little fear of interference. After all, the law around here was pretty much Sheriff Anderson—him and a few deputies working out of the sheriff's office on Main Street. They also covered Bannon, the township to the west that rarely called on the law. When they did it was usually for accidental deaths, property arguments, or hunting deer out of season.

Headlights swam through the twilight of a still evening. The road shivered unsteadily in the light.

He hit Main Street, a dead-end road on both sides bisected by Cross Street. To the east the street ended at a little white church with a sharp steeple. To the west it ended at the tavern, The Rusty Doornail.

Some saw good at one end of Main Street and evil at the other. Dax saw a kind of escape at both.

When he pulled up to Montgomery Gas and Grocery, a succession of emotions passed through him, almost too fast to latch onto as they passed: first he hoped Wyatt wasn't there; then he felt guilty for hoping Wyatt wasn't there; then he felt annoyed that he felt guilty. He wondered what he would say to him. He worried nothing would come out but a jumble of half-apologies, *long-time-no-sees*, and *how-are-you-doings*.

A little brass bell jangled as he stepped inside the store. The place seemed empty in the white glare of the fluorescent lights. He took a basket and made his way down the aisles, grabbing a loaf of bread, a bag of chips, and peanut butter and jelly along the way.

He heard movement at the back of the store—the sound of a door swinging open and shut. Probably the door that led to the storage room. Was it Beau Montgomery, the friendly man who had given him free popsicles when he was a kid? Or his beleaguered wife, who always seemed to have at least one of her five children hanging onto her throughout the day?

No matter who it was, he couldn't hide between the shelves all night. He finished loading his basket and stepped into the main aisle. At the front, behind the cash register, idly picking at something on the counter, stood Wyatt.

"Can I help—"

Before he finished his question, he looked up and saw Dax. For a second, he froze. Then he gave an incredulous grin and said, "Well, fuck me with a cattle prod. You're back."

He looked different. His face was somehow even more pocked than when they were teenagers. His hair had grown a little longer, shabbier, and he sported a layer of ash-blond stubble across his chin. His voice was deeper, gravelly. When he leaned on the counter, Dax noticed the cast on his right arm.

"Hey man," Wyatt said, scratching behind his ear, "I'm sorry about your dad."

"Yeah," Dax said. "Me too."

An awkward silence hung between them.

"Your folks have you on night shift?" Dax asked as he placed his basket on the counter.

"Well, shit, I ain't stocking anything, that's for sure," he said, holding up his casted arm. He started unloading the groceries and punching keys in the register. "It's boring as *hell* here at night, too. I keep hoping a drifter serial killer will stop in and shoot me dead."

"'Sometimes, dead is better,'" Dax quoted, not remembering what movie it was from, only that it was one of the many classic horror flicks he and Wyatt used to binge in the Montgomeries' basement, late into the night, feasting on whatever artery-clogging snacks they could pilfer from the store.

Maybe Wyatt remembered, because he started laughing, and Dax joined in. It felt easy, familiar. Like old times.

Then, without warning, he remembered his father—dead. And he stopped laughing.

Wyatt squinted intensely at the bread, looking for a barcode, or maybe reading the list of ingredients.

"How'd you break your arm?" Dax said.

Wyatt pulled out a brown paper bag and whipped it open. Suddenly, he sobered; the silent remnants of laughter disappeared from his face, and his eyes zipped around the groceries, refusing to look up. "Fishing."

"A fish did that?"

He started shoving groceries into the bag. "That ain't what I said."

In the bare light over the counter, Wyatt looked too pale, and up close, Dax noticed the bruise-colored pockets beneath his eyes, the hollowness of his face.

"Then what was it?"

"Why're you so interested?" Wyatt snapped, crushing some of the chips as he tossed them into the bag. "You been gone for, what, four years, and suddenly you want to talk about ... *fishing?*"

Dax said nothing.

Wyatt swiveled the display over the register to show him the total.

Dax fished out his father's money clip and said, "Put the rest on two."

"You're right," Wyatt said finally, apropos of nothing, as he took the money. "We should catch up. Got any plans tomorrow night? There's a party at the Willoughby farm." The till popped open, and Wyatt tucked the money inside. "Might be good to, you know, get your mind off things. Although," he said and looked up at Dax, and then finished, "this thing probably won't be nothing compared to your college parties."

Dax took the receipt. "I'm not much of a partier."

"Then I guess not much has changed." Wyatt slammed the register shut. "You in?"

Dax thought of the old house, the overgrown fields, the barn where couples snuck off by themselves. The Willoughby farm had been abandoned since the fifties or sixties after a tragedy that wiped out the whole family, but rumors of a haunting held no sway over drunk teenagers seeking freedom and debauchery.

"Yeah, all right."

Wyatt grinned. "Good. Now I don't have to go with my sister."

"Sarah?"

Wyatt made a sound of assent in the back of his throat. "Gotta be a goddamn chaperone for a girl who's always disappearing with her weird little friends doing who-the-hell-knows-what."

Dax remembered Sarah as the adolescent tomboy who used to throw mud at them when they teased her. Now she had to be about seventeen or so. Wyatt's next oldest sibling, Noah, was surely still mired in pre-pubescence, along with the twins who hadn't been more than children when Dax had left. He couldn't picture what Sarah might look like now, practically an adult, nor could he imagine her christening the hay on which so many of his peers had lost their virginity.

Wyatt winked and pulled a six-pack from behind the counter, loading it up with Dax's other stuff. "My treat. What the old man don't know won't hurt him."

As Dax left, Wyatt waved his casted arm, making ghostly smears in the darkness.

The cash he'd put in pump two yielded a quarter tank. He replaced the pump and slid behind the wheel with a sigh.

The drive back was dark and sobering. He had another beer when he got home, but it didn't take the edge off. Sleep eluded him. When he did manage to drift off in the living room armchair, he was plagued by nightmares that dissolved from memory when he opened his eyes. He woke around three in the morning, sweating and half-covered by a ratty blanket.

Unsatisfied with the armchair, he got up and started riffling through the things in the room. He needed something to occupy his mind. He went to the bookcase—still filled after all these years with his mother's old books—and pulled out a dusty volume. The leather cover creaked when he opened it, and something fell out of the binding.

A thin white joint.

The old paper felt stiff in his hands, but when he brought it to his nose he caught the faintest hint of the dry weed within. He could almost picture his mother sitting on the porch with the book, iced tea in hand, the smoke fumes dispersing into the cool evening air.

He wondered what his father would say as he found a book of matches, lit the joint, and inhaled the acrid smoke. An appendage of ash grew on the end, hanging on until he flicked the tip and sent it swirling around the room.

The heavy, anxious feeling eased and left him warm and buzzing. He coughed roughly and picked up the book of fairy tales, but it took an effort to focus on each sentence, on the way the words danced together on the page.

Unable to concentrate, and suddenly craving fresh air, he headed out back into the fields where just-planted cornstalks sprouted from the dirt. The early-morning air was cool, damp with spring dew. Insects chirped and buzzed. A lone cow lowed in the distance. The sky stretched out above him: dark, star-dusted, and clear. He lost himself in its luminous infinity. What the Lakota called the Trail of Souls made a white path across the sky, an arm of their spiral galaxy. Maybe the Lakota were right. Maybe his father's soul was soaring away by the light of these stars, sucked toward the giant black hole at the center of the galaxy. All one big accretion disk spinning, spinning toward death.

It had been dark and clear the night before he'd left for school. A night like this, with fireflies winking around him. For weeks, he'd been trying to talk to his father about his leaving, but Roy had ignored him, as if he refused to believe it. Dax had wanted to talk to him about it again that night, the *last* night, but Roy had taken off for The Rusty Doornail instead.

When Dax had finally fished him out of the bar, Roy was swimming in liquor. They had stumbled out onto Main Street, bathed in moonlight. Still clutching his drink, Roy had yanked himself out of Dax's grip. *How dare you*, he'd said, able to hide the slur in his words. He'd had a lot of practice pretending to be sober, but Dax could always tell. *Go home. We'll talk in the morning.*

I'm leaving in the morning, Dax had said.

Roy had pointed at him, said he *wasn't* leaving—how was he

supposed to run a farm all by himself? Dax had told him he'd been doing a good job running it into the ground *by himself.* His father, not usually a violent man, had thrown his empty bottle—not at Dax, just at the ground, but it had shattered at his feet into a thousand glimmering shards.

Dax remembered stepping around the glass. Whenever his fight or flight response was triggered, his instinct was flight, and that's exactly what he had been going to do just then. He had tried to leave, but his father had grabbed him and shoved, roughly, with the clumsiness of booze. A crowd had gathered in the doorway of the bar. Dax had shoved back until Roy stumbled and fell, landing in the broken glass, in the glimmering darkness of Main Street, eyes rimmed red.

Heated with fury, Dax had shouted at him as he never had before. *Go on,* he'd said, delirious with an anger that sprouted from hurt, *Go drink yourself to death. See if I care.*

Those words echoed in the haunting lens of retrospect, with a sense of finality.

Roy had gotten up from the ground and had started shouting back. Some of the other drinkers had emerged from the bar, grabbed Roy to calm him down, but he pushed them away.

Dax couldn't quite remember what he'd said; some of it had made sense, some of it hadn't. Some of it may have been about Renée. Before things went much further, Sheriff Anderson had arrived. At first, he'd threatened to toss both of them in the drunk tank for the night, but when he learned Dax hadn't been drinking, he'd given him a hard, skeptical stare, as though he were disappointed he couldn't lock him up, too. Finally, he'd told Dax to go home, and said he'd better not see him out there again.

His father had spent that night alone in the drunk tank, and the next morning, Dax had left before he came home.

Go drink yourself to death.

Had those words persisted for his father as they had for Dax? Had he thought of them over and over in his remaining years of life? Dax wished he could take them back, but now the words haunted this place like everything else.

Two eyes in the darkness snapped him from these thoughts. Two yellow eyes shining, watching him from between the low, green stalks. At first he thought it was a hallucination, the old marijuana infecting and heightening his senses—but no, the eyes shifted, followed him.

His throat crowded with cotton as the infant cornstalks rustled, cracking beneath the creature's feet. The eyes shone like stars as they moved in the night.

A cloud shifted overhead. In the pale light of the newly emerged moon, the creature stepped out of the corn and slunk away.

Only a coyote.

Dax felt dizzy and leaned back against the wall of the house, closed his eyes, breathed. He told himself not to be stupid; there were dozens of coyotes wandering around out here. It wasn't the one he'd killed. The very notion was absurd.

That one, wherever it was, was dead.

It took a moment for his heart to regain its normal rhythm. The stars spiraled around him, drove him back inside, into the warm embrace of the house. He was so tired, his limbs alien and sluggish. He fell into bed, into the cushion of sleep.

Dawn brought clouded gray sunlight into the room. Dax let his senses edge away from sleep before he opened his eyes. His throat was so dry he could hardly swallow. He padded to the kitchen, poured a glass of water from the tap, and swilled it. Everything was quiet, and he could hear the floorboards groan and the wind sigh. He felt alien here. It was home, but it wasn't.

He let himself sleep again, the merciful sleep of the depressed, until early afternoon, when he knew he could no longer postpone the inevitable. Finally he rose and drove to Eli's house.

After knocking, he stood on the stoop, staring at the fresh white paint on the banister beside the stairs, the flakes of older paint coming off like dandruff in spots that had been missed. The door swung open, and Eli welcomed him inside.

"I believe we settled on the basic urn?" the coroner said. "There's still time to upgrade, you know. Get a nice, proper piece of remembrance."

Dax declined. Something inside him detested Eli, couldn't help but think of the man with his grubby hand out, waiting for others' grief to make him rich. He knew that wasn't fair, though. Everyone had to do something to get by.

Eli disappeared into the back and left Dax alone. He wasn't sure whether to sit at one of the antique chairs or stand in the entryway, so he stuck his hands in his pockets and engaged in a staring contest with the crucifix on the opposite wall, feeling the weight of Christian mythology suffusing the room. When Eli returned, he beckoned Dax to a desk and presented him with a plain metal vessel no larger than a flower vase.

Dax wondered how his father could be in there.

"How would you like to pay?" asked Eli as he handed over an invoice with the total cost.

Why, Dax wondered, *is dying so damned expensive?*

He charged it to his credit card, wondering if he had enough to cover the balance. While Eli swiped the card and printed his receipt, Dax looked up again at wooden Jesus pinned to his cross, dying in agony beneath a crown of thorns. Eli had to tap him to bring him back to the transaction.

"Just sign here," he said, imploring Dax with a ballpoint pen. "And if you would like to make a donation to the church, or set up a memorial service, I can help you with all the particulars—"

Dax decided he hated this man.

He wasn't sure what to do with the urn when he got home. He didn't want to look at it, yet he couldn't seem to let it out of his sight. He ate a sandwich with the urn on the table in front of him. He drank a beer in the living room, staring at the urn, knowing what was inside and refusing to believe. Eventually he brought it to his father's room and sat on the bed.

In the still and quiet of the room, he opened it.

Inside were the ashes. His entire father—the man he once was— reduced to dust inside this metal vase. Dax stared into the urn while the moon appeared in the window.

This was Roy Howard. This is all that's left.

When he closed the vessel, his own reflection met him in the armoire. He pulled open the mirrored doors and set down the urn at the bottom, beneath the hanging shirts. The cold metal winked in the room's overhead light. As he straightened, he spotted another paper behind the clothing. Thinking it was another drawing of his mother's, he grabbed the hangers and shoved them to either side of the wardrobe.

Papers covered the entire back wall of the armoire. Not drawings, but articles, some on faded newspaper, some clearly printed from a computer. Dax froze, his arms still outstretched on the hangers. He tried to see the back panel of the armoire, behind the papers, but there were too many overlapping layers, as though there were no back, no end. The accumulation of papers had been taped or stuck with tacks, and their corners folded inward, curling up with age.

Dax looked down at the urn. "What the hell?"

When the urn gave no response, he leaned closer to the papers and scanned the headlines. He hesitated over the word "carnival," which appeared twice.

He reached out, not knowing which one to take first, his fingers trembling, the shock of this bizarre display unsettling his stomach—

A car honked out front.

He closed the armoire. The papers and the urn disappeared.

Headlights flooded the dark living room, and he stepped outside where the Montgomery family's Dodge idled in the driveway. When he peered into the shadowy interior of the car, however, he found it wasn't Wyatt in the front seat. With the papers still fresh in his mind, the unfamiliar shadow felt portentous, like an omen.

He squinted in the blinding lights.

Sarah crooked an elbow out the window and stuck her head into the night air. "Hey, Dax! Shotgun's yours if you want it!"

Wyatt grumbled from the back, "Aw, pipe down up there. You wouldn't even be driving if you hadn't tattled to Mom."

Dax climbed into the seat next to her, twisted around to Wyatt and said, "She wouldn't let you drive with the cast?"

"Shit, you only need one hand to drive anyway," he complained.

Sarah jerked the car around and pulled away, long ash-blonde hair spilling down her shoulders. "Not how *I* drive." She gave Dax a wry smile before taking the car off the road. Tires bumped over the rocky field.

Wyatt shouted from the back, "You trying to get us killed?"

Sarah maneuvered the car back onto the road with a laugh.

"Damn," Wyatt mumbled, leaning back in his seat. "Warn a guy next time we go off-roading." He shook his head, popped open a can of beer, and offered it to Dax.

"Pass me one," Sarah said.

Wyatt opened another and took a long slurp off the top. "Nope, not for the driver."

Darkness zoomed by on the edges of the headlights. Dax gulped down the beer and balanced the empty can on his knee.

Sarah took a sharp turn off Old Haven Lane onto Woodview, past Phil Sawyer's place, then onto Dunes Way toward the old Willoughby farm.

Gunning the engine, she said, "All right, here's your warning. *Yeeehaaaw!*" And they were off the road again, careening over mounds of dirt.

The empty can leapt off Dax's knee, clattered somewhere by his feet. Wyatt spilled beer down his front and swore. The headlights bounced, zigzagged, and Dax found himself laughing with Sarah, laughing into the oncoming darkness.

CHAPTER 3

A big farmhouse with rotting, sun-bleached wood stood in between a derelict barn and a silo. The half-octagon roof of the house cut into the sky, and the outer walls crawled with overgrown weeds. Heavy bass thumped from within. Dax felt it in the vibrations of his heart.

Sarah pulled up to the field where cars made a makeshift parking lot. "Hope you didn't mind the shortcut."

Wyatt shoved the back of Sarah's seat and threw himself out of the car.

Sarah rolled her eyes. "Don't let the sourpuss ruin the party. He's just pissed 'cause a fish broke his arm."

"I thought he said it *wasn't* a fish," Dax said.

Sarah laughed. "Well sure, he was probably flying high as a—"

A bang on her window startled them both. Wyatt's face loomed beyond the glass. "You assholes coming or what?" he shouted, muffled, through the window.

Dax swung open his door and stepped out into the field surrounding the Willoughby farm. As he did, a gunshot cracked through the air. The echo of the report rang in his ears, in his bones, and a cheer rose in the distance.

"Sounds like someone's starting target practice," Sarah said. She pulled out a cigarette and flicked her lighter a few times before it snapped to life, but she didn't even get a full drag before Wyatt yanked the cigarette from her mouth and tossed it away.

"Hey—!"

"Smoking and swearing don't make you hot shit," he said.

Sarah smirked. "You're one to talk."

"Glad you think I'm hot shit."

"Don't be an ass, Wy," she snapped as she fished the cigarette out of the dark grass. "I know about *your* little habit, so if you don't want Mom and Dad finding out, I suggest you try being a little nicer."

Wyatt had no response. He glowered when Sarah blew smoke in his face.

"I'm going to go find Savannah. Nice seeing you again, Dax," she said before taking off across the field toward the lights and music.

"So what was that all about? 'Your little habit'?" Dax said as they trudged across the field.

"I don't know, she must've found my stash of porn or something."

A cluster of teenagers stood in front of the dilapidated farmhouse with drinks.

Wyatt and Dax went inside. The wood floors were grimy and eaten through by termites, the walls water-stained. A hole in the roof revealed a jagged circle of starlight. Someone had strung blood-red lights around the interior of the rotted building and plugged them into a rumbling generator, and the lights glowed violently upon an old table that held cheap plastic bottles of vodka, whiskey, and Cherry Coke. A bag of Cheetos had split open and spilled across the tabletop.

"Beer pong out back by the keg!" someone shouted.

A few people who recognized Dax said hello, followed by the inevitable half-hearted and insincere condolences, followed by questions of what he had been doing up in Minnesota—asked in an absurd Canadian-esque accent.

"Hey, Barney!" Wyatt shouted, then clapped Dax on the shoulder. "Be right back," he said before disappearing.

"Wait—"

Dax pushed his way through the throng, but Wyatt was gone. The crowd's movements buffeted him back to the wall, where he stood looking out. No one paid him any mind. Eventually he followed the current of people out the back door, toward the keg and the beer pong table gleaming with sticky residue. Beyond this, past an overgrown field of weeds and dead grass, was a small group pointing rifles into the distance, their shadows thrown against the trees by the light of an electric lantern.

Someone bumped into Dax from behind—Mason Tesoro carrying three red cups half-filled with beer in a kind of triangle smashed between his hands. He placed them on the table, where Ezekiel Anderson stood regaling three teenage girls with a story, which resulted in a fit of giggling. Ezekiel balanced a 12-gauge shotgun on his shoulder, aimed at the stars behind him. Both Mason and Zeke were a year older than Dax, and about as hotheaded and pugnacious as they come.

Mason finished setting up the table, and Zeke handed his shotgun to one of the girls with exaggerated formality. Then he turned away, observing the table and the crowd milling around it, and spotted Dax. "Hey!" he called. "Ho-lee shit, it's the astronaut!"

Dax thought if he backed up he might dissolve into the night and escape the sheriff's son. He thought about saying he wasn't an astronaut—studying astrophysics was not the same thing—but the correction sounded stupid even in his head.

"Get the hell over here," Zeke said. "We're just about to start up a game."

Dax approached them while Zeke introduced him to the three girls. "That, ladies, is Roy Howard's son—you know, the *space cadet*. Roy Howard ... may that son-of-a-bitch rest in peace." He turned to Dax. "Goddamn shame about Roy. What a legend! He could drink me under the table any day, and hell, that's saying something."

Dax looked down at the triangular formations of plastic cups, red arrows targeting each other. "You knew my dad?"

"Shit, we were drinking buddies!" Zeke produced two ping-pong balls from his pocket and nodded at Mason, who came over to his side. "Your dad was something else. Hey, pick a partner. Me and Mason versus you and ... whoever."

"I don't know," Dax said. His skin crawled as he imagined Zeke and his father sitting together at The Rusty Doornail, trading beers and stories.

"You," Zeke said, pointing to the girl with the shotgun. He took it from her and pushed her by the shoulders until she was kneeling in the grass, provocatively close to him. "I dub thee," he said, placing the barrel on one shoulder, "The space cadet's beer pong partner," he continued, tapping the shotgun against her other shoulder. "Now go forth, and get plastered!" Ringlets of red hair curled around her face as she turned it upward, a pale moonlike oval. He swung the shotgun away from her, and Dax watched the sweep of its barrel gazing off into the dark. She stood and went to the other end of the table while Zeke handed the shotgun to the next girl, who held the barrel facing upward as if she might blow off her face. He hoped there was only birdshot in there, not that there would be much difference at that range. He seemed to remember Zeke once proclaiming birdshot was for pussies.

"I'm Avery," the redhead said.

Zeke tossed Dax one of the ping-pong balls, which bounced off his hand, and he chased it across the grass. After he retrieved it, they both stood poised to shoot while Mason counted. On three, Dax's ball bounced off the table, and Zeke's splashed into a cup.

"All right, *we* start," Zeke announced.

On the first round, Dax missed, but Mason scored. Avery put up her hands and said she was "already kind of sloshed," so Dax picked up the cup and drank it for her. The carbonation prickled his throat.

Dax missed on his next turn. Avery nailed the cup at the tip of the arrow.

Zeke whooped and clapped his hands. "Guess we know who wears the pants in *this* relationship." He lifted the cup and said, "To Roy!" and chugged until the cup was empty. "Better step it up, Dax. Make your old man proud!"

This time, both Zeke and Mason scored. Avery sipped her beer while Dax swallowed angrily, foaming tendrils slipping down his chin from the corners of his mouth. He wiped it away, his insides red-hot.

What did Zeke and Roy talk about at The Rusty Doornail? What could they possibly have in common, aside from belligerent alcoholism?

Dax and Avery both missed.

"Oh, *come on*," shouted Zeke, "I want to drink some of this fine PBR! Your old man's favorite beer, right?"

Zeke shot first, landed the ball in the center cup. Mason followed, hit the same one.

The two girls on the sidelines cheered. The one holding the shotgun waved it over her head, and Dax thought she was going to hit the trigger and crack the sky until the stars fell down and buried them. Mason bowed in their direction while Zeke shouted, "Hole in fucking *one!* Get ready to chug."

Dax's hand shook as he lifted the cup, nearly spilling it. Avery scooped up the balls and tossed them back to Mason. She glanced sidelong at Dax, her lips pursed in a frown. He didn't know if it was because they were losing or because she felt sorry for him.

Mason pointed to the other cup they had to drink, and Avery removed it. She tapped her plastic cup against Dax's and tilted it back. Dax stared down into the beer, feeling flushed and unhappy.

Zeke scored. Mason missed.

Dax chugged the rest of his beer and grabbed another. Avery scored. Dax hesitated long enough for Zeke to conspicuously check his watch, and then missed.

"Ouch!" Zeke cried. "Bet your old man's rolling in his grave." Dax's head swam. "What the fuck do you know?"

"Nothing." Zeke said. "Nothing, because you know, he talked a lot—but never about you. Wonder why." His grin took over his face, rough with stubble and sun.

Zeke and Mason won the game. They won, like they would always win. Same old Conjunction, same old kingdom of brutality.

"Eenie, meenie, miney, moe," Zeke said, pointing between the two girls. He landed on the one without the shotgun and pressed his mouth against hers, bending her over backward. Then he pulled away, draping an arm over each of their shoulders. "Who wants to play the champions?"

The girl with the shotgun raised her free hand, and he snatched the gun from her and started pointing it around and calling people out, the barrel threatening anyone who dared refuse.

"Good game," Avery said, pouring two cups of beer together into one. "Sorry," she added vaguely, carrying her drink away to the two girls that Zeke had left behind as he chatted up new competition. He slapped a girl's ass and turned away as she looked around to find the culprit.

"Better luck next time!" Zeke called out as Dax was turning to leave.

Two gunshots fired in the distance. Dax flinched.

He headed back into the house, his gut churning with beer and jealousy and guilt. His mind conjured images of Zeke and Roy and their inexplicable camaraderie while the farm rotted around him like a living thing. He couldn't help but notice loose spider web strands dangling from ceiling corners, the moldy funk of the remaining floorboards, and the spray-painted graffiti faded into some kind of ancient Midwestern hieroglyphics.

Dax poured himself a drink. The cheap whiskey burned his throat.

With still no clue where Wyatt had disappeared to, he started down a hall and found himself in the sagging doorway to a dirt-floored room steeped in candlelight. A circle of shadow-people sat along the walls. In the center sat a lone figure of a woman, cross-legged and surrounded by melting candles. Long dark hair hung over bare jutting shoulders, her bones pushing against a thin layer of skin that took on a sickly grayish hue in the dim light. Two sunken eyes bore out from the dark rings around her sockets, and her pale lips were cracked and dry, chapped almost to the point of splitting open.

Holding a glass jar filled with dirt, she said, "Some of you weren't here last week. This is how it works. We pass around the story jar, and you tell a story about yourself. Something no one else knows."

Dax took a step into the doorway, and the floor creaked beneath him, interrupting the girl and causing several of her shadow-flock to turn and glare at his interruption. One was Sarah.

"Hey, Dax," she whispered. "If you're looking for my brother, he's probably in the silo with the other tweakers."

The girl in the center brought everyone's attention back to her without saying a thing. Her presence drew them, insects to blinding light. Finally she said, "I'll go first," and brought the jar up to her mouth. When she spoke again, the glass muffled her voice.

Dax didn't listen so much to the words as to the tone—the almost hypnotic lilt of her voice, which rose and fell like the tide, the tones of storytelling that reminded him of his mother.

She said that when she was young, her family never listened to her; she was ignored, and so she decided one day to stop speaking altogether. Once she became mute, her family suddenly paid more attention to her. She realized, then, the power of silence. She began speaking again after that, but she always remembered the power she had felt in deliberately giving up her voice.

"Recently," she continued, lifting her face slightly from the jar, her breath shivering the candle flames, "I decided to give my voice to God. Yes, there is a God, but not the one you hear about in church. He is the Watcher in the Stars. He sees all; He hears all. He hears your voice when no one else does. He is life, but He is death, also—and in death, where everyone else will vanish into a silent obscurity, your voice and your story will remain so long as you give it to Him. Your story will go where all stories go: into the great, hungry mouth of Father Death. And, even in death, all of our stories will live on forever—and so will we."

Dax's mouth went dry, but he didn't lift his cup. Maybe the liquor had finally gone to his head, for the candles seemed to swim. The room was stifling. Despite the heat, his skin raced with chills. He noticed the window had been boarded up. Candlelight gleamed on the girl's yellowed grin. Unable to look at her any longer, he grabbed Sarah's shoulder and pulled her gently until she stood and joined him outside the doorway.

She frowned. "Are you okay? You look pale."

"Yeah." He tried to breathe deeply. "Who is that?"

She glanced behind her. Someone else had taken the story jar and now spoke quietly into the dirt. "That's Savannah."

"Oh," Dax said, uncomprehending.

The air from the room snaked out toward him. It had the shut-up feeling of a tomb, and the longer he stood there, the more lightheaded and muddled he felt. Yet he wasn't quite ready to leave behind the darkness, Savannah, and her soothing monologue. Part of him wanted to let it enclose him, bury him. Wanted to join them in the circle, seekers after some esoteric truth.

"Who's the Watcher in the Stars?" he asked.

"It's just a name. I think maybe she got it from her family? She's Sioux—maybe it's from that."

"No," he said, "it's not."

Sarah shrugged. Something seemed to be drawing her back into the room.

"Why don't you go find Wyatt?" she said.

Dax stood there a moment longer after Sarah rejoined the group. He felt a pang in his chest, an emptiness. Briefly, Savannah's words had filled it. Now it was back, and he drank to fill it with whiskey instead. He walked back down the hallway and out into the cool night.

It got quieter as he approached the silo, the noise of the party behind him now. The silence of the countryside enveloped him. He found the access door on the side of the crumbling tower and pulled it open with the creak of metal against cement staves.

The round interior was lit by an electric lantern sitting crooked on the rocky soil. Its harsh white glow revealed the vines that snaked their way up the grimy walls to the domed ceiling. A faint chemical smell pervaded the area. Two figures sat around the lantern and one paced the walls. One of the sitters looked up and Dax saw, in the lantern light, Wyatt's face glowing through the darkness.

"Hey man, what are you doing here?" Wyatt asked, his eyes darting around the room as he tried to hide the glass pipe in his hand.

Dax froze in the doorway. "What are *you* doing?"

The other guy, who sported a scruffy beard, stood and said, "Who invited *you?*"

Wyatt leapt to his feet and held out a hand to pacify him. "This is Dax. He's cool," Wyatt said, handing him the pipe. "Come on, let's all just chill out."

"You're smoking meth," Dax said.

"Let's talk outside." Wyatt pushed him back out the doorway. Dax could see it now, and he didn't know how he hadn't noticed before: the nervous knuckle-cracking, the hollow gauntness, the yellowing teeth. He whirled around as soon as they exited the silo and tossed his drink into the grass, plastic cup and all.

"What the hell happened to you?" Dax said.

Wyatt's face went cold. "Nothing, man. Nothing happened. Hell, we can't all get full rides and go to college, can we?"

"That's not an excuse for being a junkie."

A peal of wild laughter escaped Wyatt. "This coming from you? Give me a break. Your mom was a pothead for chrissake, and your dad was a drunk."

"Shut up."

"What the hell do you care, anyway? You'd never have come back if your dad hadn't kicked off, admit it. You'd have let us all rot if you could, huh?"

Dax opened his mouth but found no words that comprised an adequate response—because Wyatt was right. He stood there with an open mouth filled with damning silence.

"Oh shit," Wyatt murmured. He had already moved on from the conversation and was staring into the distance, at the forest that lay beyond the boundary of the farm. "Oh shit, I knew it, that fucker followed me, how does it know? How does it know where I am?"

Dax followed his gaze. Far away was a shape with eyes that gleamed in the moonlight. He swallowed down his own unease and said, "It's just an animal."

"A fucking *animal*," Wyatt whispered manically. "What kind of *animal* follows you around like that? It's too smart to be an animal, get me? I think it's something else. No, no, listen. It just wants us to *think* it's an animal, right? Those yellow eyes, man, they see right through you. I been seeing it everywhere, ever since ..." His voice trailed off into the whisper of the wind and the distant echo of music from the house.

"Ever since what?"

Wyatt shook his head. "No. No, no."

"Come on, Wyatt."

"No way, man, I don't want to talk about it. Let's talk about something else."

Wyatt was vibrating with drugs, with nervous energy, with fear.

"Fine," Dax said. "Forget it."

"It was at the lake," Wyatt finally spat out. "When I ... you know ..."

"When you were fishing?"

"Yeah. When I was fishing, yeah. I mean, no, I wasn't there to fish, not really, I was just there to light up. Well, I guess I was fishing, too. It was cloudy, I remember. Looked like it was gonna rain. You know how it looks, when it gets like that? How the water looks all dark, almost black? Like, you can't even see through it at all, you don't know what's under there." He chewed nervously on his lip, staring. "You don't even know what's under there."

After a moment he snapped out of it and continued. "So I was out, on the lake, you know, and I saw that thing—the coyote, well, the thing *pretending* to be the coyote, I'm telling you—standing at the edge of the lake. Just standing, staring at me. Goddamned creepy. *Staring* at me. With those fucking *eyes*." He shook his head. "So I sat back in the boat, you know, trying to ignore it. I don't know how long. I lost track."

Dax thought he was going to have to prod Wyatt to continue, but as abruptly as he trailed off, he started talking again.

"So then I look up, and I see something in the water. Floating, you know. Mostly, I see the dark hair—like this long black hair all fanned out, all tangled and floating at the surface. But, hey, I hadn't seen nobody at all since pushing off. I would've noticed somebody drowning. I would've *noticed*. She was already dead."

"Wait. It was a body?" Dax asked.

"A what?" Wyatt snapped. "Oh, yeah. Yeah, it was a fucking body. Facedown in the water. Totally still, or, well, like floating with the current, you know, what's it, *undulating*."

"Undulating?"

"Yeah, undulating. That's what she was doing. I guess that's how I knew she was dead. Wasn't trying to swim or anything. But, still. What am I supposed to do, you know? Just, like, ignore the dead body floating in the fucking lake? How'm I supposed to enjoy myself with it right over there? So I paddle closer, maybe to turn her over or something, see if I recognize who it is. And I'm just reaching down into the water, you know, to grab her and turn her over, but—"

He stopped.

"But what?"

Wyatt fixed Dax with impossibly wide eyes, his pupils vast and black.

"But *she* grabbed *me*."

Dax let the words settle.

"So she wasn't dead."

Wyatt's eyes locked onto Dax's, searing him. "How? How could she not be dead, huh? Took longer'n a few minutes to paddle over. Whole time, she was facedown. Dead. Had to be dead. Fucking *dead*."

Dax shook his head and, at last, decided it was time to speak aloud what he'd been thinking throughout the story. "You were high."

"Yeah, I was high. So fucking what? You think I hallucinated this shit? You think I hallucinated *this?*" Wyatt shoved his cast in front of Dax's face. "She grabbed me—hard. Cracked my bones with one hand. You tell me: if she wasn't dead, then *what the fuck* was *she?*"

Dax had no answer, and he watched Wyatt lean back against the silo and then stand up straight again, as if he couldn't decide what to do with his body.

"That's not all," he said finally. "After she breaks my arm, and I fall back onto the boat, and I start paddling back to the bank like crazy, I look back ... and the top of her head is rising from the surface of the water. Just *rising*. I paddle, but, you know, I only got one good arm, and every time I look back, she's a little higher outta the water. All I saw was that long black hair and her wet dress dripping. I get to shore and look back and she's hanging in the air like a goddamn skeleton, I swear to you, hovering *a foot above* the lake. I took off and didn't look back, didn't stop running, 'til I was *gone*."

CHAPTER 4

The night hung heavy and oppressive around them, suffused with an uncanny chill that worked its way deeper into Dax's skin.

"And you don't think it was the drugs?" he said.

Wyatt's face darkened. He spat into the grass. "Knew you'd say that." His eyes flicked to the trees in the distance, searching out the coyote.

Dax didn't turn to look, and said, "Let's just find your sister and get the hell out of here."

Wyatt gave a jerky nod, drumming nervous fingers on his cast. He muttered something under his breath, kicked the wall of the silo, and started off across the grass.

Dax followed, and they walked in silence back to the house. He led them down the hall to the room where Savannah and her group had been, but it was empty and dark. The hairs on his arms prickled as he fumbled for his cell phone and lit the room in a quiet glow. Wyatt, walking backward down the hall, stumbled into his back and jarred the light around the floor.

"Hey," Dax said, catching his balance and steadying the light. He spotted a dark groove in the dirt floor, the width of a finger. It looked deliberate. "You see that?"

Wyatt's voice came out a whisper. "Is it her?"

"No. A drawing, maybe." Dax bent down and followed the line with his phone as it arced across the floor. "Sarah isn't here."

"I didn't mean Sarah," murmured Wyatt, a silhouette in the doorway. "I meant *her.*"

Dax felt uncomfortable in the small dark room. He pushed past Wyatt, through the doorway, into the hall, and back to the main area of the house. Loud music hit him, shuddering his heart. He didn't see

Sarah when he scanned the red-tinged room. Bodies writhed against one another. A circle of stars pierced through the hole in the roof, the jagged edges of broken wood planks jutting into the sky. He forced his eyes back to the people around him and recognized someone from Savannah's group—a nondescript brown-haired boy with glazed eyes. "Hey," Dax said, making his way to the table of drinks where the boy stood. "Have you seen Sarah Montgomery anywhere?"

The kid hiccupped a laugh, sloshing some of his drink out the sides of his plastic cup. "Sarah Montgomery!" he slurred with a grin. "Bitch can *drink*."

Wyatt grabbed the kid by his collar and yanked him close to his snarling face. "The hell you saying about my sister?"

"Whoa, take it easy," Dax said, prying Wyatt's fingers off the startled teen's shirt.

With a glare, Wyatt released his grip and stepped back.

Before the stranger could scramble away with his drink, Dax held up his hands, placating. "She was here?"

The kid nodded.

"Where did she go?" Dax said.

The kid shrugged. "I dunno. Out back?"

The cool night air greeted them again, though now the stars hid behind oncoming gray clouds. A cluster of people stood around the beer pong table, cheering and booing as the balls bounced into the grass. Sarah was not among them. He didn't see Zeke or Mason either.

Dax peered into the distance, to the line of trees at the edge of the farm. A lantern gave off white fluorescence in front of the trees, where several shadows huddled. A gunshot cracked through the air, followed by the tinkle of exploding glass.

The moon vanished behind a cloud.

There seemed to be a part of Wyatt missing—thrown deep into himself, or off into another reality. He clenched his jaw, breathing shallowly. His eyes were wide, perhaps seeing more in the night than was really there. He whispered to himself, the same word over and over.

Dax gave Wyatt a shove. "Snap out of it."

When they drew closer to the trees, Dax searched the silhouettes for a sign of Sarah.

Four boys and three girls egged each other on as they shot into the darkness. He didn't recognize them. "Any of you seen Sarah Montgomery out here?" he asked.

A gangly teen with long hair spat a line of brown saliva into the grass, then resumed chewing his tobacco. "Yeah, I mighta seen her," he said, "but she ain't here now."

"Where is she?"

He turned his head to the side and snorted as the moon returned, shining on teeth bared in a grin. "That her brother?" he said and nodded at Wyatt.

Dax shoved Wyatt forward, breaking his chant.

Wyatt glanced around. "It's following us," he murmured.

"Yeah, that's him," Dax said. We need to find her and take her home. She got really drunk."

The teen chuckled. "No kidding. She bet me she wasn't too drunk to hit a bottle." He nodded toward the fallen log in the distance, backlit by another lantern, where a line of glowing brown beer bottles perched. "Zeke gave her his 12-gauge. She could barely lift the thing, but damn it if she didn't get one, all right, after a few tries."

Wyatt kept mumbling.

"Where'd she go?" asked Dax.

In the space between words, he realized what Wyatt was saying: *devil eyes.*

The boy grinned. "That's something her brother might not wanna hear."

"What?" Wyatt snapped, rounding on the group. "*What?*" He turned from one to the next, staring into their faces.

One of the girls spoke up. "She went to the barn."

Wyatt's eyes locked onto her, sharp and deadly. "What'd you just say?"

"She looked like she saw something and took off toward the barn. Didn't even give Zeke back his gun, so he followed her. Wasn't more than a few minutes ago."

She didn't need to say more. They all knew what people went to the barn for.

"I will rip his *balls* out of his fucking nut-sack," Wyatt snarled. He tore off and Dax hurried after him.

"Wyatt—"

They sprinted across the field, stumbling over uneven ground.

Wyatt was ahead of him, going faster than he'd ever seen him run. As they approached the lightless barn, Dax slowed, letting Wyatt ride the wind alone. The moon flickered in and out of existence beyond the clouds. He opened his mouth to call out, to tell him to slow down, but a gunshot overtook his voice, this one from just ahead of them, *unmistakably* ahead of them, not from the group at their backs.

Dax stopped cold, even as Wyatt burst into the barn, banging the wooden door on its hinges. Dax couldn't move. His feet felt nailed to the earth. It wasn't until Wyatt let out a strangled, guttural yell that Dax snapped out of it. He entered the barn slowly, cautiously, stepping into the darkness with his arms out.

Wyatt stood near the doorway, staring inside.

The moon washed in through the windows, revealing blood pooling on the floor; it spread, a dark red puddle that was almost black in the night, seeping into the dirt. He followed the puddle to the shadowed figure lying there, unmoving, beneath the network of wooden beams that crisscrossed the ceiling.

Then a shaky voice said, "Is he dead?"

Dax looked up from the body.

A shadow resolved into Sarah, still frozen with the shotgun held out in front of her. The moon made her face deathly pale. Her arms trembled.

"Sarah!" cried Wyatt, rushing to her in the dark. He tripped and sprawled in the dirt, then let out a panicked sound as he shuffled away from the body.

Dax stepped closer.

Zeke stared glazed-eyed into the darkness above.

Breathing deeply through his nose, Dax reached down with two fingers and felt the still-warm neck for a pulse. A mess of red in Zeke's chest where the buckshot had entered. The realization he was touching a dead person turned his stomach, and he stepped away, wishing he wasn't enclosed by shadows, wishing he had a light.

Sarah bent over, fingers still locked around the gun, and vomited into the hay. When she stood, her cheeks glistened with tears. "I didn't mean to do it," she murmured.

Wyatt struggled to his feet and turned to his sister, chest heaving. "What the fuck did you do?" He grabbed the barrel of the gun, yanked it out of her hands, and tossed it to the ground. "What the *fuck*, Sarah?"

Hands now empty, Sarah brought them up to her face and covered it from view. Then she sank to her knees, shaking all over.

"She wasn't here," Sarah said. "I thought I saw her, but she wasn't here. I couldn't find her. She wasn't here, and Zeke started ... touching me ... I told him to stop. I tried to ... He didn't listen. So I ... so I ... oh god."

Dax could barely see her in the dark. He didn't *want* to see her. Let her voice ride bodiless on the night, disconnected from the hand that had pulled the trigger. The tang of blood filled the air, and Dax swallowed to stop from gagging. If he looked away, he could almost pretend Zeke didn't lay dead on the floor but for the smell reminding him that this was real.

"So you shot him?" Wyatt snapped. "You fucking *shot* him?"

"I didn't mean to. I didn't mean to," Sarah whispered. "I tried to tell him. He didn't listen. I told him I would use it. But he ... he laughed. He didn't believe me. He didn't believe me ..." Her voice trailed off. "He kept laughing. He just kept laughing!"

Wyatt stood over his sister, looking down at her. Dax wanted him to say something. This unnerving quiet was somehow even worse than his yelling.

Unable to take the heavy silence and the feeling of death hanging in the air, Dax stepped through the doorway. Out here, the night was cool, calm. The stars watched over the dark landscape from their perch in the sky. He looked around, expecting to see couples stumbling toward the barn, but the field was deserted.

After a moment, he went back inside. He looked around, dazed, at the blood on the floor, at Sarah curled up in the hay, at Wyatt hovering over her, at Zeke's corpse, the smell of gunpowder and alcohol pervading the barn.

"The sheriff," Dax said, then stopped as dread filled him. "What are we going to do? I mean, it was clearly self-defense. He knows what his son is like. He'll have to believe—"

"Just how stupid *are* you?" Wyatt snapped, rounding on Dax. "Zeke gets away with plenty of shit, and his dad always looks the other way. You think he'll fucking look the other way for Sarah?"

"If it was self-defense, the law—"

"Damn the law! You think Sheriff Anderson'll give a rat's ass about the law when it comes to Zeke? This is my fucking sister!" Wyatt roared.

"I'll turn myself in," Sarah said from the floor, her voice so quiet it seemed to be coming from far away.

"The hell you will." Wyatt's voice was hard, uncompromising.

Dax looked out the doorway again, across the field. This time there were two shapes moving toward them in the distance.

"Someone's coming," he said.

Throwing himself past Dax, Wyatt leapt out the doorway and went silent. The figures drew closer, moonlight etching their silhouettes against the ground, the silence beating on to the tempo of Dax's heart.

Then Wyatt flapped his arms and bellowed, "Occupied, motherfuckers!"

For a long moment they stopped walking, just stood there, dark and featureless on the plain. They didn't seem real, just undefined shadows, standing still and staring, alien-like, across the vastness of the field.

After a moment that dragged into infinity, the shadows turned and headed back the way they'd come.

"That's right, and don't come back," Wyatt mumbled. He pushed past Dax and went back into the barn. After a moment, Dax followed.

He avoided looking at the dark patch on the ground. He thought about the sheriff and realized, with a slow and viscous dismay filling his veins, that Wyatt was right. And now, more than a witness, he felt like an accomplice. Finally, he spoke, almost disbelieving his own suggestion as he said, damning himself with the words: "We have to get rid of the body."

A wild, awful laugh escaped Wyatt. "Throw it in the lake," he said. "Throw it in the lake, it'll come back to life! It'll come back!"

"Fine," Dax said, trying to keep himself calm. "We'll take him to the lake. Dump him there." He swallowed and thought of dragging Zeke's dead body out to the lake, rolling him into the water, his blood staining it red. Eventually, though, he would float back to the surface—like that body Wyatt may or may not have encountered. Float back to the surface, maybe keep floating when he got there, floating up out of the water ...

"I ain't going back there," Wyatt said.

Sarah curled in a ball on the hay, head between her knees.

Dax sank into the shadows of the barn, eyes adjusting to the darkness. Moonlight slanted in through the windows, thin and ghostly. There were some old rusted tools piled in the corner: a dull saw, a twisted pitchfork, a shovel. He grabbed a handle, tested its strength. "We'll bury him," he said. He turned around and looked back at the Montgomery siblings. The moon glinted in Wyatt's eyes, reflecting weirdly when he nodded. They managed to get Sarah on her feet and to the doorway so she could keep watch. Wyatt took Zeke's feet, Dax the arms. The weight was solid, but they were able to drag him to the back of the barn before stopping. Then they dragged him farther still, away from the barn, far enough that the echoes of the party vanished into the night. They were met only with the chirp of crickets and the occasional owl's hoot.

Dax tried to ignore the feeling of cold flesh in his hands. Zeke's head lolled back and stared up at him with blank, unblinking eyes. He shuffled backward, glanced behind him at the copse of trees off the edge of the property. Within those trees loomed a thick, unbroken darkness. When they made it there, they lowered Zeke onto the grass, and Wyatt left to retrieve the shovel. Dax leaned against the bark of a tree to catch his breath.

Eli the coroner's words came to him then, about the sanctity of the body in burial, and he forcefully shook off the whisper of the old man's voice. He thought of Zeke abandoned in his unmarked grave, a victim of time. He thought of spring turning into summer and the heat baking the dry soil all the way through to the tatters of his face—summer sliding into fall and yellow leaves that were the bounty of death—fall plunging into winter where beneath forgetful snow a bare skull lay frozen in an eternal grin—winter melting into spring and seeds sprouting up out of the mulch, blooming from empty sockets and between ribs, breeding lilacs out of the dead.

Dax trembled in the chill of night as years spun through his mind, all the tortured years before Zeke would finally, at the end of an age, collapse to dust and be no more. Until then, he would lie here, and Dax would always know. Zeke would grin, as he always grinned, unable ever to stop.

Dax stared into the dark of the forest, the shadows full and thick with nameless secrets. Here was another for time to keep, a secret guarded by the woods, perhaps one of many lurking among the roots and shotgun shells. If he walked through the forest, he might step on hundreds of mysteries buried in dirt, a host of cold denizens laid to nameless rest. He looked at his feet and stepped to the side, then back again, feeling as though there were things beneath his shoes upon which he dared not tread.

His eyes found Zeke again and could not look away. Irrationally, he found himself watching for movement, expecting the body to twitch and shudder. He knew Zeke was dead, but it did not seem possible that he was not also still alive somehow. He rubbed sweaty palms on his jeans, staring, staring at the immobile form. At last, he looked away to see two shadow-beings approaching from the farm. They seemed insubstantial, less real than the body, as though life itself were merely a play of shadows rehearsing for whatever came after the final curtain.

At last the shapes of Wyatt and Sarah manifested in the moonlight. Wyatt carried the shovel in his good hand.

"Turned over the dirt in the barn," he said when they got to Dax. "Lot of blood."

The shovel wasn't the only thing Wyatt carried; he dropped the gun onto the ground beside Zeke's body.

Dax reached for the shovel, thinking Wyatt couldn't dig with a broken arm, but Wyatt shooed him away and, with a grunt, speared the ground. He hacked feverishly into the dirt, attacked it with a violence Dax had never seen in him before. Dax looked away, at the ground. Something glinted in the grass near his feet, and he stooped to pick it up—a silver watch with a broken clasp: the watch Zeke had been wearing. He slipped it into his pocket so that he wouldn't forget it there on the ground, to be found by anyone.

After a while, Wyatt paused, and Dax took the shovel from him.

They took turns digging until Dax was sweating, dirt-stained, straining his arms.

Wyatt, on the other hand, seemed incapable of tiring. He didn't stop to catch his breath, just tore at the dirt, pulling up great chunks and tossing them away despite the poor grip he had with the bit of cast running between his thumb and pointer. When Dax tried to take the shovel back, Wyatt snarled at him and kept digging with that unnatural energy. The moon crested the sky as midnight slipped away into morning.

Sarah hadn't moved or spoken since the digging began. Dax thought she must be in shock, and he didn't dare disturb her.

At last the grave was done, and they rolled Zeke to the edge. Rigor mortis had begun to set in. His limbs jostled stiffly as he toppled into the pit.

Dax tossed in the shotgun—gently, not wanting it to hurt when it thumped onto his stomach, yet simultaneously knowing, knowing horribly, that Zeke wouldn't feel it, would never feel again. They started piling dirt back into the hole, covering the face he remembered alive, the face he'd seen laughing only a few hours earlier, when they were playing beer pong. He dropped dirt onto the congealing hole in Zeke's chest, then onto his face, over his open eyes and mouth, until the body disappeared beneath the soil.

CHAPTER 5

Sarah gave Dax the keys to the Dodge, and together the three of them made their way, tired and dazed, back out to the field filled with cars. Dax got behind the wheel, Wyatt in the passenger's seat. Sarah curled up in the back and fell asleep, her body offering the only coping mechanism it could. Dax sat there for a moment, put the key in the ignition.

"What have we done?" Dax said.

Wyatt's pupils seemed too large, too black, filled with the secrets of the forest. His face was stretched tight. He stared out the windshield, his jaw twitching.

"Just drive," Wyatt said.

Dax started the engine and drove across the bumpy field, onto the road. They wound their way through the countryside in silence, through darkness lit only by headlights, through the emptiness of early morning, toward the Howard farm.

Wyatt spent the ride chewing on his lower lip until it was a mess of torn skin, and when they pulled into the driveway, he looked up in surprise. They got out, and Wyatt opened the back door and reached in for Sarah. Dax tried to help, but Wyatt shrugged him off and picked up his sister, draping her knees over his cast. She didn't stir as he carried her into the house and deposited her on the couch.

Exhaustion ached through Dax's threadbare nerves. He started down the hallway, past his old bedroom, heading instead for the room at the end with Wyatt trailing along behind him. He opened the door to his father's room and stepped inside.

In the still of the early morning, the abandoned bedroom felt like a tomb. He faced the mirrored doors of the armoire and saw Wyatt manifest behind his own reflection. Ignoring the haggard shell-shocked looks they both wore, Dax pulled open the doors.

"Shit, man," Wyatt said as he took a step back. "Are we going to Narnia?"

Dax picked up the metal urn. His throat went dry, and he tried to swallow.

"Is that ...?"

Wyatt didn't need to finish. Dax nodded. He clung to the cold urn, willing his father's presence to deliver some kind of comfort, but there was nothing here. It was just a container holding ash—ash that could once have been anything.

Wyatt stepped up beside him, peering into the armoire. Dax thought about shutting the doors, shutting his mother's memory into the dark where it belonged, but he couldn't bear to look into his own accusing reflection in the dusty mirrors.

"Hey," Wyatt said, reaching for the clothing. He pushed the hangers further to the sides, the shirts swinging, exposing the collage of newspapers Dax had nearly forgotten was there. "Whoa," he said, reaching forward again, fingering the curled edges of weathered newspaper. "You know this was here?"

"Not until today," Dax said.

"You looked through it yet?"

Dax shook his head as Wyatt tore off one of the papers and frowned. At an angle, Dax saw his mother's name and the word "missing." It was a local paper.

This one may have started the whole thing, he realized.

He imagined his father sitting at the kitchen table, reading newspaper after newspaper after newspaper. He imagined him disappearing into his bedroom alone, carefully cutting articles with the pair of rusted scissors Renée had used to cut fabric for the quilt she'd made. He imagined his father crouching in front of the armoire, smelling her herbal scent, enveloped in her clothing, as he taped articles together and stared at his design, drinking and thinking of ... *what?*

What had he been thinking? Surely it wasn't just a bizarre method of grieving. He had been looking for something. Had he found it?

Wyatt leaned forward to read more of the articles. "Look at this," he said, but Dax didn't. "It talks about a carnival."

Dax shook his head. He didn't want to know.

Wyatt pulled back and turned to him. "You think ... the one, you know ... with your mom?"

"That must be what this is all about," Dax said. "I mean, they never found it. Sheriff Anderson said he tried. It was just gone, and no one knew where it went, so he gave up. But I guess ..."

He guessed his dad hadn't given up. The sheriff hadn't seemed convinced the carnival had anything to do with Renée's disappearance, though others in town whispered that it was a pretty funny coincidence for her to disappear at the carnival, and then for it to disappear, sucked up into the wind like smoke. The sheriff had given up, and for that, Roy never forgave him.

Dax swallowed, feeling shivery. "He was looking for it, wasn't he?"

"Maybe," Wyatt said.

Dax looked into the armoire, and the bits of newspaper swam before his eyes, swirled together. His heart pounded. He felt sick.

Wyatt reached in and started ripping down the papers, one by one.

"Hey—"

He turned to Dax, papers clutched in both hands. His eyes held a feverish gleam. "I'll figure it out," he said, nodding to himself. "I'll figure out what he was doing. Don't you want to know? Don't you want to know what he found?"

Dax stepped back and sat on the bed while Wyatt dropped to the floor, his back against the foot of the bed, and spread out the articles before him. Dax glanced into the armoire and the bare back wall, its papering dislodged. Tiny holes punctured the wood from the tacks that now littered the floor, giving the back of the wardrobe a naked and diseased appearance.

As Wyatt started flipping through the articles, Dax found himself staring through the armoire, staring back in time at Zeke, in the ground. He blinked and gazed into the vaguely reflective surface of the urn. He saw the blood on the barn floor. He saw pieces of newspaper in the recycling bin.

Wyatt murmured to himself as he read.

"Buckland, Ohio. 1973," he mumbled, his voice drifting across the room to Dax as the latter, limbs heavy and raw from digging, collapsed onto the bed. He set the urn onto the bedside table and lay on his side, staring at it. "Woodburn, Iowa. 1964. Bellflower, Missouri. 1988. Fairfield, Oklahoma. 2001."

The litany continued as Dax closed his eyes. Zeke was there again, pale and still.

"Crescent Valley, Louisiana. 1952."

Zeke's eyes snapped open, and they were a sickly jaundiced yellow. Dax jerked awake as Wyatt continued mumbling and moving papers. He turned over, staring out the window into the predawn dark, and then closed his eyes.

When he woke next, it was morning. Sunlight filtered into the room, landing warm on his face. He lay on top of the covers, still wearing his jeans and shoes. Something dug uncomfortably into his thigh, and he rolled over and extricated the metal object from his pocket. The silver watch dangled from his hand, ticking away. He had forgotten to bury it, he realized with dismay, and dropped it on the bed.

When he sat up, he was surprised to find Wyatt exactly where he'd left him last night.

"Did you sleep at all?" Dax asked, running a hand over his face, which was rough with impending stubble.

"No," Wyatt said, shuffling papers. "I don't need sleep."

Dax sat on the edge of the bed, peering over the top of Wyatt's head.

"Find anything interesting?"

"Murder. Tornados. County fairs. And carnivals, poking their heads in everywhere."

"Carnivals?" Dax said. "Or carnival, singular?"

"Hell," Wyatt said, scratching under his cast, "I don't know. Could be the same, could be a dozen different ones. Who knows?"

As a child, Dax had been almost as obsessed with the idea of carnivals as his father. Their cranking machinery and leering residents carried over an uncanny quality into his nightmares. As the years had passed, and his dreams receded behind him, he'd begun to mull it over more rationally and come to side with the sheriff. There simply wasn't enough proof to blame the carnival. Renée could easily have been taken by a drifter. Perhaps a certain dread had lingered in his subconscious, but that didn't make it logical. And now what did they have, anyway? A jigsaw of conjecture compiled by a lonely alcoholic? It wasn't the most compelling argument.

Maybe she'd been murdered, right here in town. Maybe she was buried somewhere, unmarked and forgotten, like Zeke.

"Here," Wyatt said, pointing to the map he'd spread across the floor. "He found all the places—from the articles, you know—and marked them on the map. Small towns, all of them, like here. Not all of them are listed, but he must've figured out where they were, anyhow." Dax leaned forward to see the circles drawn in black ink.

"He went seriously old school with this whole thing," Wyatt continued. "Did he have something against a little thing I like to call *the internet?* Aside from the ones he printed, helluva lot of these are the real thing. Must've been a job for him to track down all these papers. Except this one, from here in Conjunction."

Wyatt brandished an article dated 1968 with a picture of a family grinning black-and-white from the page and the headline: "Willoughby Massacre's Lone Survivor Runs Away."

With a jolt, Dax realized who the people were in the picture.

The Willoughby family had been slaughtered one night, their bodies tied to crosses and left in the fields like scarecrows. Scavenging birds had been pecking at empty eye sockets when a visiting neighbor discovered the bodies. He wasn't sure whether the birds had eaten the eyes or whether it was something else, but he remembered the detail about the eyes being gone. The image of those vacant sockets had haunted him when he'd first heard the story. It was equally possible, however, that none of this was true, as stories have a way of distorting the truth when retold time and again for the macabre curiosity of children.

Either way, Dax thought the entire Willoughby family had been wiped out that night. He scanned the article Wyatt handed to him. Someone named Luther Crane had spotted the youngest Willoughby— little Maybelle, age six—running through the fields beside Dunes Way, heading into the western sand hills, chasing after the caravan of a traveling carnival.

"Get this," Wyatt said, pointing to a paragraph in the middle of the article, "says this Luther guy was out that way visiting his girlfriend, Frieda Redding. That crazy old bitch must've been, what, eighteen, twenty?"

The narrow dirt road dead-ending at Frieda's cobblestone cottage wound through Dax's memory. "She lived at the end of Hells Hollow Road way back then?"

"Probably lived there her whole life," Wyatt said. "Don't know why you'd move to that kind of place. Unless you want to grow up to be a hermit. Can't say how many times that road floods a year."

"She still alive?"

"Far as I know. I think kids still dare each other to touch that old well."

Dax had touched the stone well in front of Frieda's place once when he was young. People in town whispered that she talked to it, heard voices inside. *Crazy Frieda.* The mean ones said she threw trespassing children down there. Naturally, that made children want to sneak onto her land and look for bones at the bottom.

He'd gone not long after his mother disappeared. Angry and defiant, he'd convinced Wyatt to dare him to touch the well. The stars had been out that night, a nearly-full moon bulging overhead. Her wind chimes had clinked in the breeze—*crafted of the bones of children?*—and he'd crept up to the well, the stone cold against his palms, and peered into its dark, fathomless depths. And then she had appeared at his side—a frightful old hag to his child's mind riddled with fairy tales. She'd grabbed his wrist and yanked his hand away, spun him around to face her.

Moonlight had deepened her frown as she bore down on him. "The hell you think you're doing out here, boy?" She'd pushed him until he felt the edge of the well pressing into his back. She'd pushed him until he bent backward so far he heard his spine creak, and then the sky tilted overhead. Somewhere below, the cold air of the well had reached up for him, prickling the back of his neck, and he'd wanted to turn his head to see what ghosts exhaled that cold dead air, but could not. Whatever had lain below, he could not see—could only see the stars etched in black above, and Frieda looming closer. He'd felt his heartbeat quicken. "You want to end up down there?" she'd said. He'd felt a wave of vertigo, that at any moment he would tip over, plummet into the blind infinity below.

Dax shook his head, wishing he'd seen what was down there. His young mind had conjured all manner of impossible horrors explaining what had reached up for him.

"Don't you know that well is haunted, boy?" she'd whispered. "Can't you *hear* it?"

His breath had come out in harsh pants as he'd tried to wriggle free, but it was no use. He'd gazed up into the darkness between stars, the deepest reaches of outer space, and had wondered if it was the same darkness from the well.

Then he'd heard it. Something sloshing through the water, far below. The echo of a splash ricocheting up the walls. An impossibly deep groan, like the sound of the earth shifting. Whispers, perhaps, of many voices tangled together as they fought to escape the endless chasm. Dax had gripped the edge of the well and had pushed forward, unbending his back and surging straight into Frieda, desperate to escape from that sound and whatever lay below. He'd found himself momentarily cushioned by her bosom, and then she had stepped back to let him fall. He'd stumbled, landing on his knees in the damp grass.

"I catch you out here again," she'd said from somewhere above him, "you'll find out what's at the bottom of that well, boy."

As soon as he'd found his feet, he ran, expecting the ghosts of the children she'd killed to rise up from the well. He'd thrown glances over his shoulder, feeling as though something were following on his heels. The memory of his footsteps carried him through time, back onto the Hells Hollow Road of distant memory, back into the daylight of his father's bedroom.

"We should talk to her," Dax said now as he made for the door.

Wyatt sprang to his feet. "Are you out of your goddamn mind? She'll pitch us down that creepy well of hers for sure. There's something not right up here," he said, tapping his temple. "Schizophrenic, or some shit."

"Are you scared of an old woman because she's mentally ill?" Dax said, trying to forget the adolescent fear that had kept him away from her house ever since that encounter.

"Hell, that's not—She's *crazy*. Besides," he added, "I gotta go back to the Willoughby farm."

"What? Why would you want to go back there?"

"That was my pipe I left in the silo." Wyatt shrugged. "I want it back."

The idea of returning to the Willoughby farm turned Dax's stomach.

"You think he left it there?"

"That's what I would do," Wyatt said, looking defensive. "Barney's cool. He wouldn't jack my shit."

Dax crossed his arms. "Fine. We'll go back. But first we're going to talk to Frieda."

For a moment, Wyatt seemed to wrestle with himself. Then he nodded.

Dax headed down the hall, but the couch Sarah had been sleeping on was empty. He looked around and flinched when he found her sitting stone-still on the rocking chair, knees curled up to her chin, staring blankly into space.

"You're awake," he said as he entered the living room.

She blinked slowly.

"It wasn't a dream." Her voice was little more than a rusty croak.

Dax looked down at the wood floor, tracing the grain with his eyes.

"Hey. Wyatt and I are going to go meet someone. You're welcome to …" He couldn't finish the sentence, realizing he wasn't comfortable leaving Sarah alone. "Maybe you should come with. You can hang in the car if you want."

"Okay," she murmured.

Wyatt emerged from the hallway, and they went out to the Bronco.

Dax started the engine, headed west down Old Haven Lane. Sunlight and clouds made sharp shadows against the morning glare. He turned onto Dunes Way, the edge of Sandpiper Lake just visible in the distance, a blue glimmer outlined by a vast forest.

When he pulled onto Hells Hollow Road, a cloud of dirt rose behind the back tires. They passed through a cluster of trees and emerged as grass and weeds began overtaking the road. It disappeared altogether when they pulled up to the stone cottage. He parked in the grass beside what remained of the road. Behind the house, an old windmill spun lazily against a pale blue sky.

He and Wyatt got out and went to the front door, Sarah trailing behind them.

Dax banged the rusted brass doorknocker once, twice, the echo loud in his ears. Heavy footsteps trod within. Wyatt fidgeted, cracking his knuckles.

The door swung open, and Frieda Redding stepped into the threshold. Long white hair wisped like gossamer over her shoulders. Her eyes were two wounds in the wrinkled flesh, gashes that opened onto darkness behind half-moon glasses. Gravity dragged the corners of her mouth into a frown.

"Well?" she said.

"Frieda? I'm Dax. This is Wyatt—Sarah."

The wind picked up. The mill's blades spun faster, and a chime jingled through the quiet.

"Who?" she snapped, peering over the rims of her glasses.

"We're just—"

Wyatt elbowed Dax out of the way and held up the newspaper

article he'd brought along. "We want to talk to you about Luther Crane and the Willoughby massacre."

Frieda's frown deepened. She looked from one to the next, the loose skin of her neck quivering. When she spoke again, her voice whistled through the spaces between her teeth.

"Just who in the hell do you think you are? I'm not talking to you about nothing," she snapped and made to close the door on them.

Wyatt thrust his good hand between the door and the jamb, and for a moment Dax thought she was going to slam it shut and break his fingers. She stopped just short of fully closing the door, peering at them through the four-inch opening she'd left.

"You get off my land right now. You want to see the killing end of my rifle?"

"Please," Dax cut in. "Or, maybe you can tell us where we can find Luther Crane."

One beady eye squinted at him through the opening. "Sure, I can tell you," she said with a huff that sounded almost like a laugh. "Six feet under for some forty years, that's where you can find him."

"What happened to him?"

Her one visible eye darted from Dax to Wyatt to Sarah. "Dug himself a grave and lay down in it, that's what." Her eye slid away and refocused somewhere behind them. "Why you want to know about Luther?"

"In the article," Dax said, stepping in front of Wyatt, "he said something about a carnival."

"You would want to know about that, wouldn't you?" She opened the door wider. "Well, if you won't let it alone, you'd best come in. Kettle's on."

She stepped aside to admit them, and they followed her down the cramped front hall and into the living room, where a picture window overlooked the browning fields to the south. They took seats at the worn sofa that had bits of fluff poking out the seams.

"How do you take it?" she said.

It took Dax a moment to realize she was offering them tea.

Sarah said, "Milk and sugar."

Frieda banged around the kitchen for a few minutes, muttering to herself, then returned with two mugs. She sat down in an armchair and stared across the coffee table at them.

Dax cleared his throat and said, "We're here because ... well, my mother disappeared when I was a kid."

"I know," she said, taking a sip of her tea. "I know who you are: Dax Howard. Think I would've let you in if you'd been some journalist or other, shoving old newspapers in my face?" Without transferring her gaze, she added, "Put down a coaster, we ain't animals."

Sarah grabbed a coaster and slid it under her mug.

"Could you tell us about Luther?" Dax asked.

Frieda studied them, sipped her tea. "That was a long time ago. Nothing to tell about old Luther."

Wyatt jumped up, started pacing the room.

Frieda quirked an eyebrow at him and pursed her lips, but he didn't seem to notice.

"He died forty years ago, you said," Wyatt offered. "So what happened to him? Not old age. He saw something, that's what the article said. He saw that little girl. Did it have anything to do with that?"

"Boy, you sit your ass down 'fore I take a cane to it," Frieda said.

Wyatt returned to the sofa, but instead of fidgeting, he sank into the cushion as if dead and didn't move.

"If he saw something," Frieda said, "I don't know anything about it." She spoke directly to her tea. The steam fogged her glasses.

The woman who sat before them was hardly the fearsome hag from Dax's youth. It wasn't that she had changed, though. *He* was the one who had changed, and by his changing, he had changed *her*—the way he saw her, at least. He wondered, if he had one last opportunity to speak to his father, how different it might be from that night four years ago. Would his father have changed, too, with Dax's changing? He decided not to get lost in thoughts he didn't altogether understand. The speculation only enlarged his regret. A faint buzzing sound drew him out of his thoughts, but he couldn't place where it was coming from.

His silence, as he fought himself free of this web of rumination, had given Frieda the space to conjure forth her own thoughts into words:

"He was always a tough one, my Luther," she mused. "Liked to drink more than his fill. One spring, he went down to New Orleans for Mardis Gras. Nearly drank himself to death, the fool. I had to march down there myself and pick him out of the gutter in Bourbon Street. Smelling to high heaven. Told him he'd better clean up his act or I'd leave him, right then and there." She smiled grimly. "Did he listen? 'Course not. You know how it is. Spent a year trying to get clean, only to go right back to the bottle every few months, as if he couldn't help it. As if he'd find himself somewhere at the bottom, underneath the beer." Her dark eyes pierced Dax. "It takes all kinds, don't it?"

He looked at the floor.

"That it does," she said, answering herself. "And it always takes them, in the end. Drank too much one night, wrapped his car around a tree, and that was the end of Luther Crane."

Dax had to dredge the words out of himself before he got stuck thinking too much of alcoholics. Frieda seemed to have that effect on him, her words burying him with their texture, ripe with meaning.

"What about ..." he said, "the Willoughby girl?"

Frieda slammed her mug onto the table, dark tea sloshing over the sides. "What about her?" Her hands trembled. She clasped them together and pursed her lips as she stared resolutely out the window. "He saw what he saw, and that's that. I don't know a thing about it. Whatever it was, he shouldn't have gone talking to reporters about it. Wasn't a few years after that he wrecked his car." She frowned. "I guess we'll never know if it was an accident or not."

There was the buzzing sound again, bringing an audible anxiety into the room.

Dax leaned forward. "Did *you* see Maybelle Willoughby?"

It was a long moment before she said, "I don't know what I saw." Her eyes gleamed with something dark and nameless. "But it wasn't Maybelle."

Outside, the wind chime gave a sudden, wild rattle, and Dax glanced out the window. Clouds stirred in the distance, approaching at the edge of the plain.

"What about the carnival?" he asked. "The one Maybelle was chasing?"

Frieda picked up her mug and held it close but didn't drink. "What about it? They set up here, on the land just south of my home, but I didn't go, of course. Sounds like Luther's Mardis Gras. Such debauchery usually leaves nothing but hangovers and heartache in its wake. You should know, I guess. You know what the word 'carnival' means?"

Dax shook his head.

"*Carne vale,*" she said in what must have been Latin. "Farewell to flesh."

A chill sank into his skin. He looked around at Sarah, holding her empty mug, and Wyatt, unexpectedly silent and still. Wyatt didn't look too good: his skin pale and slicked with a faint sheen of sweat, his eyes sunken into shadowed rings, and his lips cracked and dry. A scab had formed on his lower lip from chewing it.

When Dax stood to leave, Sarah blinked as though surprised to realize where she was. Wyatt took a little longer getting to his feet. He squinted even in the low lighting and pressed a hand against the wall for balance.

They stepped onto the porch, and Frieda stood in the doorway, washed with gray light. Her eyes lit on the well, unblinking and glazed with the kind of stare that fixes without seeing.

"It's quiet today," she said to no one.

Then she closed the door, leaving the three of them alone on the porch, wind chimes clinking in the stormy breeze. Darker clouds inched ever-closer to the pale gauze that made a ghost of the sun.

As they stepped off the porch, Dax heard the buzzing again.

Sarah pulled her vibrating cell phone out of her pocket. She held it, staring vacantly, not reading the ID. Finally she took a breath, hit a button, and held it to her ear.

"Hi, Mom," she said. "Oh, really? No, I didn't hear it. I was asleep. Yeah. His must have run out of battery, you know it never holds a charge." She glared at Wyatt. "Sorry. Yeah, sorry ... Dax's house. We just woke up. Okay. Be home soon." She gave Wyatt another sharp glance. "They're pissed we didn't come home."

Wyatt shrugged, slouched off to the car, head hanging low.

Heavy clouds crept over the sun, casting the world in gray.

Dax paused beside the well and gazed down the tunnel into earthy, unforgiving darkness. The whisper of the wind seemed to echo up at him, what might have been a flurry of ghostly voices chittering somewhere far below. He stumbled away, willing his mind to stop playing tricks, and hurried to catch up with the others as they climbed into the Bronco.

"Home?" Sarah said.

"My pipe," Wyatt grumbled, leaning his cast against the window and laying his face on it. "Get my fucking pipe."

"We're not going back there unless Sarah wants to," Dax said as he started the car.

Garbled curses streamed from Wyatt's hidden face before he finally picked up his head and snarled at them, "You want Sheriff Anderson to go snooping around the farm and find my pipe?" When neither Dax nor Sarah responded, he lay his head back down.

With a glance at Sarah's resigned face, Dax drove off toward the Willoughby farm.

Sarah cracked the window, lit a cigarette, and closed her eyes as she smoked, the heady scent of tobacco filling the car.

They peeled off down the road as Dax tried chasing a sun drowning in clouds.

The closer they got to the Willoughby farm, the harder Sarah smoked her cigarette. She got down to the filter and tossed it out the window, lit a second with no pause in between. Her hand trembled; the smoke shivered as it drifted from the smoldering tip.

Dax parked on the same field that had been filled with cars last night, but this morning was empty, tire tracks zigzagging across the trodden ground. The stillness was ghostly, a stark contrast to the loud, throbbing party that had surely seen the last of its stragglers stumbling away only hours ago.

When it became apparent Wyatt wasn't going to get out of the car—or move at all, for that matter—Dax wrenched open his door and stepped out into the stinging wind. He was surprised when Sarah followed him, and he opened his mouth to tell her she didn't need to come, but she shook her head, finished her second cigarette, and crushed the still-smoking butt under the heel of her shoe. Dry grass crinkled where she stepped.

"Come on," she muttered. "He's coming down. Means he'll be useless for a while."

They trekked out to the farmhouse, still trashed with empty half-crushed cans, chip bags, and red plastic cups, then kept going, out to the silo looming on the horizon. Against the bleak sky, it looked like the ruins of an ancient castle turret. They ducked inside.

Sarah pulled out a third cigarette and flicked the lighter against her palm. Dax searched the ground—shadowed in the silo's interior, lit only by the faint gray glow of the sky above—but it was bare. He was just about to give the pipe up for lost, to tell Wyatt his so-called "friends" had pilfered his pipe after all, when Sarah managed to get a flame on her lighter, which glinted off the glass pipe half-buried in the dirt. Dax dug it out and wiped it on his jeans.

"Well, Wy'll be happy," Sarah said, bringing a trembling cigarette to her lips.

Dax studied the clouded glass of the pipe. He thought of Wyatt's yellowing teeth, his pockmarked skin, and then the girl from the center of the circle the night before—grinning into the jar of dirt with that same rotten smile.

"Hey ... does Savannah smoke meth?"

"No!" Sarah blinked and shook her head. "No. She doesn't." She sounded less sure now. Her pleading blue eyes met his. "She's got the look, though, doesn't she?"

He shrugged.

"She didn't used to. She's ... *changed*." Sarah didn't make a move to leave the silo, just stood there smoking her cigarette. "I guess it doesn't matter. She's still Savannah, right?" She paused long enough for Dax to wonder whether he was supposed to respond. "I mean, sure, in some ways she's changed. But in some ways, she's the same. I still ... feel the same about her." She turned her eyes skyward, searching for something, some divine peace that could not exist in this place.

"I wanted to tell her, last night," she finally continued, her voice soft and distant. "I wanted to tell her how I feel about her. I needed some ... liquid courage, I guess. But I couldn't find her. It was like she disappeared after the story circle. Then I thought I saw her, by the barn—but when I got there, she was gone again.

"You know, the girls at school call me a dyke. Savannah's different, though. She's the only one who's ever..." She trailed off, forgetting even about the cigarette, which burned slowly in her fingers. "She saw me. I know she saw me. But she left me there. With *him*."

She closed her eyes. "I shouldn't've dragged you into this," she said. "I keep thinking ... I shouldn't have pulled the trigger. I should've let him do whatever he was going to do." Her voice wavered, and she took another pull on her cigarette. "Maybe if I let him do it, I wouldn't be ..." Her voice shook violently and choked off.

"No," Dax said. "Don't say that."

Perhaps her throat had closed with tears, for she didn't seem able to smoke anymore. She let the cigarette fall to the ground, half-finished.

They exited the silo and started walking back to the car, but Dax hesitated beside the farmhouse. Something nagged at him—that mysterious drawing in the dirt floor of what he had come to think of as

Savannah's room. By the light of his cell phone, he hadn't been able to see much, and now an intense curiosity overcame his desire to escape the deserted farm.

"Here," he said and handed Sarah the pipe. "Give me two minutes, I want to go check something."

He left her gaping at him as he took off toward the deteriorating house.

The main room reeked of beer and sweat, echoes of the departed partygoers, and he slowed as he crept into the hall, musty with muted light. The door to the room hung crooked and ajar, and he pushed it back with a creak of its rusty hinges. Cloud-shrouded sunlight snaked into the room through the cracks in the boarded-up window, fell over the dirt floor where Savannah had sat last night, and Dax breathed in sharply.

A huge eye spanning nearly the entire length of the floor had been etched into the dirt. Whoever had drawn it made no pupil: instead, within the oval of the iris were two strange symbols. Along the outer edge of the iris lay a series of characters: *68.816664 hr 93 ly.*

He didn't know what he'd been expecting, but it wasn't this.

What disturbed him even more than what had been grooved into the dirt was what he found missing on the floor of the room.

No footprints.

Not a trace of the weightless creator despite the great size of the eye, like a ghost disappearing through fresh and undisturbed snow.

How had the artist conceived this cryptic vision?

There was nothing, not even the candles that had perched around the clandestine group. Nothing but the vast blank eye staring up at him through the sightless enigma of symbols that meant nothing to him, but which must mean something to someone.

The shadow of that meaning crept up Dax's spine like the feeling of eyes on the back of his neck—the dark and unfathomable presence that seemed to gaze up at him from the bottom of Frieda's well. He thought of his old classmate from college, a girl named Lailani, and all the fantastic mysteries she believed the universe held just out of sight, and he felt now the cold shiver of his ignorance to the vast multiplicity of things beyond his own comprehension. He felt the utter smallness of himself, and the hugeness of this eye, and he wondered if he should even want to know what it meant, or if it was in fact the dark eye of Savannah's Father Death: The Watcher in the Stars.

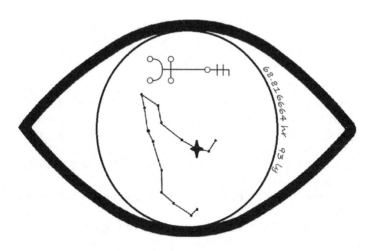

CHAPTER 6

Dax might have wiped away the image with his foot, stamped out the inscrutable iris, but he didn't move. Motes of dust haloed by narrow shafts of gray sunlight floated in the air, turning the quality of the room to one of thickness and perpetual motion. The slowly swirling dust preserved, tomb-like, what lay below, and Dax couldn't bring himself to destroy it despite his ill feelings.

He stepped back into the hall. Footsteps approached behind him.

"What's the holdup?"

He turned to find Wyatt, one hand braced against the wall. His voice sounded as though it had been raked over gravel.

"Come on," Wyatt said, "we got the pipe. Let's get the fuck out of here."

"I was just ..." Dax trailed off and gestured toward the room.

"The hell?" Wyatt said as he peered past him. He squinted and shook his head. "What is that?"

"This is where Sarah was hanging out last night with her friend Savannah." Dax pulled out his cell phone and snapped a photo. "I don't know what *that* is, though."

"Bitch sounds like bad news," Wyatt muttered, turning away. "Figure it out later. Let's go home."

Dax followed Wyatt back outside to the field where long grass blew slanted in the wind. Sarah waited in the car, smoking her fourth cigarette of the morning.

When Dax dropped them off outside his house, and they climbed into the Dodge and took off in a cloud of dust, he felt suddenly deserted. The house swelled with memories of his parents, and outside heavy clouds threatened rain. He walked from room to room, unsure what to do with himself. His father's absence manifested in all the empty corners and quiet doorways of the house. Here and there he found an empty bottle, and his heart sank.

He showered. The water came out cold. He stood waiting for it to warm, until his skin prickled and numbed, and then realized the hot water must have been shut off. After the shower, a threadbare towel provided little comfort as icy water streamed down his legs and puddled on the floor. He might as well have gone outside and waited for the rain to pound him clean.

Shivering and damp, he dressed and went into his father's room. Newspaper articles lay strewn about the floor where Wyatt had left them. The urn sat on the bedside table. He momentarily envisioned himself carrying it around with him all the rest of his life, never letting it out of his sight, as if to make up for the four years' distance he could never take back. He imagined the urn in the passenger seat of the Bronco, gleaming in the sun; the urn on his desk at some future—and now perhaps impossible—research job, his coworkers leery of the dead man that cohabited his cubicle; the urn on a front row seat during his marriage to some faceless woman; the urn alone and abandoned in the eventuality of his own demise, when its meaning would cease to exist and it would transform back into a plain pewter receptacle filled with nameless ash.

In that moment, he wondered whether he might have been better off buying a plot at the county cemetery. Then he remembered Zeke in the ground, rotting slowly, slowly, and he put the thought to rest.

Dax wanted to say something to his father, but speaking to the metal container struck him as absurd. Instead he opened it and peered at the pile of gray dust, then reached inside, the vessel's neck just wide enough to fit his hand. His fingers plunged into fine particles of ash. Faintly repulsed, and tinged with an inexplicable embarrassment at such intimate contact with the remains, he sifted through the material. Eli hadn't done a thorough job; he came across small chunks of bone and something with ridges he couldn't identify. He pulled it out, and in the palm of his dirty hand was a tooth. He dropped it back into the ashes and closed the urn.

He couldn't un-see the tooth, couldn't un-feel it in his hand.

With the urn safely ensconced in the armoire once again, Dax went to the kitchen and sat at the table. Above the sink, the window draped itself in old blinds. One was missing, leaving a three-inch gap that let in the darkness of the coming storm.

He set about sketching the image of the eye onto a sheet of paper after examining the picture on his phone. Though he hadn't inherited his mother's artistic skill, he managed to copy it down as it looked in the photo. The eye stared back at him.

Thunder rent the air, and Dax looked up with a start from the hypnotic drawing.

A pale face peered in at him through the gap in the blinds—one eye pressed up to the window. He tensed with a shuddering gasp of fear that made his whole body cold.

He only saw it for a flash before he blinked—and the face was gone. The only thing beyond the window now was darkness.

Goosebumps erupted across his arms as the cold rush of misplaced adrenaline washed over him, and he found himself shaking. He could have sworn he'd seen that sliver of face watching him from the window—Savannah gaping in at him—but it was gone, and now he wondered whether it had ever been there.

After a while, his heart slowed. Wind whistled through the cracks in the house. A spike of lightning cleft the sky and flashed through the gap in the blinds. Then, at last, the rain fell.

The storm hadn't let up by nightfall. He slept deeply and dreamlessly until morning.

He awoke to a sharp knock at the front door.

Rain drizzled down the windowpanes, but the clouds had lightened against the risen sun. The knock came again, and Dax scrambled out of bed.

The front door didn't have a peephole, and he stood there for a moment, his hands sweaty with trepidation. He swung open the door to find Sheriff Anderson on the stoop.

"Dax," the sheriff said, tipping his hat. "Mind if I come in?"

"Uh," Dax looked around, heart pounding. "Sure." He stepped back to let the sheriff walk past him into the living room, where he took a seat on the couch.

The sheriff lowered his head, removed his hat, and held it between his knees. The hunch of his back and low hang of his head bespoke a kind of unfamiliar dejection and weariness.

Dax sat in the opposite chair, suddenly aware of his oversized pajama pants and bare feet.

"My condolences about your father," the sheriff said suddenly. It wasn't what he had meant to say, Dax could tell, and it sounded forced, blurted out of guilt or regret. The sheriff sighed and fixed blue-gray eyes on Dax, his face haggard. "I know this isn't a good time for you, but I— I've been calling around town and heard you were at a party on Friday. At the old Willoughby place?"

Dax tried to conceal the mild trembling in his hands by clasping them together between his knees, mimicking the sheriff's posture. His heartbeat echoed in his ears.

He wondered how guilty he would look if he denied even being at the party. Did the sheriff have proof? Would denial be proof enough?

Distrusting his voice, he finally nodded.

"No need to look so scared," the sheriff said. "I'm not here to bust anyone." He fiddled with the brim of his hat. "My boy Zeke's missing. He was at the same party. Never came home. You didn't see him there, did you?"

Before he could stop himself, Dax shook his head. Then he said, "Yeah, in passing." A rush of panic washed through him when he realized Mason would have told the sheriff about their game. He thought of Zeke slinging his gun over his shoulder, then lying in the dirt covered in red. "I mean, we played a quick game of beer pong. I was pretty drunk. The whole night's kind of a blur, to be honest."

A long pause between heartbeats.

The lines around the sheriff's mouth deepened. "Anything else?" he said at last, and this time his voice was hard and cold.

Dax shook his head again. "I'm sorry," he said, and realized he *was* sorry. Maybe he hadn't been the one to pull the trigger, and maybe he had hated Zeke that night—hated him with a potent jealousy—but he was sorry. He was sorry Zeke was dead at twenty-three. He was sorry he couldn't tell the sheriff his son was never coming back. He was sorry the sheriff had to wander street to street, house to house, searching desperately for his son and wondering endlessly what had happened, wondering the same way Dax still wondered about his mother. He bit his tongue, and a warm, coppery taste flooded his mouth.

"Well, thanks for your time," the sheriff said, professionalism creeping back into his tone. He stood and put out his hand.

Dax did likewise and shook it, hoping the sheriff couldn't feel his pulse thrumming in his wrist. The man's hand was large and rough, and his grip was strong. Dax couldn't help but notice the gun holstered at his belt, and he tried to keep his eyes off it.

They walked to the front door, and the sheriff paused in the threshold to don his hat. He looked at Dax.

"Word to the wise," he said, a sharp edge in his voice. "I suggest you keep off the hooch. Didn't do your daddy no good, and it'd be a shame for the apple to fall too close to the tree."

A deadly silence stretched between them.

Finally the sheriff touched the brim of his hat again and walked off the porch to the cruiser. The car started, made a three-point turn, and peeled away.

Dax closed the door and stood with his back against it, breathing a long sigh of mingled dread and relief. He closed his eyes and pressed his palms against them until the backs of his lids erupted in gray stars.

The stars over Conjunction were the same as those over Minneapolis—the difference being that they were visible in the Nebraskan countryside. If you went out to the middle of a deserted field, nothing but cornstalks swishing at your ankles, and looked up, you might even see the dark trail of the Milky Way. Constellations drew patterns, which vanished in the city's eternal incandescence. On summer nights, Dax had spent his midnight hours lying on his back in the dirt, making his own mythologies out of the pictures he saw in the sky as ants crawled over his legs and owls called their low, ghostly hoots.

Aside from the trafficked streets, the jagged skyline, and cramped housing, the absence of stars had been the first thing he'd noticed about the city. He'd been too busy to give it much thought at first. He'd quickly found ways to use up his free time with work, and even some of the time he should have spent sleeping. He'd gotten jobs at a hardware store, a fast-food joint, a movie theater, and even an internship with the school doing research for one of his professors. He'd spent hours staring out the telescope, collecting data, and using different equations to create simulations on the lab computer. That had ended after his junior year, leaving him barely able to pay his phone bill.

Not that he used his phone much. He hadn't made many friends, and the ones he had he wouldn't call more than acquaintances. He could have called up Wyatt, but part of him had been hoping his friend was long gone from Conjunction by then, northbound to Iceland, even while another part of him knew, deep down, that Wyatt was right where he'd left him.

Those long hours spent inputting data into computer simulations might have made the internship a lonely endeavor had it not been for Lailani Castillo. They'd sat side-by-side well into the night, talking as they worked. One night, she'd asked where he had grown up.

"Small town in Nebraska. You?"

From behind her thick-framed glasses, her eyes had flitted across the computer screen. "I lived in the Philippines 'til I was six. I don't remember a lot of it. I think I might appreciate it more if I went back. We lived in this shoddy house on a forest road—my three brothers, parents, and Lola: my grandmother." She'd pressed her lips together in thought for a long moment. "Did you ever have anything ... *weird* happen to you, when you were younger?"

He might have said no, but she'd turned to look at him then. Her eyes were so dark that he couldn't see where the iris ended and the pupils began. Somehow that gaze had startled him into saying, "Yes."

"I think kids are magnets for weird stuff," Lailani had said. "When I was three or four, people used to follow me around. People nobody else could see."

"What, like imaginary friends?"

"The funny thing is, I don't really remember. My parents tell me I used to hide in closets and when they would find me, I'd tell them I was hiding from the shadow people. Lola took me to a medicine man—*Mananambal*, they called him. She told him I was haunted by spirits. I don't remember what he did, and Lola never went into detail about it. She died five years ago. But after that, I guess I was cured. No more shadow people. My parents are kind of superstitious, so they believed the medicine man did it—but for all they knew, I was just a kid making shit up, and I grew out of it." She'd laughed. "When I tell people that story, they look at me like I'm crazy. You're not looking at me like I'm crazy, though. Which makes me think you've got stories, too. Come on, spit it out. You're stuck with me for the next two hours, anyway."

He'd hesitated. "I grew up in a place called Conjunction."

"Any shadow people live there?"

"Just rural people," he'd said, shaking his head. "Which I guess are different from city people, in a way."

"Sure."

"I went to school in this tiny brick building, in the curve of a street called Deerlicker Lane. The freshman classroom was in the basement. It was always cold down there, year-round. You never saw a freshman walking out of school without a sweatshirt—except for the ones who thought they were hard. You know, the ones who smoked weed in the bathroom and rented different guns from the shop in town every week to show off their shooting."

"I don't actually know anyone like that, but sure."

"Well, anyway, the basement of the school was pretty bad. By the end of the year, the whole class was barely clinging to sanity. We all walked around like the dead. It was way into summer before any of us managed to shake off that chill. Any longer, and we might have turned into shadow people ourselves."

"Harsh," Lailani had said. "Your parents never tried to get them to move the class?"

"My dad was always busy with the farm," he'd said. "My mother disappeared when I was eight." He'd chewed the words before managing to get them out. "No one ... *really* knows what happened to her."

"I'm sorry," she'd said. "It's funny, though."

"Come again?"

"How people like us are drawn to the stars." She'd turned to him, and when she spoke next, it was with the voice she'd used in class: the calculating voice of someone deep in intellectual reflection. "When people experience things they can't understand, they look to the sky for answers. Which is so ironic, because that's the place you're least likely to find them. What's more mysterious than outer space?" She'd leaned forward and double-clicked to open something on her computer—an image from the telescope. Stars had filled the shot. "I think that's why people like us are drawn to astronomy. Trying to understand the unknowable. Of course, the more we know, the more we realize how much we *don't* know."

She'd zoomed in on the image, and the stars had resolved into the tiny spirals of distant galaxies, filled with even more stars too distant to make out individually, and beyond that, more galaxies too faint and too small for the telescope to catch.

He hadn't known how to respond; Lailani was able to navigate a certain gray area—to think in ambiguities. Math and lab experiments had filled most of the astrophysics major with the need for hard answers, but Lailani had existed within complexities. She'd believed all answers were merely questions no one had thought to ask yet.

She'd always reminded Dax of his own duality; his left brain craved logic and solutions, but his right brain was not satisfied by science alone—it needed stories, the myths his mother had shared with him as a kid. *But if science demystifies, how can the two ever really coexist?* Perhaps it was for this reason he was never quite satisfied with any answers, needing to find meaning from *both* sides. Lailani had been the first person Dax met for whom science and myth seemed to converge.

Over the course of that semester, the two of them had become friends.

Few guys paid much attention to her—perhaps intimidated by her intelligence, or more likely put off by her squat stature and bookish looks—but Dax thought about her often. Once, after a late night doing tedious work, they'd had a few drinks together and ended up in bed. It was an awkward, fumbling affair they never bothered to repeat. The next morning, after they'd smiled ruefully at each other, she'd pulled out a pill bottle. "I have an overactive mind," she'd said. "This helps."

Lailani was a year ahead of him, then, already accepted into a graduate program.

That summer, she'd attempted suicide.

He'd heard about it from someone else in the department. The news had ignited a slow, burning dread deep within him. He'd thought about getting in touch with her, but every time he prepared to dial her number, he was struck by panic. He'd spent the summer under a thin guise of calm, coming up with different scenarios in which death seemed like a good option to her. The world had become foggy and inscrutable to him, then, and the mysteries of the universe had seemed only to provide a great cosmic void indifferent to the minor plight of human beings. He'd felt sluggish and hollow, filled with the emptiness of all he didn't understand.

And when fall semester of his senior year began, he'd found he couldn't concentrate. All he could think about was Lailani—on the verge of success and in the infancy of her career—wanting nothing more than to die.

Sometimes the panic had consumed him; other times it seethed, low and hot, in the pit of his stomach. But it was always there. He'd failed out of one class halfway through and had dropped another before the professor could cut him loose. He'd picked up a few lower-level classes: Astronomy Appreciation, Early-American Lit, but neither had counted for his major. He hadn't even bothered enrolling in the right classes for spring. Instead, he'd sat back and watched himself destroy his future, not really understanding why. He'd ended up too short on credits to graduate, just in time for his four-year scholarship to end.

Dax never knew what had happened to Lailani, though he still thought about her sometimes. These memories of her had become almost more real than whoever she might be *now*, the way memories have a habit of usurping reality, preserved long after crumbling.

Memories spin on ...

Whenever he looked up at the stars, he knew some had already winked out long ago. He was seeing dead lights: ghosts in the great universal graveyard. Spinning, even in death, while they waited for the end of time.

⸺⚬⸺

Dax stared at the eye, and the eye stared back.

The symbol at the top of the iris left him clueless. It sort of resembled a key, but he could not imagine what it was meant to unlock.

Below the sigil was a crooked shape of lines connecting dots, and this he immediately recognized as a constellation, though he couldn't tell which. One of the dots near the right end had been drawn into a four-pointed star.

He stared at the images, awaiting clarity that never came.

When he was eleven or so, he and his father had sat out back one late autumn evening, and Dax had tried to point out the visible constellations. He'd picked an easy one—*see, those three stars make up Orion's belt, and the two square above them, his shoulders. The red one is called Betelgeuse.* But his father said he didn't see it, so Dax had tried again: the same constellation, only what his mother had taught him—what the Lakota saw. The belt became the spine of a bison; the rectangle of stars became the bison's ribs; the Pleiades became its head. *I don't see how you're connecting those dots*, his father had said. Dax had tried to show him the shape, how the stars came together into either animal or man, but Roy had shaken his head with a dismissive grumble. Dax had frowned, then, and said, *Mom knew this one. She knew both versions. She called it 'Orion the Bison.'* The friendly evening had turned quiet and cold. Without a word, Roy had gone inside, leaving Dax alone with the constellations, and when he looked up again, Orion had assumed his usual shape: a man with a club and shield. He'd played a trick with his eyes, then, where Orion transformed into a bison and then back again, over and over, until the stars had all but disappeared and he could only see the illusions they'd created.

Now, try as he might, he could not see the illusion behind the constellation within the drawn eye. He could only see what his father had seen years ago: random dots connected arbitrarily, signifying nothing.

He went into his father's room, still carpeted with a disarray of newspaper articles. While he idly gathered them, he couldn't help glancing at the headlines, then skimming paragraphs. Before he knew it, he was sitting on the bed reading an article from 1886, clearly printed from a computer. He had to squint to read the text—a spotty font that reminded him of the Old West.

The paper was from a place called Silvertown, Colorado and detailed disturbances following a vaudeville show gone wrong. Apparently, a boa constrictor had gotten loose from a minstrel show and had strangled an onlooker; in the chaos, several shots were fired from a booth with a display of guns, injuring three townsfolk. The fourth bullet fired had hit the minstrel square in the chest, but horrified onlookers had claimed he never broke character—just danced into one of the covered wagons and never reemerged. In addition to the chaos, some of the people at the show had become inexplicably mute afterwards, a mystery no one could explain, but the townsfolk all seemed to believe witchery was afoot. The Winking Eye Vaudeville company had apparently made a hasty retreat after that disaster of a show, packing their things overnight and vanishing by dawn. The mayor had posted a reward if anyone could bring in the scandalous troupe for the injury they'd done to Silvertown, as well as for the known bandit, Wild Willie Clayton, who had run off with the show after breaking out of the local jail. His crimes appeared numerous: theft, disorderly behavior, and a few gunfights.

Dax didn't see any more articles from that long ago. The next oldest was from 1927. The headline read, "Early Harvest for Pastor's Grove Yields Fresh Fruit, Fun at Fair."

The first line brought him to a stop:

"Crow County's own Pastor's Grove enjoyed an early harvest this year, launching its eleventh annual summer fair with a plentiful bounty of fresh fruits, nuts, and mushrooms."

He read the name again. The only towns in Crow County were Conjunction and Bannon; he'd never heard of Pastor's Grove. He hadn't even heard of it in connection with any of the nearby ghost towns. As a teenager, he'd heard plenty of stories about the surrounding abandoned settlements: overgrown places with little more than half a schoolhouse and a rusting grain elevator. Places where people were said to have died in horrific farming accidents and now haunted the empty landscapes. But he hadn't heard of Pastor's Grove. The place seemed to no longer exist, forgotten sometime between the summer harvest of 1927 and the present.

Dax skimmed ahead, past several lengthy descriptions of the economic boost promised by the good crops, and finally to the paragraph describing the fair. The festivities seemed rather ordinary: food, livestock, cooking competitions, music, and ... a traveling carnival.

He read on but found little else of value in the article—no mention of the carnival's name. He considered that his father might have decided it was the same one because he *wanted* it to be the same one. There was no evidence to suggest he'd been onto anything but a beer binge. He might not have been able to see the patterns in the stars, but he seemed to have created a pattern here where Dax was not convinced any existed.

Growing discouraged, he made to put the article aside, but paused to glance at the grainy picture beneath the text. He discerned food stands where indistinct figures crowded, and in the lower right corner a wagon with an image painted on the side. He held the paper close to his face, blinking. The image was unmistakable: a leaf-shaped eye with a black four-point star instead of a pupil, and faintly within that star, the white outline of the key-like symbol.

Dax picked up the eye he had drawn and compared them. The likeness was uncanny.

Winking Eye—it was the same name as the vaudeville show from Silvertown, now converted to a traveling carnival.

What was this doing at the 1927 fair in the now-lost Pastor's Grove?
He dared not allow himself to believe; his heart pounded.

Dax pulled out his father's map, running a finger over the marked roads and towns of Nebraska. There was Conjunction, smack in the middle of little Crow County. Then he noticed a hand-drawn star just above Conjunction, in what he thought was only woods, and beside it, in his father's neat scrawl: "P.G."

Pastor's Grove.

No major roads led through the area, but Pastor's Grove had to exist, even if it wasn't on the map—and he would find it. If he could follow the trail of breadcrumbs, maybe he would find what his father had been looking for. Something that would lead him to the truth.

He spun his phone in his hand a few times before waking the screen. There was only one person he could imagine calling for help. He put the phone to his ear and waited for Wyatt to pick up. The phone rang.

Dax glanced down at the two images of the eye: the one he'd sketched and the one in the article. The pair stared up at him as the phone rang and rang.

CHAPTER 7

Dax told Wyatt to meet him at the railroad tracks, where they used to drink whiskey from bottles hidden in paper bags during their teenage years and where, as kids, they imagined phantom trains gliding along the rusted tracks. Weeds had grown over the metal lines, and the railroad ties had rotted out. The spot they picked was the intersection of the tracks with an equally-disused and nameless dirt road that branched off from Hells Hollow Road. A wooden pole stood to the right of the intersection, with two crossed white planks in the shape of an X that read "Rail Road Crossing." About a mile northeast, the tracks ended with a shrug, breaking off into weeds and dirt. Dax didn't think the line had been in use since some time in the early 60s.

He was already waiting at the crossing when Wyatt arrived. The rain had brightened the dying grass, and the sun peered out over trees in the distance.

Wyatt looked as if he'd tumbled through the laundry inside of his blue flannel shirt with holes worn through at the elbows.

"So?" he said as they converged at the obsolete signpost.

"How's Sarah?"

"*That's* what you dragged me all the way out here to ask? 'How's Sarah?'"

"No," Dax said, "but how is she, anyway?"

"Hard to tell," Wyatt said, fidgeting with his cast. "Haven't seen her eat much. I don't think she's slept, either. Keep having to clean up her fucking cigarette butts everywhere." He picked up a small stick from the ground, tossed it away, chose another, and dug it into his cast to scratch his arm. "So why are we here?"

"You know what's up that way?" Dax asked, pointing down the dirt road. Hells Hollow Road also ran north, curving around the edge of a lake. When the road reached the other side of the water, he thought it hit the forest, so this dirt road, and maybe Woodview Lane on the other side, were the only ones he could think of that went north into the unobstructed wilderness.

Wyatt shrugged. "The hell should I know? Trees?" He champed down on the stick with his teeth like a dog and savagely shoved his longest two fingers into the cast, scratching desperately.

Shaking his head, Dax opened the door of the Bronco and pulled out his father's map. Unfurling it so that it revealed Nebraska, he held it up for Wyatt and pointed.

"You ever hear of a place called Pastor's Grove?"

Wyatt opened his mouth and the stick fell out. "Nope." He turned from the map to the road and back. "Hate to break it to you, but I don't think there's anything up that way. At least, not anymore."

"I want to make sure," Dax said, folding the map again and heading for his car. "If we follow this road, we should be able to cut around the forest to the other side—"

"Whoa, hold up. Clue me in here. The hell is so important about this place?"

Dax recounted what he'd read in the article.

"Winking Eye, huh?" He chewed on the words. "Pastor's Grove. Pastor's Grove. Remember that time we drove ... to Pastor's Grove ..." He snapped his fingers as if he were singing a song he'd just invented, grooving to the beat, and when his eyes met Dax's they were black: pupils eclipsing iris, ringed only by the slightest band of blue.

Dax frowned.

"Are you high?"

With a giggle, Wyatt snapped one more time, pointed at Dax. "I ain't *low.*"

"Are you fucking serious?"

"Well ... well, shit. I mean. After everything that's ... You expect me *not* to ..."

Dax unknotted a tangle of frustration in his throat. "How are you supposed to help me if you're like *this?*"

"Hey man," Wyatt snapped, the levity vanishing from his voice. "I didn't hear you complaining when I was digging that grave all by myself, *like this.*"

"Jesus, shut up, will you?" Dax said, looking around even though he knew they were alone. "What are you trying to do?"

"What are *you* trying to do, huh?" Wyatt was buzzing now like a mosquito zapper, sickly-bright and electric. "You show up here and, what, expect me to change my life? You show up after all this time and think you can just tell me what to do? You know, nobody needs you here. We've been doing just fine without you. The cows still crap and the sun still shines. Why don't you just go back to college?"

He reached into his pocket and pulled out the glass pipe, but before he got a chance to light up, Dax shoved him. Wyatt wheeled, curled his fingers into a fist around the pipe and threw a punch, but he listed and his hand whizzed through air.

When Dax hit back, something burst under his knuckles, and red sprayed down Wyatt's face. The pipe flew out of his hand, landed with a clink on the ground.

After a stunned moment, he smacked Dax on the side of his head with the cast, and Dax fell onto his back. His ears rang; his head throbbed. Birds chortled past overhead. He found he couldn't get up—not because of any physical injury, but something deeper in his limbs that weighed him into the ground, pinned him there.

Wyatt stood over him, clutching his nose. After a moment, he prodded Dax with his toe and said, "Hey?" When Dax still didn't get up, he said, "I didn't scramble up your brains, did I?"

Dax shook his head, half-wishing Wyatt would get fed up with him and leave him there on the ground. What was he doing here, anyway? In Conjunction, that is, not in the dirt. His dad was taken care of. No one was going to buy the piece of crap farm. There was no reason to stay, but he didn't have anywhere else to go, either. Except, maybe to Pastor's Grove, wherever the hell that was.

"I failed," he mumbled finally.

"What?"

"I failed. I can't go back to school because I failed." He tasted dirt in his mouth. "I should have been here. My dad died thinking I wanted nothing to do with him." A hollow void seemed to be filling him as he lay there on the ground. "He was right. I didn't."

Clouds whispered across the sky.

"We should go find this Pastor's Grove place," Wyatt said at last, voice muffled by his clogged nose. He nudged Dax again with his shoe. "I'm serious. Get up already. Let's go."

When Dax still didn't move, Wyatt made a sound in the back of his throat, grabbed him with his good hand, and hauled him off the ground.

As soon as Dax was standing, he cringed at Wyatt's bloodied face.

"How's your nose?" he asked.

Wyatt poked it gingerly, then shrugged. It had stopped bleeding. "Not broken. I've had worse. Hell, I don't even feel it, that's the beauty." He bent down to retrieve the pipe from where it had landed, the dirty glass intact. He looked at Dax from slightly-narrowed eyes. "You got that out of your system now?"

Dax shrugged.

"Good," Wyatt said as he shoved Dax out of the way and leaned against the crossing sign, squinting over his swollen nose. He pulled out a plastic bag with small white crystals.

"Shut up," Wyatt said.

"I didn't say anything."

"Yeah, well, I can hear you thinking." He closed the bag, flattened it, and shoved it into the crevice between his cast and arm. "I'm about to go search for the Lost City of Pastor's Asshole. And someone just punched me in the fucking face."

From his jeans pocket, Wyatt produced a lighter. It was strange watching him heat the pipe and inhale—a practiced move that seemed so easy, and so unfamiliar. A plume of smoke ejected from between his lips and dissipated into the air. Then he held out the pipe to Dax and said, "You want a hit?"

A notion came to him, then, that he might just get high with Wyatt and wander down the train tracks into the oblivion of the smoke snaking up from the dusty glass pipe. But it was only a fleeting notion, and he declined.

It took a few minutes to convince Wyatt that Dax should drive, but he took it in stride, hopping in the Bronco and snatching the map.

"Want me to stop for some ice?"

Wyatt's laughed. "I just had some! Oh, you mean for ..." He pointed at his nose. "Nah, man. You punch like a five-year-old." As they pulled away down the road, he looked out the window, over the tracks, and off through dead fields. He started flipping through radio stations in short, static-filled snippets, refusing to land on one for longer than three seconds.

They rambled around for an hour, encountering nothing but empty fields.

Wyatt opened the map and studied it, mumbling and pointing to random spots.

When Dax realized they were almost to the county line, he doubled back and tried a different road, this one rockier and narrower than the last. He zigzagged through prairie and sand hills, finding the exact nothingness he had expected, the sort of raw unclaimed land like a wound with the bandage ripped off.

At one point they doubled back on Hells Hollow Road, and Wyatt gave a startling bark of laughter, pointed out the window, and said, "Hell is real! Get it?" Dax thought he was referring to the billboard out on the highway heading into town.

The sun dipped low to the west, casting a reddish glow over the edge of the plains and onto the fluttering grass.

Dax released a frustrated sigh and pulled to the side of the road.

"Let's go home. There's nothing here."

Wyatt gave no response, as if not listening, too busy staring out the window. Finally, he said, "Maybe we should go *through*."

At first, Dax didn't understand. They'd crisscrossed over miles of open land north of Conjunction and had come up empty. Then he followed Wyatt's gaze to the forest around which they'd driven, the trees throwing long shadows in the settling dusk.

Dax was about to tell him they couldn't go that way when he noticed an unpaved one-lane road leading to the woods.

He squinted at the map. It wasn't much help. He pulled back onto the road and turned, carefully maneuvering the tires over the bumpy soil. Then they were rolling along past fields of prairie grass, the woods approaching as a wall of trees. The sun wavered on the edge of the horizon, its top cresting the rim of the earth while plunging the east into twilight.

Dax slowed when they approached the place where the road cut between the trees, just wide enough for the car to get through. Branches scraped by on either side. As soon as the canopy closed above them, the red sun disappeared, and he had to turn on the headlights.

He drove slowly, tires crunching over dirt and fallen twigs. Trees rustled around them. The buzz of insects melded with the murmur of wind in the leaves.

Dax looked at Wyatt, ghostly pale in the darkness, and found him staring out the windshield, eyes wide and unblinking, then he flinched and shouted, "Stop!"

Dax slammed the brakes.

"It's a body," Wyatt whispered.

A dark shape was in the road ahead of them.

Dax sucked in a breath. He was reminded of Zeke—of standing at the Willoughby farm with the body, of digging the grave, of rolling his corpse into the dirt.

He inched the car closer so the headlights flooded the area, lighting up a fallen log that stretched from one end of the road to the other.

"Get a grip," he said, unsure whether he was talking to Wyatt or himself. "It's just a tree." To prove his point, he opened the door and stepped out into the gathering night.

The log was almost three feet thick. Too big to move.

After all that—defeated by a log.

The futility of it all made him kick the fallen tree. Pieces of rotted wood fell away. He turned around, blinded by the headlights.

For a moment, he couldn't bring himself to go back to the car. If he gave up now, there would be no turning back, no trying again. Eventually, what he didn't know would consume him, as it had consumed his father. Then he had another idea.

Dax went back to the car, turned it off, and the headlights died. "What the hell, man?"

he said and pocketed the keys

He stepped out of the car again and slammed the door shut. He started walking.

Wyatt opened his door and called out, "Hey, what are you doing?"

"Going on foot," Dax said. He stopped at the log and turned back to Wyatt but couldn't see him in the dark.

"Are you out of your goddamn mind?"

"Maybe," he said. "You coming, or what?"

"Hell no."

"Fine." Dax stepped over the log. "Sit in the car, in the dark, by yourself."

"Hey!"

Dax kept walking, but heard Wyatt get out of the car and shut the door.

"Hey, come on—*fuck!* This is bullshit, man! I ain't going on a hike in the middle of the goddamn woods in the middle of the goddamn *night!*"

"It's not even eight o'clock," Dax said, slowing for Wyatt to catch up. He pulled out his phone and turned on the flashlight app, pointing it up to Wyatt's wild, glittering eyes.

"Get that shit out of my face," Wyatt said and swatted. He took out his own phone, but the cracked screen faintly illumined only a few inches around it and switched off after about three seconds. He grunted and pressed a button to relight the screen, but it kept shutting off. He swore and put it away.

"Here," Dax said, handing Wyatt his phone.

Wyatt narrowed his eyes and took it, pointing it forward so the white glow washed over the trail ahead of them and repelled the encroaching darkness.

They started walking.

The woods stirred with nocturnal creatures, but Dax ignored them. The trail narrowed and curved, low branches dangling over them, some still naked with winter. A chill gathered up from the ground and diffused the last echoes of daytime. The longer they walked, the more aware Dax became of his own heartbeat, and each beat brought him closer to the vast edge of panic—*now*, they would find it, *now*, or *now*. The longer they walked, not finding what they sought, the more convinced he became that this path led nowhere.

He stepped out of the light and looked around.

Wyatt had stopped behind him, staring into the distance, the phone dangling at his side, uselessly illuminating the ground.

"What is it?" Dax said.

Wyatt did not move. "The stars are watching."

Dax followed his gaze and saw two yellow specks of light among the trees. From here, they looked almost like stars against the black forest.

Then the stars winked out.

"Come on," Dax said, feeling weird and uneasy. "It's just an animal's eyes reflecting the light."

They kept going as the path narrowed and narrowed. Trees pressed ever-inward, as if contemplating the strangers, swaying and gossiping in the breeze, until the path nearly disappeared beneath overgrown shrubs and dangling branches.

"End of the line," Wyatt said. "Better go back."

Dax stood there, staring into the obstructed path. Then he caught something within the trees which did not appear to grow naturally there. He took the phone from Wyatt and pointed its light to a wooden sign protruding from the undergrowth. Vines snaked up over the surface and partially obscured it. He stepped closer, pulled away the covering of leaves, and moved the light over the weathered grooves of carved letters.

Welcome to Pastor's Grove.

Beyond the sign, the trail disappeared into the thick dark of the forest.

"I can't believe it," Dax said. "This is it."

"Great, we found it." Wyatt said and snatched the phone. "Let's go home." He turned around to start walking but froze. Two yellow eyes watched them from just down the road.

"Come on," Dax said. "We're here. Let's go through." He pushed away branches that reached across a path buried by undergrowth. "What *is* this place?"

"I don't know, and I don't want to know," Wyatt snapped. "Now let's get the hell out of here before that *thing* catches up."

The shining eyes drew closer.

Wyatt held up the light, but the creature was too far away to see clearly.

"Do whatever you want," Dax said, taking the phone. "I'm going to check this place out."

Wyatt scowled. "Oh sure, make me walk back in the dark."

"Then come with."

Wyatt backed up a step from the yellow eyes, and a low-hanging branch dragged across his shoulder. He flinched and whirled, punching at leaves. The branch snapped back and whacked him in the face. He dropped his arms to his sides.

"If we don't survive this," he said, "I'm going to kill you."

"Uh huh."

Dax ducked around branches and crept forward, the growth climbing up past his knees. The prickly edges of shrubs bit into him as he waded through plants, Wyatt close behind him.

At last, the path opened up again, this time into a clearing.

Dax raised his phone and illuminated the area as best as he could. In the dim glow, he could just make out several crumbling structures that might once have been houses. He approached one, shined the light over it. Tall grass crept up the walls. He couldn't see which direction the road continued because the ground had grown tall and shaggy with plant life. Several large trees interspersed the open area where the dead buildings kept their vigil. When he looked around for Wyatt, he realized his friend was not beside him. Shadows pressed in around the small circle of light. He called out his name as he walked, with spots of Pastor's Grove coming into view as the phone shifted aim, leaving the rest in darkness.

He swung the phone and found Wyatt mumbling to himself.

"What?" Dax asked.

Wyatt turned from the woods to Dax and said, "Devil eyes."

Two yellow orbs floated in the darkness.

The creature had followed them.

"It knows what we did," Wyatt said. "It sees everything. It saw us bury the body."

"Shut up," Dax said, not willing to admit he was spooked.

He wanted to peek inside the buildings, to see if there was any evidence of what had happened here. Before he could look away, the yellow eyes moved closer, seeming to glide straight through the trees.

Wyatt shouted and took off.

Dax followed, trying to keep Wyatt in the swinging light of the phone, but he kept disappearing, swallowed by shadows.

"Slow down!" Dax called. "Damn it—stop running!"

Panting, Dax stopped and looked around.

The animal was gone, and so was Wyatt.

He called his name and turned in a slow circle, the silent dark of the woods pressing around him. Trees thickened this part of the town, growing around the dilapidated building before which he stood. The high peaked roof was partially collapsed, but it still bore a cross at the top. The church was tilted, sagging into its foundations, as though the ground had begun to swallow it up. What remained of the wooden structure was choked with weeds. A tree intruded upon the side of the dead husk, caving it inward.

Dax turned away when he heard movement. The phone's light shifted over columns of trees casting long shadows against the ground. He moved the light, and Wyatt appeared.

"Jesus Christ," Dax said.

"Yeah," Wyatt said, looking up at the church. "Amen."

Dax stepped closer and found that the door blocked by a felled tree. It had landed in the fork between two branches on the other side of the church. Two windows sat high on the front wall, but the glass was so dusty it had become opaque, a tarnished gray color.

"What happened to this place?" Dax murmured.

"Maybe they got sick of living in a goddamn forest."

"Here, help me out." Dax handed the phone to Wyatt. "Shine the light up there. I want to see in the window."

Dax climbed onto the bottom of the crooked tree, where thick roots curled into the ground like tentacles. Testing the solidity of the wood, he crawled up about a foot, the bark scraping his hands.

"Okay, give me the light," he said, but Wyatt shined it away from him.

"Oh *shit.*"

Wyatt scrambled onto the tree, knocking him to the ground. In the chaos, the phone fell, and the light shut off. As Dax rolled across the grass, he heard the sharp crack of breaking glass and the thump of Wyatt leaping into the church.

"Hey!" Dax shouted.

A growl issued through the air beside him, and he turned, staring blindly into the dark. The eyes hovered only feet from his face. He blinked, but couldn't quite make out the creature's silhouette, and in the trickery of sightlessness envisioned a much larger animal—a hulking savage beast. It growled again, and an irrational fear invaded him. Those sharp eyes seemed to glow with their own unearthly light, and he wondered for a wild moment whether this was even an animal at all, or something else—

Stop it. That's what Wyatt would say.

Dax got to his knees and crawled away, his hands spidering frantically across the grass. Any moment now, it might attack him, and he couldn't find the phone, had no idea where it had fallen. His heart was reaching a critical speed when he finally found it and climbed blindly onto the tree by intuition and adrenaline alone.

He felt his way up to the window, now broken open with shards of glass protruding in vicious arrows from the frame.

A howl cut through the night, guttural and strange.

The back of his neck prickled as he dislodged a few shards of glass from the window before jumping inside. He landed hard on a groaning wooden floor. Gradually, his heart regained a normal rhythm, and he fumbled with the phone to turn on the light.

Rows of pews lay tilted in the sunken floorboards, which creaked deeply with every step. Some places were rotted through, with weeds sprouting up into the sanctuary.

"Wyatt?" he called, his voice carrying in the quiet.

He walked down the center aisle, shadows closing him in.

"Here," Wyatt's disembodied voice floated from somewhere ahead.

Dax continued down the aisle, watching his footing as he passed an area where the pews lay a foot or more beneath the level of the floor, burying themselves in whatever lay below. He shined the light up to the vaulted ceiling, where rafters showed bare. Spider webs shrouded the corners of the room.

He was about to call out again when his friend's pale form appeared facing him in the darkness beyond the last row of pews—or the first row, for Wyatt stood on a raised dais where the altar would have been.

"It can't get in here, right?" asked Wyatt, his eyes darting around.

"That coyote? No. It'll go away."

Wyatt stared at him disbelievingly. "It's not a coyote," he said.

Dax ignored him and raised the light behind his friend to see where the building ended.

Crucified upon a wooden cross on the wall behind the pulpit was a mummified skeleton in decaying priest's garb. Nails driven between the wrist bones pinned the body in place. A bare skull lay crooked on the neck, no longer able to hold itself up in death, and its black sockets bore into Dax. As he stumbled back, away from the body on the wall, the floorboards groaned beneath him, echoing through the hollow building.

"What?" murmured Wyatt as he turned around. He let out a cry as he whirled fully toward the thing. "Holy shitfuck."

Dax spun the light away from the skeleton and around the sanctuary. A dusty debris littered the ground beneath the pews. He stared at it for a moment, uncomprehending, before he faintly recognized what lay there—recalling the urn with his father's ashes—and realized with mounting horror that the floor was covered in human remains. The bones of long-dead churchgoers had collapsed into a tangled heap of rubble extending through all the pews. Here lay the townspeople of Pastor's Grove: fragmented, indistinguishable, forgotten.

Wyatt stared transfixed at the crucified priest and whispered, "It sees us. It has the coyote's eyes." His voice quickened and wavered in pitch, growing louder and higher. "It has the devil eyes! The eyes! Oh god, it's watching us!" Wyatt raised his hands and clawed at his own eyes, his voice reaching hysteria. "The eye! It sees! The stars ... *The stars are watching!*" He dragged his nails down his face, scraping as though trying to dig his eyeballs from his sockets and screaming unintelligibly.

The light wavered over him as Dax retreated, heart pounding, the screams drowning out the floor's cries. The smell of decaying wood reached up through the dark. As he stepped back without looking, the rotted floor sagged and gave way beneath his feet, and he fell down into the darkness below the church.

CHAPTER 8

Dax crashed to his knees. Pieces of floorboard and bone clattered around him. He lurched forward on his hands, digging his palms into the ground littered with slivers of wood. When he inhaled, his lungs filled with dust, and he coughed, feeling around for his phone. The light had gone off again during the fall. He could see nothing. Wyatt's screams echoed in the church above, but the sound was distant.

Dax tried to ignore the ache in his knee and wrist as he reached forward blindly, heart going wild in his chest.

I must have fallen into the cellar.

With no idea what lay before him, he held his breath and ran his fingers over the ground, pleading with the darkness to reveal his phone. When he found it, he exhaled shakily and tapped until the screen came to life. It was a moment before he registered the silence above him. Wyatt had stopped screaming.

Using the dim glow of the phone to take stock of his surroundings, he discovered the floor was made of stone and the ceiling was partially caved-in.

He crawled forward, away from the hanging floorboards, and rose to his feet. His knees throbbed in response.

Particles of dust drifted through the beam of light, and he moved the phone slowly, seeing nothing but an empty cellar webbed with dusty corners where spiders had built their nests. He wiped dangling strands from his face as he walked through a web, cringing; he felt a light, crawling sensation on his arm, and he brushed at it frantically.

He directed the light onto the ground to better watch his footing, and there he noticed a thick blackish line made of what looked like long-dried paint. He followed the curve across half the length of the cellar, where it came to a point and sharply changed directions to curve back the other way.

"Wyatt?" he called out as recognition hit him.

He followed the curve again, this time spotting the circle painted inside the leaf shape. Then he stepped back, taking in as much of the painting as he could. It was the same one from the Willoughby farm: a great eye with two symbols inside its iris; one that looked like a key and one that looked like a constellation, although these had chipped and faded until they were almost unrecognizable.

"Wyatt?" he called again, hoping his voice carried up into the church.

He knelt on the stone floor and touched the substance that didn't quite strike him as paint. It flaked off in his fingers, and he brought it up to his face. This close to the light, it gave off a reddish-brown shine. Standing, he wiped his hands on his pants and backed away from the eye.

It wasn't paint. It was blood.

"Wyatt!" he shouted, turning in a circle as he tried to find where he'd fallen through. The air of the dank, imploding cellar felt heavy in his lungs.

He found the rotted hole in the floorboards and reached through, shining the light up into the church. Wyatt's face appeared, scratched and utterly blank. Dax tossed him the phone and scrambled for purchase on the edges of the opening. He tried, and failed, to get out of the hole. Wyatt reached down for him, straining for a solid grip, and hauled him back into the church.

"You okay?" Dax said, catching his breath on the floor.

Wyatt stared down at him with an expression of horror so deep that all he could do was stretch his mouth in a long line and stare unblinkingly.

"The priest said it's time to leave," he said in a deadened voice.

"The ..." Dax saw only darkness. He knew the priest was there, somewhere in the shadows, crucified above his pulpit, and he could not control the shiver that shook him. "The priest is dead. There's no one here. Get your head out of your goddamn cloud of meth and back to reality. *Please.*"

"I don't know what reality is anymore."

Dax refrained from agreeing. Instead, he looked up at the broken window, just out of reach, and Wyatt shined the light where he directed. He jumped and missed—jumped again and grabbed the edges of the window frame as a shock of pain sank into his palms. Bits of glass dug into his skin as he gripped the ledge, strained his arms, kicked his legs. He grunted and almost let go, but Wyatt grabbed his feet and pushed from behind with surprising strength, sending him up and through the window into the outer darkness. He hit the fallen tree and rolled off onto the ground, landing hard on his back in the weeds. Moonlight filtered faintly through the heavy cover of treetops.

A moment later, Wyatt joined him, swinging the phone in all directions so the light zigzagged wildly.

Trying to ignore the pain throbbing in his palms, Dax shoved himself to his feet and started forward.

"What's that?" Wyatt said. "What's that? What is it?"

Two yellow eyes slinked forward.

Light fell over the mangy fur, the rabid face, the half-collapsed ribcage—and Dax couldn't deny it anymore. It was the same coyote. The coyote that was supposed to be dead.

Lips retracted from glistening fangs, and the coyote lunged.

Wyatt and Dax took off running.

They ran blindly through the remains of Pastor's Grove, through the swishing overgrown grass and back to the thicket separating them from the road.

Dax dove through the shrubs, twigs tangling in his clothing and pulling him back with clawed fingers while the wind raked furiously through the leaves. He disentangled himself and ran forward, down the long dirt path.

His heart thumped in his throat as he heard the patter of paws approaching.

Wyatt's feet had carried him far ahead, taking the light with him, leaving Dax sprinting through the darkness with low-hanging tree branches slapping him in the face, and the coyote just behind.

The path curved and the light disappeared around the corner. Dax shouted through his ragged panting, but his friend didn't respond, and so he stumbled in the darkness over branches and roots, panic zinging through him.

A growl erupted from directly behind him, so close he thought the coyote—*the dead coyote, the thing that could not be*—might sink its fangs into the back of his neck.

When he came around the curve, he saw Wyatt's shadow just ahead of him.

Dax's shins hit the massive log in the road, and he started to scramble over it until the bottom of his jeans tugged him back. For a terrifying moment he thought the coyote had him.

"Wyatt!" he shouted, and his friend turned around.

Dax threw him the car keys, which landed with a tinkle on the ground. He turned back to his attacker and realized it was only a sharp bit of wood that had snagged his pants. He pulled himself free, and then he was over the log, racing for the car.

Headlights beamed through the darkness.

Wyatt sat in the driver's seat, so Dax jumped in beside him and slammed the door.

The coyote stood in the path, the headlights shining fully over its bloody disfigurations, its snarling mouth and wild eyes. Long tendrils of saliva hung from its jaws. White bone protruded from its sunken chest.

Wyatt fumbled with the gearshift as the creature took a step forward. He hit the gas pedal, and the car lurched backward. The phone slid wildly across the dash as they careened down the road, the coyote receding from them even as it took chase.

Behind them, trees leaned in to whip at the car, appearing as if out of thin air as they shot in reverse through the forest. Before them, the headlights bounced as the car rocked over uneven ground, the path to Pastor's Grove fleeing the retreating light.

The coyote kept chase, but it was farther in the distance now, a dark shape running down the path at the edge of the headlight beams. Soon it, too, would be swallowed by the darkness.

Branches scraped the edges of the car, which swerved dangerously as it rocketed backward, barely missing trees lining the narrow road. Something clanged against the side-view mirror and knocked it out of place.

The thump of branches smacking the doors seemed to beat in time with Dax's racing heart. His stomach leapt with every lurch of the car, which suspended him in the air for long seconds as he clung to his seatbelt, breathless.

Finally the trees gave way and they were out of the forest, back into the flat fields surrounding it. Wyatt swerved sharply, the tires screeching, almost doing a donut as he wheeled the car all the way around and away from the woods.

They started forward, and the sudden change disoriented Dax. His hands began to throb, and he used what little light there was in the car to pry shards of glass from his skin. Blood filled the grooves in his palms, feathering out over the flesh like flooded riverbeds. He watched as blood welled over the crevice of his lifeline, which had been severed.

They made it to the railroad tracks where Wyatt's Dodge sat parked alongside the deserted road, and only then did Dax finally get out of the car and breathe a sigh of relief.

Wyatt cradled his bum arm and started laughing—a gasping, borderline hysterical sound.

"Did you see the priest?" he said through mouthfuls of laughter. "Deader than dead. Hoisted up on his own bullshit. Him and his fucking hellhound." His laughter took on a note of gasping horror. "But they're not really dead! They *see everything.*"

Hands shaking, Wyatt reached into his pocket and pulled out the glass pipe. The moon shone down on rusted tracks waiting for a train that would never come, on Wyatt's dirtied cast and swollen, purple nose, on the chipping blue paint of the tree-beaten Bronco.

Dax tried not to think about the coyote—or whatever it was. Instead, he looked up and tried to calm his shivering nerves.

Stars spattered the sky around the ethereal halo of the moon. Each star a massive orb of flame and fusion, the miniscule distances between them actually vast, unthinkable stretches of empty space. From Earth's perspective, the patterns made pictures of bears and scorpions, *and coyotes.* From elsewhere, they shaped into otherworldly images. Maybe the sun itself was a part of someone else's constellation.

He tried to tune out the crickets and the low swish of wind in grass. He tried to ignore the echo in his mind of the coyote's unnatural howl. The night sky took up his entire field of vision, horizon to horizon. He spotted Virgo. Ursa Major.

What if the Winking Eye's constellation couldn't be seen in the spring? Or from the northern hemisphere? Or even from Earth?

Wyatt flicked his lighter to life, and Dax snapped out of his daze.

"Hey, come on, put that shit away," he said, but his voice was tired, defeated.

Wyatt paused, lighter halfway to the pipe. He seemed to think about it for a moment, then let the flame go out. He didn't put the pipe away, though, and said, "Your dad was right,"

"He was right about *something*," Dax said after a moment. "I'm just not sure what."

Wyatt still hadn't taken a smoke or pocketed the pipe. He seemed frozen.

Dax asked if he would get home okay, and Wyatt shrugged him off in a way that was not at all reassuring. Realizing, though, that he couldn't babysit him any more than he could convince him to quit cold turkey, he let Wyatt go.

He drove through the country dark, the low whirr of tires the only sound in his car. As he turned onto a road that would take him past town, the headlights moved over a figure standing off to the side like a hitchhiker. It was a girl, arms at her sides, long dark hair falling around her moon-washed face. Her eyes seemed to pierce him through the glare of the headlights.

Savannah.

He hit the brakes and turned around, but she was gone. The prairie grass rustled just beyond the empty space where he'd sworn she'd been standing—*an animal creeping off into the night?* Unsettled, he turned back around and started driving again. The lonesome sound of the Bronco making its way down the road lulled him back to calm. The wind whisked over the rolling car. There was no one out there. He was alone.

His phone buzzed, and Dax fumbled for it on the nightstand. His palms ached dully, and he took a moment to stare at the congealing scabs in wonder. He turned them over to find that the knuckles on his right hand were also slightly bruised from when he'd punched Wyatt.

"Hello?" he mumbled, staring at the reddish lines on his left hand.

"*Dax?*" Wyatt's voice was a harsh, muffled whisper.

"Yeah. What is it?"

"The sheriff was just at my house," he said. "Asking about Zeke. I think he knows. I think he knows what we did."

Dax's stomach bottomed out. "Okay, calm down. Who'd he talk to? Just you?"

"Yeah. My parents are both at the store, and everyone else is at school. Well ... almost everyone. He asked about Sarah. I told him she was at school, but that was a lie. She ditched. She's been upstairs all morning. He said he'd come back."

Dax tried to retrace the trajectory of that night in his mind, tried to recall all the faces he'd seen and who had seen them: the two alien figures that had tried to reach the barn; the gun-happy group that had directed them there in the first place. He didn't know their names.

Had Sheriff Anderson spoken with them?

"All right, I'm coming over."

After he hung up, he searched for some fresh clothes—at least, clothes not covered in the grime of Pastor's Grove. He found a pair of jeans in his father's room and sat on the bed, but he stood again when he felt something on the mattress beneath him.

Zeke's watch.

He'd almost forgotten about it. He gazed at the watch, transfixed and filled with dread, and finally pulled on the jeans. Seeing it now, he didn't want to leave the watch here.

What if the sheriff came back?

He grabbed the watch and tucked it into his pocket.

When he was dressed, he stumbled out to the Bronco, glad for the seclusion of the farm. No close neighbors meant no one to see him fumbling for his keys, which he dropped twice. His hands shook as he started the car and peeled away down the long drive. He barely paid attention as he drove into town and parked in front of the white-trimmed brick house with its towering chimney and peaked roof. He killed the engine and headed for the porch.

The door swung open before he could knock, and Wyatt ushered him in, peering around at the empty street before he shut the door behind them. The front hall was long and dark. Upstairs, Dax remembered, there were three rooms: one for Mr. and Mrs. Montgomery, and two others shared in some combination by Sarah, Noah—who was a few years younger than his sister—and the fraternal twins, Dallas and Adelaide. Wyatt lived in the basement, which was converted to a bedroom despite its tendency to collect bugs and dampness. This was where Wyatt led him first: to the end of the main hall, down the stairs, and into his dim, wooden sanctuary with

Metallica posters on the walls and piles of dirty laundry in the corners. Once inside, Wyatt whirled around at Dax with only a thin veneer of composure. He looked ragged. His swollen nose had turned a dark shade of purple.

"How's your ...?" Dax pointed to his nose.

Wyatt waved him off. "Fine. Whatever. What are we gonna do?"

"We should probably talk to Sarah."

He shook his head. "She ain't talking to *no one*. Not even Addie, and they share a pair of bunkbeds. I think Addie and Dallas have been talking about her, but they're too smart to say anything to the rest of us. At least Noah seems oblivious, but that's probably because he's always holed up in his room, and I'd rather not think about that. I remember what *I* was doing by myself when I was fourteen." His foot started tapping on the wood floor. "What do we say if he comes back? Shit, people saw Sarah go to the barn with Zeke. Someone's gonna say something—and then we're fucked."

"Maybe no one paid attention," Dax said, feeling uneasy. "The sheriff came to my place yesterday."

Wyatt rounded on him, incredulous. "And you didn't think to tell me?"

"He didn't suspect anything."

"Yeah, well, who knows how long he'll keep not suspecting anything?" Wyatt pressed his fingers into his eyes. "Never seen him like this before. He was *scary*. Not himself."

"His son just disappeared. You can't expect him to act like everything's normal."

Wyatt lifted his head, eyes bright and sharp. "He's out for blood."

"We should talk to Sarah," Dax said.

The watch felt heavy in his pocket.

Wyatt released a long, slow breath and said, "Fine."

Dax followed him out of the basement and up the groaning stairs.

A gray miasma of smoke suffused Sarah and Addie's room. Two bunkbeds stacked on wooden frames sat against one wall. The window was open a crack, where smoke slipped through and fled to the sky. A socked foot dangled over the side of the upper bed, joined soon by a hand that flopped over the edge with a half-burned cigarette wedged between two fingers.

"Sarah," Wyatt said. When she didn't respond, he slapped the bed frame. "Hey!"

"What?" Her voice drifted down from the ceiling.

"Hell, can you get down off a there and put out that damn thing?"

The pale hand disappeared—smoke blowing and curling down languorously—then reappeared. Sarah pressed the glowing butt to the bed frame and then dropped it.

"Aw, come on," Wyatt grumbled, stooping to pick up the filter before tossing it out the window. The cigarette had left a small, burnt circle on the dark wood. Wyatt rubbed at it with his thumb, but the smudge remained. "Goddamn, do you *have* to do that?"

Sarah sat up. "What do you want?"

Tangles of blonde hair dangled around her pale face. Her sharply freckled cheeks supported gray half-moons lying on their backs beneath her eyes.

"Sheriff Anderson was just here," Wyatt said.

"I know," she said, no inflection to her voice.

"Well, what are we gonna do about that?" Wyatt looked from Sarah to Dax. "In case you forgot, we helped you bury a body a few nights ago—you want to fuck up your life, that ain't *my* problem, but if that's the way you want to go, you'd best keep your shit out of my toilet, thanks."

Sarah jumped down from the bed. "There's already plenty of shit in your toilet."

"This is *not* a joke," Wyatt snapped. "You *killed* someone."

"I know what I did."

"Well, you don't sound too sorry about it."

She pierced Wyatt with a stare glazed with loathing. "Maybe I should have just turned the shotgun around after I did it. Would *that* be sorry enough for you?"

"No, Jesus—"

"You said you saw Savannah near the barn," Dax said, keeping his voice low. There was something volatile behind the distance in Sarah's eyes and the faint frown dragging down her mouth. "Do you think … did she know you saw her? Did she know you were coming?"

Sarah's gaze didn't waver, but seemed to gaze momentarily inward.

"I thought she did," she whispered.

"You think she was there?" Wyatt said. "You think she knows? You think she saw? Oh, God." He paced back and forth. "Is she a witness?"

Sarah shook her head. She seemed hardly to be listening to her brother. "Then why didn't she do anything?"

Dax thought of Savannah's luminous voice tracing its way around the candles, the flicker of light and shadow on her face—*rotten with meth, it was the only explanation*—and the way the room's stale warmth had imbued him with its narcotic hypnosis.

The face in the window ... the figure on the side of the road ...

A thrill of dread crawled up his spine.

"Have you talked to her?" Dax asked.

Sarah shook her head.

"This bitch might have seen you go into the barn with Zeke and you haven't figured out what she knows?" Wyatt snapped.

Outside, the lowing of a cow was carried on the wind from a distance, then the clang of a bell—maybe from the cow's neck, maybe from a chime hanging off someone's roof. Smoke still saturated the stagnant air of the room, and Dax went to the window and pushed it all the way open, inhaling the cool breeze and trying to cleanse himself of that slow creeping dread.

Sarah fished around under her sheets until she found a crushed, half-empty box of Marlboros. "Savannah's homeschooled," she said. "She should be there now." She tucked her cigarettes in her back pocket and tugged on a pair of well-worn sneakers. "If we're going to go, let's go."

Wyatt pulled the keys to the Dodge from his pocket, and Sarah snatched them from his hand. "I'm driving," she said, and started for the doorway.

Dax and Wyatt trailed behind her down the stairs and out of the house.

As the car backed out of the driveway and sped off down the street, Dax stared out the window at his ghostly reflection pasted over the backdrop of fields and houses sliding past.

"Where does she live?" Wyatt asked, rolling down his window and leaning his casted arm over the edge.

They turned off Cross Street south of town, cutting west toward the sand hills.

"Her family's got a ranch out this way," Sarah said, driving over a pothole that made Dax's stomach pirouette. "I don't know what I'm going to say to her."

Outside, motionless cows whipped by on the still landscape.

"I do," Wyatt replied. "Hello, did you happen to see my sister shoot someone while you hid conveniently in the shadows, and if so, do you get off on that, you twisted cunt?"

Sarah reached over and punched him on his good arm.

They were quiet for a moment while Wyatt massaged his arm.

"She's got you wrapped around her little finger," Wyatt said, "doesn't she?"

"At least I'm not a slave to meth."

"Uh-huh. Why don't you go chain-smoke another carton of cigarettes, then?"

"If you say one more word, I swear to God, I'll break your other arm."

"One more word."

"Jackass."

"Murderer."

Sarah slammed the brakes. Tires squealed, and they skidded off the road and jerked to a stop in a thicket of weeds. She panted, white-knuckling the wheel.

"Shut up," she breathed. No one said anything. "Shut up!"

Wyatt's voice was small when he spoke. "I'm sorry. I ... I didn't mean it."

Harsh, shallow breathing filled the car.

"That was a shitty thing to say," Wyatt continued. "I know. I'm an ass. Hit me again."

She didn't let go of the wheel, but her breathing calmed.

The car started rolling again, and she steered it back onto the road. They drove, slowly this time, with a deliberateness that drew itself from the tension inside the car. Wyatt and Sarah both faced forward, and Dax couldn't see either of their faces from the back.

Eventually they turned onto a narrow dirt road leading to a ranch house with a wooden fence snaking out from behind it. They drove beneath an arched signpost, its chains rattling in the wind and its carved black letters welcoming them to Prairie Rose Ranch.

CHAPTER 9

Dax craned his neck to read the sign out the window as they drove beneath it and into Prairie Rose Ranch. The wind picked had up, and a vastness of gray clouds crept across the sky. He wouldn't have been surprised if one of them turned into a wall cloud; it was tornado season, after all.

The tornado alarm had gone off more than a few times when he was a kid: a high, unnerving note that rose and fell in protracted waves. That sound meant the approach of something terrible. The winds would be high, swirling the sky gray and green. Everyone at school would pile into the ice-cold basement with the freshmen. Or, if it wasn't a school day, Dax might hear the siren while riding his bike. He would pump his legs until they ached, flying along the road with his shirt billowing, the siren propelling him home. His father would be waiting for him outside when Dax careened up the drive. Together they would descend the rickety stairs to the cellar and close the doors above them. The darkness there was earthy and dank. Roy would slap a flashlight against his palm with a few muttered curses, always surprised that the batteries were always dead. Dax would find a candle and some matches, and they would sit around the small flickering flame and play gin rummy while the wind beat against the doors and threatened to burst into the underground chamber.

Often tornados had just skirted the edges of Crow County. Once, when Dax was maybe four or five, a low-grade tornado had cut a swath right through town. It had lifted shingles from a row of houses and pitched them across uprooted vegetation. Dax had walked around in the aftermath while rain pattered the torn-up ground, debris littering the street. He'd been in awe of this great, mysterious power that came down from the sky, wondering what a more severe tornado would have been like. The thought had terrified him.

His mother had explained it to him, but he couldn't now recall what she'd said to give tornados any reason to a child. Perhaps it was because they had *no reason*. They were senseless and mindless vortices of destruction that came and went with no regard for little human lives.

Despite his firsthand view of that minor destruction in his youth, he'd never seen a tornado in person, and he didn't want to now. He hoped the weather would hold, at least until they left the ranch.

Sarah parked in front of the house.

The windows were dark and exuded a kind of emptiness.

"How many people live here?" Dax said.

"Savannah," Sarah said. "Her parents. Three siblings. And her grandparents."

There was no one in the fields around the house. Maybe they were all inside avoiding the weather.

Dax wondered what it was like to have a big family, like Wyatt and Sarah. Like Savannah. So many people crammed into one house, all fighting for their place. For most of his life, it had just been him and his dad, usually in two separate areas of the farm entirely, alone and disconnected.

Dax followed Sarah up to the covered porch while Wyatt stood leaning against the car, picking at his cast. The wood of the house looked old and discolored, creaking like a great beast in the wind.

Sarah rapped her knuckles on the door. The light of day turned from yellow to gray while a cloud crept across the sun. She waited, then knocked again.

"I don't think anybody's here," Dax said.

"What, they all got up and left? And went where?" She walked to a window shaded with blue curtains. They were parted slightly in the middle, and Sarah cupped her hands over her eyes and leaned against the glass to peer inside.

Remembering the eye he'd seen peering in at him from between the kitchen blinds, Dax suppressed a shudder and looked back at the car.

"What is that?" Sarah said.

He turned back to her. "What?"

"Holy shit."

"What?" He stepped closer to the window, trying to see around the curtains.

Sarah pulled back, blinking and pointing to the glass.

Dax leaned forward and cupped his hands to block out the slanted glow of vacillating sunlight behind him. Through the part in the curtains, he could see the dark interior of a living room with a sofa pressed against the far wall and a hallway that led back through the house. At first, he didn't notice anything strange. The fireplace was dormant, and there seemed to be no life within. Then he spotted a dark shape on the floor. A net of gray hair fell in wavy strands from the head, concealing the turned-away face.

"Is that her grandmother?" Dax guessed, trying to spot any movement from the body, any gentle rise and fall of a chest. All was still.

"I think so," Sarah said, jiggling the doorknob back and forth with a rattle that told him it was locked. She swore.

His eyes roved away from the body and across the wood floor, over a woven rug, around the rest of the silent room. Nothing, but for a man's brown shoe on its side by the entrance to the hallway, not far from where the grandmother lay.

Then he saw it: a socked foot poking out from the dim hallway. The foot—like the shoe, like the grandmother—lay still.

When Dax stepped back, the wind mustered up a hearty gust that teetered him off-balance.

Sarah leaned around the side of the porch, looking for something.

"There's got to be another way in," she said.

The sky, graying over with thicker clouds, was taking on that telltale greenish hue of an impending storm. Dax could smell it, too— that damp, musty smell—and the air was hot and sticky and still but for those occasional fierce bursts of wind. He was sure if he grazed his eyes over the horizon, he would see a distant line of rain coming down. Instead, he looked around at the desolate ranch. If a storm were approaching, the animals should have sensed it, grown skittish and sought shelter. They must have already done so because he didn't see them—only the grass within the dilapidated fence.

"Hey!" Wyatt called to them. "What's the holdup?"

Sarah ignored him, hopped over the porch railing, and went around the side of the house.

Behind Wyatt, the clouds roiled ominously and the wind died.

"There's a stable over there!" Sarah called. She pointed beyond the house and field, to the wooden building nearby. "She loves her horses. Maybe she's in there?"

"You sure she's not in the house?" asked Wyatt, peering around Dax to the impenetrable window with its blue curtain pulled almost closed.

The air felt warm, oppressive. Too still.

They followed Sarah around the house, trying to see in through the shuttered windows. When they reached the back, they found another porch looking onto the gently rolling fields.

Sarah tried the door, and the knob turned with a soft click. She pushed, and the door swung inward with a creak to reveal a dark and silent hall, filled with a sweet sick stench.

They found the kitchen, and in it, on the floor caked with a layer of dirt, the body of a girl. The smell was nearly intolerable. Wyatt stepped back from the doorway and gagged, but Dax pressed forward. The girl was young, maybe eleven or twelve, but her wet skin, blotched coal-black and green with decay, had grotesquely deflated around her thin frame. She lay on her stomach with her head turned to the side, a pool of blood dried and black outlining her head and neck, the latter of which looked torn open. The whites of her eyes writhed with movement. After a moment, he realized he was wrong—she didn't have any eyes. Maggots filled the empty sockets. Flies landed and flew, landed and flew around her.

Sarah turned away with a shudder, her throat convulsing.

"Savannah?" she called frantically.

Wyatt shushed her immediately, looking around in horror. She did not heed him. Instead, she stumbled down the hallway, searching the other rooms.

"Savannah!" she called again.

Dax followed the hallway to the living room he'd seen through the window. At the end of the hall, cloaked in darkness, lay an old man: one shoe kicked off, limbs sprawled crooked, old blood on the front of his shirt beneath a ravaged throat shredded open as if by animal teeth. His sockets were empty, and his mouth hung wide on a broken jaw, revealing an abyss where his tongue used to be. Someone—*or something*—had ripped it out of his mouth.

Retreating, Dax found Wyatt standing frozen in the doorway of a bedroom inhabited by two male corpses: one on the floor, one on a bed. Dax backed away, down the hall, past another room with the bodies of Savannah's parents. He couldn't breathe. Flakes of dead skin floated on the air. The hallway tilted around him strangely.

He found Sarah standing in another bedroom.

Dried blood covered the walls, not random splatters but designs: crude mysterious stick figures with too many limbs, arcane geometry, cryptograms that looked like nothing ever translated before. The radio on the desk was on but not tuned to a station, instead issuing a low static buzz. Long plain dresses hung in the open closet.

Savannah's room.

The smell pervading the house thickened the air, and Dax tried to suppress the nausea steadily rising in his gut, the panic steadily rising in his throat. Wherever he turned, a new dizzying series of blood-drawn sigils confronted him, and he breathed deeply through his nose, trying not to look too closely at them, until he spotted a familiar shape.

The key.

Radio static buzzed in his ears.

The key from the eye at the Willoughby farm, and at Pastor's Grove.

Sarah stood at Savannah's desk. Her eyes contained empyrean nightmares, and her head shook slowly, perhaps unconsciously, back and forth. Her fingers touched the top of the desk—smooth solid wood, an anchor to normalcy—and landed on a pocket-sized notebook sitting beside the hissing radio, and she picked it up wonderingly.

"Jesus," Wyatt whispered from the doorway. "Jesus, God. What the fuck?"

Sarah clutched the little notebook to her chest.

Even the ceiling was covered in symbols.

Dax thought he might throw up. He backed into Wyatt and nearly knocked them both down. Instead, Wyatt stumbled into the closet and lost his footing, grasping at the curtain of dresses and tearing some to the floor.

Distracted from the sigils, Dax noticed a shelf on the opposite wall and upon it a fluid-filled jar, with grotesque whitish orbs and pink lumps of flesh floating within.

The white noise of the radio crackled in his ears as he fled down the hall. He burst onto the porch, and leaned over, hands on his knees. After a moment, the nausea began to recede.

Wyatt yanked Sarah by the wrist through the doorway behind him.

She struggled and pulled herself free, still clutching the notebook. Wyatt made a sound of disgust and spat.

"Where is she?" asked Sarah, staring around. "Where is she?" Tears crystallized her eyes. "Is she dead?"

"We saw her a few days ago," Dax said. "Those people … have been dead a while."

"No," she said. "*No.*"

"Jesus, Sarah, you saw her room!" Wyatt jabbed a finger at the notebook. "Read her goddamn diary, then. Maybe she wrote about how she killed her family and painted their blood—"

"Stop it!" Sarah's voice shrilled.

Her voice lingered in Dax's eardrums, even after it echoed into oblivion.

Wyatt wouldn't stop: "She ripped out their throats—"

"An animal!" Sarah cried out.

"An animal didn't take out their eyes," Dax said quietly. "Their eyes and tongues. I saw them in a jar in Savannah's room."

They stared at him wordlessly.

Dax felt a sudden pressure in his head, the world somehow hot and cold at the same time. His ears hurt. He couldn't loosen his jaw.

Dark clouds hung low over the waving prairie grass.

When his ears popped, Dax knew what was coming a moment before the warning siren wailed in the distance.

"We have to get inside!" he shouted over the long, whining note. Another sound rose, something that sounded like an approaching freight train. He thought of the ghost train he and Wyatt always half-expected to see barreling along those abandoned tracks outside town, even as the sound of the tornado met his ears.

"*Fuck* no, I am *not* going back in there!" Wyatt yelled.

"There's got to be a storm cellar somewhere," Dax said.

They started moving along the side of the house, looking for a trapdoor leading down, but Sarah broke away from them.

"What about Savannah?" she cried.

"Fuck Savannah!" Wyatt snarled.

"I need to find her." She bolted across the field toward the stable.

As she ran, growing smaller and smaller in the distance, the wind rose to monstrous strength. Wyatt took off after her, and Dax followed.

Sarah disappeared inside the stable.

Wyatt ran ahead of him, but Dax quickly caught up, and by the time they reached the open door—swinging back and forth in the heavy wind—they were side-by-side. Dax couldn't hear the sound of his own panting over the wind, the roar of the lowering tornado, or the siren rising and falling, rising and falling in waves.

They stumbled into the semi-dark interior, feet sliding on the straw coating the floor.

Sarah stood with her back to them, silhouetted by the dusty gray light that seeped through the heavy clouds and reached into the stable.

The horses stomped, threw their heads and whinnied, agitated and trapped in their stalls.

Savannah stood in the center of the stable ... but she wasn't really standing.

Wind came in through openings in the wooden walls, swirled around the room in its own miniature version of a tornado, and whipped Savannah's long dark hair around her cracked and cratered face. Her ragged gray dress lifted and fluttered around her.

She hovered above the ground.

Dax thought it must be an optical illusion, some slant of the floor and the whirl of the wind, but her bare feet were dangling, her toes were dangling. She floated, surrounded and swept up by the wind, arms flung out like featherless wings. She floated.

The deafening howl of the tornado filled the room.

Even though Dax could see Sarah open her mouth—the edge of her parted lips and the gleam of her teeth in profile—and knew she was screaming, he couldn't hear it. Her voice vanished, carried away by the wind.

Like the snap of a rubber band, Savannah dropped several inches until her feet hit the floor. Her cracked lips moved with unheard words. The roaring of the storm lessened, and what Dax heard in its wake made his skin crawl: a deep, unearthly voice, some low utterance in an unfamiliar tongue, coming from Savannah's mouth.

Wyatt had backed up against the wall.

"It's her," he said, just loud enough for Dax to hear.

Wind pummeled the stable, eddied around Savannah or whatever she had become.

"Who?" Dax said.

"The body from the lake," Wyatt said, his voice high with terror. "It's *her.*"

Savannah stopped speaking in that dark inhuman voice, and reached both hands up to her face, digging dirty fingers into the edges of her eyes. They came away and left her sockets hollow. She held her bloody eyes in the palms of her hands and then hurled them into the air.

Dax lost sight of them somewhere near the beams of the ceiling, and for a moment, he thought they had vanished.

Savannah stared, eyeless, her tongue peeking out between her teeth. Then two small round objects fell, landed in her waiting palms, and she pushed them one after the other into her empty sockets. When she looked up again, the eyes she wore were not her own. They were yellow, with round black pupils. Animal eyes. Coyote eyes.

Devil eyes.

When Savannah grinned, Dax expected to see long canines, but they were her normal teeth, rotted—not from meth, but from *death*—and yellow, like her new eyes.

She took a step forward, and Wyatt threw himself at his sister, grabbing Sarah around the waist and hauling her back to the door.

Dax found himself moving, though he could barely feel his own limbs. He followed Wyatt, who dragged Sarah along with him, as they ran back out into the wind, to the house.

Rain fell, slowly at first, then in earnest.

From the corner of his eye, Dax spotted the long black funnel of the tornado raising a cloud of dirt as it plowed through a distant field, but he didn't stop to survey it, didn't stop to determine its trajectory. He just ran ... ran from the thing in the stable, ran to the side of the house where two wooden trapdoors led into the ground.

Dax grabbed the iron handles and threw open the doors while Wyatt pushed Sarah onto the staircase that descended into the black pit. Dax jumped in after them, catching a glimpse of a figure standing in the doorway to the stable, a dark shadow-figure with long hair whipping in the wind and slanting rain.

That was the last thing he saw before he pulled the doors shut over them, encasing them in the cool quiet of the cellar while the storm raged above.

CHAPTER 10

All was darkness.

Dax fumbled for his phone and turned on the light. In the small white glow, Sarah and Wyatt's faces were pale and ghostly. They huddled together, shivering and soaked, their hair plastered to their skin. Sarah's eyes gleamed wetly. Bruise-colored circles deepened beneath Wyatt's bloodshot eyes. Their breathing sounded a hairbreadth from hyperventilation, loud and rough. Dax thought of wind, of moving air, the whirling tornado, the ragged drag of breath to desperate lungs. Oxygen: life-giver; destroyer of worlds.

Rain pounded on the doors above. They rattled and let in an eerie wail.

Dax's throat tightened.

Any minute, he thought, *Savannah will throw open the doors, stand above us with the tornado whirling around her, stare down with her ancient yellow eyes.*

He watched the wooden doors and waited for her to descend.

Nothing happened. The wind howled overhead, whistled through thin cracks around the edges of the doors, tried to beat its way underground.

Dax lit the area, and they retreated further into the dark, away from the doors. The cellar was a small room with an earthen floor. They settled into a circle with the phone's light in the center—a paltry beacon against waking nightmares.

Sarah gripped the little notebook in her hands hard enough to bend the cover. At last her fingers loosened, and she flipped it open.

What dreadful literature, Dax wondered, *had Savannah scrawled onto the page?*

He feared the answer would only reveal more enigmas, more cryptic hieroglyphics whose dark and abstruse meanings threatened to crumble reality.

"What does it say?" he could not help but ask.

She leafed through the pages. "Last entry is dated a few weeks ago," she said, then started reading.

"*I saw the coyote again yesterday when I was out feeding the calves. Didn't tell anyone. Followed it almost all the way to the lake. Gone all afternoon. Mother was furious. I turned back when I saw the water up ahead ... wonder if it knows I can't swim? Is it a Trickster? I am determined to find out what it wants. Next time, I'll follow it all the way.*"

"The coyote," Wyatt whispered, his voice echoing in the dark. "It led her to the lake. Turned her into ... whatever she is now."

Sarah snapped the little notebook shut and shoved it into her pocket. She crossed her arms over her knees and hugged them close.

"Sarah," Wyatt said, taking a breath. "I need to tell you how I really broke my arm."

Dax stood—the ceiling a few inches above his head—and walked to the end of the cellar as Wyatt's voice drifted around him, invoking images of the body rising from the black water of the lake, rising barefoot and dripping.

Several wooden crates stood against the far wall. Dax grabbed one and tried to lift it. It was full of something heavy. He found the lid and pried it free, finding a heap of potatoes within. Turning the crate on its side, he let them roll out onto the floor. He did the same with the next crate, which was full of onions, and a third, which turned out to be empty. Then he moved them in front of the small staircase that led up to the doors, piled one atop another until the crates blocked them entirely. Anyone above would still be able to open the doors, but at least now they might be deterred by the wooden barricade.

He sat back down with Wyatt and Sarah, the white light from the phone illuminating the horror etched onto their faces. It cast shadows behind them, just barely held at bay by the light. Savannah's demon wind held at bay only by the pile of empty crates. Dax felt appallingly unprotected, and wished he could rid himself of the chill in his bones.

Wyatt reached into his pocket and produced the glass pipe. He pulled a flattened plastic bag from the sliver of space between his cast and arm, then sprinkled some crystals into the bowl. When he was done, he put away the bag and took out a lighter.

"This shit … This is …" He left the sentence hanging unfinished in the air and raised the pipe. Flicked the lighter. Inhaled. Smoke trailed from between his lips, and he held out the pipe.

Sarah took it with trembling hands. She had gone quiet after Wyatt's story, and mimicked his movements. Deep breath in. Smoky exhale. She held out the pipe when she was done.

Dax took it from her. The glass was warm from the flame, cloudy with use. He thought of the swollen corpses inside and the smell that still haunted his senses; he thought of Savannah floating in the stable, plucking her own eyes from their sockets; he thought of those impossible yellow eyes fixed into her skull.

He lit the bowl and breathed in.

Harsh and foul-tasting smoke entered his airway. He tried to hold it in, tried to let the strange tingling in his throat infect the rest of him, but it burned, and he coughed wretchedly. Handing the pipe back to Wyatt, he hacked into his elbow, eyes watering, the sting of the smoke filling his throat and lungs.

At first, nothing. Then, as he watched Wyatt inhale again, he started to feel strange. Despite the cold rain still trickling down his arms, he grew warm, pleasurably warm, and the phone's light took on a mellower glow, white and comforting. The edges of darkness softened and bled. The pipe made its way to Sarah while Dax grew light and giddy. She handed it back to him, and he took another hit, this one with less bite, and the warm, buzzing sensation intensified.

Dax felt himself start to shake—the kind of shivering that comes with a prolonged chill, even though he was sweating. Hot and cold flushed alternately through him. His heart galloped along, pumping adrenaline through too-thin veins.

One more go-around and the bowl was killed.

Dax's gaze narrowed on the phone, on the light, which spread to him, beckoned him, a point as bright as a star, and he felt himself rushing away through the dark until the light became a star. He saw it through the cosmic space of many dimensions, a light simultaneously dead and alive—the light of beings ancient and otherworldly, beings outside space and time.

Darkness raced forward to greet him, and he found himself clinging to a desperate, hectic exhilaration. His pounding heart urged him to get up and run, but there was no room, so he stood and walked to the end of the cellar. He touched the cold wall, feeling every groove in its surface like fissures in reality. Here his eyes met only darkness, and they sharpened and tried to see what lay beyond the dark.

Can I see the very molecules that make up the air?

No, he knew that was impossible, yet still the darkness bubbled minutely around him.

He turned and hit the wall—turned and hit another wall—and felt abruptly stifled and anxious. If he lay down, he might relax, and so his back sank into dirt or the cushion of nothingness. He lay on his back in the dark, staring up at the dark as it shifted and changed, revealed pinpricks of light that his eyes made appear. They spiraled into shapes, they twirled as motes of lighted dust on a breeze, they flickered in and out and always dazzled brightest at the periphery. When he looked at them straight on, they faded away. He never could look at anything straight on.

When you look at things straight on, you see their awful truth— that's why it's best to look at things from the edges. Maybe that's all anyone ever sees. Maybe if we looked at the world straight-on and saw things for what they really were, we'd lose our minds.

At last, the starry dance of light coalesced into the constellation from Savannah's drawing of the eye. Indecipherable and meaningless, but familiar: a twitch of déjà-vu, a long-remembered but unspecified scent, the face of an old acquaintance without a name.

"What is it?" Dax said.

"What's what?"

"The constellation," he said to the mysterious voice who had replied. "The one inside the Winking Eye."

"You're high," a female said, and another voice laughed.

The constellation twisted and convulsed.

Dax thought he was turning to stone; his skin vibrated but he felt paralyzed with nameless dread, unable to move under Medusa's gaze, despite his strong imperative to move.

The constellation resolved.

An outline of Perseus drew itself around the stars: Perseus holding Medusa's severed head. And one of the stars in that head dimmed, closed, winked.

No, not a star.

Two stars orbiting each other—an eclipsing binary that flickered every time the dimmer star passed before the brighter. Ancient civilizations hadn't understood the trick as modern astronomers did, and so they had built mythologies around it, but science had settled the mystery of what people throughout history had called the Demon Star.

The star appeared to be falling toward him now, and that star was an eye: a great yellow eye in the dark, staring him down as it raced forward, engulfing him in its light until that was all he could see, until the eye consumed him and threw him violently down the dark hole of its pupil, into a place where reality broke and he broke with it.

His heart spasmed in his chest; he could feel every arrhythmic beat sending twinges of panic racing up his throat. His lungs ached, deprived of air, and he coughed. The wild joy of the high transformed into terror. He couldn't seem to breathe, his heart beating faster and faster, and he was sure, in that moment, he was going to die.

Against the starless dark, Dax conjured the skeleton on the cross, staring out with its black eye sockets. He felt as if he were staring into one of those empty sockets, down the long black tunnel of a well, or a wormhole to another dimension, where dead things and creatures from the stars roamed. Maybe his mother was there, a shade of herself. Maybe his father was there. Maybe Lailani was there—dead or alive, he didn't know. He'd never gotten in touch, never opened the box, so she was both dead and alive, a Schrödinger's Cat.

The weight of the cellar pressed him to the ground.

His chest was on fire.

"Help," he gasped.

"Dax?" came a voice from far away.

He clutched his chest. "I'm having … a heart attack."

Wyatt laughed.

The sound sent another burst of panic through him, and his vision exploded with gray stars, which slowly dissolved when he blinked.

"Sit the hell up, then." Wyatt said, and grabbed him by the shoulders.

Gravity tugged from strange angles as Dax tilted through the dark. The luminous white of the phone reappeared, and in it he saw Sarah. The black of her pupils leaked out to the edges of each iris like ink spreading in water.

Wyatt patted him on the back. "Better?"

Dax's mind sprinted through blurry, half-formed thoughts. His heart thudded, pumping blood through his overheated body. Though reality reasserted itself, the feelings intensified.

Shouldn't it be wearing off soon?

He thought it must have been full eternities since they'd smoked. He checked the phone. It had been ten minutes.

"I think my heart is going to explode," he said.

"It won't," Wyatt said.

"I think my head is going to explode," Sarah said.

Wyatt hesitated, then said, "Maybe it will."

"Goddamnit, Wyatt!"

Sarah stood quickly. She paced, fidgeting. Then she started creeping along the rough wall, trailing her hands over the surface. She walked all the way around the cellar once, then twice. Trapped. Crates blocked the only exit above them.

"Is it getting smaller in here?" she whispered, almost to herself, her voice carrying ethereally through the cellar. She crept around the edge, crept around the walls, kept creeping. "They're closing in. Just a little at a time. Don't you notice it? I have to keep going, or they'll keep moving in until it's the size of a coffin."

Dax bent forward and breathed deeply.

"Perseus," he murmured. "Medusa. The Winking Eye. Savannah."

"Savannah's not here anymore," Sarah said as she circled the room.

"Her eyes," Wyatt said. "Her *eyes*."

Dax's mouth felt dry, inviting a wave of nausea. In the next moment it passed, leaving his stomach swooping, his mind spinning, his eyes tricking him in the dark.

"All of their eyes," he said, remembering the jar.

"It's getting smaller in here," Sarah said, this time with certainty. She gazed from Wyatt to Dax, her eyes impossibly huge. "We have to get out."

"I think we should stay down here," Wyatt said. "It's safe. There are no tornados down here. No coyotes. No sirens. No Savannah. No eyes. No bodies. Nobody. Nobody but us. It's just us. There isn't anyone else. We go up there, who knows what we'll find? Maybe the apocalypse is happening up there. Right now. Yeah, and everyone's dead but us. Think about that. We should stay down here. Where it's safe."

Everyone's dead but us.

Dax's heart skipped.

117

His mother. His father. Zeke Anderson. Savannah's whole family. Everyone dead. Everyone but them. They were alone in the storm cellar, alone in the cosmos, alone in the dark.

His breathing quickened again, and he understood without words Sarah's certainty that the room was getting smaller.

Everything's closing in.

His flesh started to crawl, and he rubbed at his arms, seeing in his mind's eye the charcoal body of Savannah's sister with her writhing eye sockets. He was sure maggots had crawled up blindly, searching from the dirt below—perhaps from a grave, perhaps they were in a grave, perhaps they were dead.

That's why the maggots came. To feast on our dead flesh.

Dax rubbed his skin to be sure he was still alive.

He had the sense of time passing, but his internal clock stalled. He reached for the source of light keeping them sane in this pit of darkness and checked the time. They had been in the cellar for an hour. He kept expecting the high to fade and lose its sharp defining edge, but the drug didn't let up, even a little. He whirled with the demon wind.

Wyatt and Sarah were talking. Their voices grew louder and harder as they spoke. Sarah stood beside the tower of wooden crates, hands pressed to the side of one, eyes wide and deranged, hair drying in ragged shapes around her face.

"I have to get out," she said. "You can stay down here if you want, but I'm getting *out*. I don't want to be buried alive." The words tumbled out, rapid and uneven.

Wyatt grabbed her by the shoulders and pulled her back from the tower of crates. "You can't," he said. "There's only death up there."

"There's only death in *here*." She broke free of Wyatt's grip and shoved the top crate off the pile. It collapsed to the ground, the sides splintering on impact. She gave a sound of triumph and pushed the next crate, which toppled beside the first. She scrambled onto the final crate, stood, and reached up for the trapdoors.

"No!" Wyatt shouted, throwing himself toward her.

With only one good arm, he couldn't get a hold of his sister. She wriggled out of his grip and heaved, but the doors did not open.

She tried again, the jerky movements of her arms betraying panic, and when the doors refused to give, she started pounding wildly against the wood.

"Let us out! Let us out!" she screamed. "Oh my god, we're trapped! Help! Help!"

Dax staggered closer, not knowing how to help.

Wyatt grabbed Sarah around the waist and pulled her away, thrashing. He threw himself against the doors once, twice, and then the doors flew open.

Dax expected the roaring freight train sound of the tornado, the low howl of the wind, the demonic voice of whatever had been speaking through Savannah, the wail of the siren, but instead there was only silence. Even the rain had stopped. He shielded his eyes in the sudden brightness, despite the hidden sun. He grabbed his phone from the floor, turned off the light—the battery nearly drained—and put it in his pocket.

They stared up through the square in the ceiling at the sheet of gray light that washed down on them. Slowly, the threesome crawled out of the trapdoors and into the gray daylight, blinking and squinting as though new to the world. They had been in the storm cellar for eons.

They emerged, gazing around at the gray-cast ruin. A heavy tree branch lay just beside the cellar opening. Dax guessed it had rolled free when Wyatt had burst through.

The house had partially collapsed. Its roof had been shorn off, and most of its outer walls had imploded. Whatever horrors resided there now lay buried in a heap of architectural carnage. The stable, too, had been torn apart; only the skeleton of the structure remained. Pieces of the field were overturned. Mounds of dirt lay scattered among the debris of branches, flung across the distance from the remains of murdered trees, and bits of hay that must have come from the floor of the stable. The world a chaos of stillness, the sleeping aftermath of destruction—all filtered through the brightness and the gray, the cloud-covered light.

An eerie, almost ghostly, quality settled over the wreckage. Not a breeze moved the air. Not a voice broke the quiet. All around—the hush of death. The carcass of a cow, the shape of another farther off. Not even the animals had escaped.

The temperature had plummeted, and Dax felt cold. Whatever internal fire had been keeping him warm had gone out.

Sarah and Wyatt's faces took on a waxy hue in the discolored light. The faces of shades wandering among the living; only here, amid this desolation, it was just them and the dead.

Sarah started moving forward with purpose, Dax and Wyatt trailing behind her, until they came to the front of the house, the car now in sight and mercifully still right-side-up. They moved quickly, but the Dodge seemed to draw farther and farther away. The flat world stretched out around them, stretched endlessly to the horizon. Everything seemed so far away.

When at last they made it, Dax threw himself into the backseat while Sarah and Wyatt spent a moment arguing over who would drive. Sarah once again took the wheel.

"Should we call someone?" Dax said.

Wyatt turned around. "Who?"

"The police?"

"Don't be an idiot. Let's get the hell out of here." He turned around in his seat and asked Sarah what she was waiting for. She snapped to life and put the car in Drive.

They made their way down the road, through fields where cornstalks were just shooting up from the dirt, alongside a gnarled copse of scraggly, bare-branched trees ravaged by the storm, past the rusted water tower looming in the distance, and back toward town.

No. Past town.

They headed up Cross Street and kept going, past Main Street, up to Dunes Way and eastward. The tires rolled on. Dax wanted to ask where they were going, but the scenery outside the window kept streaking past, they kept moving, and he couldn't get out the words.

"Wrong way," Wyatt said. Then again: "Hello! You're going the wrong way!"

Sarah shook her head.

From his sharp angle, Dax could see her clenched jaw, her white-knuckled grip on the steering wheel. The road doubled and blurred ahead. The car swerved.

Wyatt made a grab for the wheel, but Sarah swatted him away.

"Where the hell are we going?" Wyatt asked.

In another moment, Dax knew the answer. The long road led away from town, out into the middle of nowhere, out where the abandoned farm waited. Where Zeke lay buried. Where the eye watched from the floor, called to its counterpart in the sky, begged Medusa's gaze to turn the town to stone. He shuddered and felt sick again. Leaning his forehead on the cool glass of the window, he closed his eyes.

Wyatt figured out their destination as well and said, "Wait—wait. Why the hell ...? What are you doing?"

Ahead, the Willoughby farm came into view. The house had shucked off planks of wood, leaving empty holes in the walls.

"We can't go home," Sarah said. "We can never go home."

As they drove down the final stretch of road, another vehicle came into view: a police cruiser parked out front.

"Stop! Stop!" Wyatt shouted as he slammed a hand on the dashboard. "It's the sheriff! Fucking *turn around!*"

Sarah jerked the wheel, swerved, and hit the brakes. Tires slid over mud, and the car spun and bounced as it veered off the road.

The thick trunk of a tree leapt out in front of them, filled the windshield, filled the entirety of Dax's vision. Breath escaped him. A branch reached forward, reached through the parting glass of the windshield and toward him, reached with its sharp impaling spike.

The world exploded.

CHAPTER 11

Everything was crooked.

Sarah's hair hung over the side of the driver's seat, strewn with bits of broken glass that glimmered like seawater in sunlight. Dax blinked as the image resolved. His mouth felt wet and tasted of blood.

He was tilted forward, kept upright by the seatbelt tight over his chest, which he clicked to release himself. Immediately, he slid forward and hit his head on the seat in front of him. Righting himself, he swung open the door with a creak and stumbled onto the grassy slope.

Nothing had exploded. He'd been sure they were all dead, but that earsplitting sound had been only the shattering of the windshield and the crunch of contorting metal.

Wyatt stirred through the window, shook his head, reached for his sister. The car was tilted forward down the incline, its front end hugging a tree. The back right tire didn't quite reach the ground, and spun impotently.

Dax wiped a trail of bloody saliva from his chin and thought he must have bit his tongue. He turned away, still feeling as though the earth had canted off balance.

The other two climbed out through Wyatt's door, the driver's side dipping low against the ground. Dax pulled out his cell phone, but he wasn't sure who to call. In the end, it didn't matter; the battery was drained, and a thin crack ran down the middle of the black screen. His dim reflection gazed back at him, a fractured phantom.

"When I said 'turn around,'" Wyatt muttered as he stumbled to the front of the car, "I didn't mean *into a goddamn tree.*"

Sarah held the side of her head.

"You were shouting," she said. "What was I supposed to do?"

"Not drive us into a fucking tree!" Wyatt tried to lift the crumpled hood, failed, and slammed a hand down on it with a clang. Something clicked, and he managed to pry it up.

Sarah started forward, but instead tripped and rolled down the incline until she came to a stop near his feet.

Wyatt bent to peer beneath the hood. He reached in with his good hand, and his fingers came out black and greasy. "Perfect," he said, straightening. "Engine's a goddamn pretzel." He kicked the screwed-up bumper, and the warped hood came crashing back down. He beat his fist on the hood until it dimpled further, then seemed to realize what he'd done and put both hands on it as if to mold it back to shape.

Dax looked up at the mottling of leaves in twisted branches overhead, an overlapping maze of wood and cloud. The leaves, still glistening with rainbowed beads of rain, threw him a fluttering wave. Veins ran through those leaves, and he imagined blood pumping through them, a forest pulsing alive. Wind sifted through the leaves. He heard the creep of insects.

"The sheriff must have heard the crash," he said.

They all turned toward the cruiser, dark and quiet in the distance.

"Make a run for it?" Wyatt said.

"And go where?"

He shrugged. "Anywhere! Let's just get the hell out of here."

Dax considered taking off down the road. He thought he could do it—just run and run, away from here, away from Conjunction until it turned to dust behind him. He couldn't look back. If he did, maybe he would turn to dust himself and blow away on the wind into nothing.

Nothing.

The thought shivered his heart with cold enchantment. How he desired to run, to leave, to scratch this place and all its ghosts from his consciousness for good. It was too late, though. He'd tried that once, and he'd looked back.

He thought of the sheriff's somber search for his son, and knew he would search forever, with an ever-ebbing hope, until love and grief expired and left only the burning desperation for an answer or an end.

Behind them, seven corpses occupied the damaged ranch where Savannah lived.

Like it or not, they needed help.

"You two stay here," he said.

"Stay—what?" Wyatt said. "Where are you going?"

Dax climbed the grassy slope back onto the road. "I'm going to talk to him," he said. "He's still the sheriff. Someone has to tell him about Savannah's family, right?"

He ignored Wyatt's protests as he walked toward the Willoughby farm.

The empty field that had been a parking lot on Friday stretched beyond the left of the farm, dirt torn up in clumps. The gray light cast a ghostly pall over this limbo.

As he walked, an image manifested in his mind: the Willoughby family strapped to wooden crosses and left in the fields, crows circling overhead; their eyes gouged out of their skulls, just like Savannah's family.

What did it mean?

He shut his eyes and took a breath of cool air, and when he reopened them the field was bare. No scarecrows, no bodies. Just the rustle of tall grass as a small figure ran away, the youngest Willoughby chasing carnivals all the way to Frieda Redding's place and beyond.

The sheriff was nowhere in sight.

It was dusky inside the farmhouse, and he understood now why people thought the place was haunted: dust floated strangely in the air, the discolored walls peeled like scabrous skin, and he felt as though ghosts were peering at him through each crack in the wooden panels. There was a cross on one wall he hadn't noticed before, old and cracked. The Willoughbies must have prayed to their savior, begged to be saved. They must have looked to their cross and to the crosses in the field where they were nailed and left to die and thought, *God, why have you forsaken us?* All except the little girl, Maybelle. The one who got away.

Something compelled him to walk down the hall to the room with the eye.

Is it still there in the dirt? Has it been wiped back into a blank slate?

Every footfall cracked the silence, and suddenly, he felt he wasn't alone.

Movement behind him.

Dax froze.

The floorboards behind him groaned, and then—

"Hands where I can see 'em!"

His hands flew into the air.

The sheriff told him to turn around, and he did, and he found Sheriff Anderson frowning at him, exhaustion etched into the lines in his face, into the rings beneath his eyes.

"Dax Howard, what the hell are you doing here?" he asked, sounding genuinely surprised, tired, annoyed. He holstered his gun.

What am *I doing here? Am I here to save the Willoughby family from slaughter? To go back in time to the party, get to Sarah and Zeke sooner, stop the inevitable? To dig up the grave? To beg for mercy?*

Sheriff Anderson's eyes narrowed. "You can put your hands down."

"Savannah," Dax said at last.

Yes, that's why I'm here.

"It's Savannah."

"Georgia?" the sheriff said.

"No, *Savannah.*"

Dax blurted out as much as he could—about her ripping out and throwing up her eyes, rising out of the lake after the coyote made her drown, her whole family dead.

He thought he had gotten his point across, but the sheriff's face was unreadable.

"What kind of drugs are you on?"

Dax thought he had completely missed the point.

"Well?" The sheriff stepped closer, his bulk menacing in the half-light of the boarded-up building. "It's meth, that it? Don't give me that look, I can smell a user a mile away."

"But—"

"Should have known. Like father, like son, huh?" He grabbed Dax by the upper arm and steered him through the room, toward the front door and the cruiser beyond. "Booze not enough for you, though, is it? Need the harder stuff. I'll bet you got it from that rat Barney Higgs, that right?"

"You have to—"

"That's enough out of you," the sheriff snapped, shoving him into the cruiser. The door slammed, and he was trapped, the wire mesh separating him from the front where the sheriff sat and started the engine. "Christ, what now?" he murmured after a short drive.

Dax craned his neck to see out the front window. He spotted the back end of the Dodge off the road ahead. They slowed, pulled to the side, stopped. Sheriff Anderson stepped out and scanned the area.

Wyatt and Sarah were gone.

After a minute, the sheriff reached for the radio on his lapel, pulled it to his mouth by the spiraled cord, and spoke rapidly into it. Then he got in the car, glanced back at Dax long enough for him to feel scrutinized, and started driving.

They had been driving just long enough for a lull to fill the car with the pregnancy of introspection when the sheriff spoke up again.

"I know this is hard for you." His eyes appeared, disembodied, in the rearview mirror. "But this ain't how we deal with our losses, son. Don't go down that road. That's the road cowards take. That's the road of giving up. You want to give up?"

Dax shook his head.

"Your old man was a blight on this town," he continued. "It's a hard pill to swallow, I know, but it's the God's honest truth. He was disruptive and mean. Started bar fights he couldn't finish. You already know that." His eyes looked up again, searing into him. "He used to harass me about reopening your mother's case. Did you know that? Wouldn't let it go. Came into the station, drunk and aggressive, telling me I'd gotten it all wrong, that she was still out there." He shook his head. "He was unhinged. Addiction will do that to a man. You want my opinion—I'm not one bit sorry he's gone, and you shouldn't be either. You were right to get away from him."

Dax's gut felt painfully tight.

"Are you sorry Zeke's gone?"

The sheriff's eyes flashed dangerously, two steely orbs. "He isn't *gone*. My boy is coming back."

Beyond the window the fields rushed by over the lonely road, under the gray weight of the sky. Then they slowed, and Dax looked up to find them behind a slow-moving vehicle dragging a trailer on a hitch.

"What the hell is this?" Sheriff Anderson murmured to himself, and he swung the car into the opposite lane. They sped up to pass the red pickup that wore its age in rusted flecks of paint, but there was another trailer in front of that one, hauled by another truck. "Is the goddamn freak show in town?"

The poor beleaguered vehicles groaned past in an endless creeping parade.

Suddenly he was seized by a cold terror.

"No," Dax said. He gripped the door handle and yanked, knowing there was no way out of this small metal cage. "No."

The sheriff ignored him as he pulled ahead, almost to the front of the caravan.

"Keep driving," Dax cried out, that unbearable foreboding flooding through him. "Don't stop! Just keep going!"

The sheriff smacked the mesh that separated them, rattling the metal, and Dax thought he heard the faint, off-key tunes of deranged circus music embedded within the metallic echo.

They pulled up alongside the first trailer in the queue, which bore on its side a horribly familiar emblem painted in gold—the logo of Winking Eye Amusements.

Somehow, trying to find them from a distance felt safe. It was an intangible mystery, one that, deep down, Dax hadn't truly believed he would solve.

But now they had found *him*.

They were *here*.

Sheriff Anderson rolled down the passenger window to speak with the driver: a man with bulbous, insectile eyes and a tattered top hat.

They crept along at fifteen miles an hour

"You'd better tell me you're just passing through. We're not interested in whatever you're peddling," the sheriff called across to him.

"Oh, we've acquired the necessary permits. We're on our way to speak with the owner of a parcel of land we wish to rent." The man's black, portentous eyes grazed over the cruiser, and his lips pulled back into a ghastly grin. "This is a show you won't want to miss."

"Listen, pal—"

In the distance, a car approached, honking its horn.

Sheriff Anderson made a sound in the back of his throat. "Send your paperwork to the sheriff's office," he called out the window before rolling it up.

He sped past the truck and cut in front of it. The approaching car shot past them in the lane they'd occupied only moments before.

Dax turned in his seat, watching the front of the caravan recede behind them. It rattled along deliberately, bearing down with painful, inexorable slowness upon the town.

And when the caterpillar emerged from its cocoon into a phantasmagoria of lights and carnival rides, what terrors would it bring with it into Conjunction?

Dax had been biting his tongue without realizing it, until tasting blood in his mouth.

They pulled onto Main Street, where buildings stood resolute while tree branches littered the grass. The remains of a rusted bicycle had wrapped around a streetlight in a twisted jumble of metal and deflated tires. He stared, transfixed, at the bike, which hung five feet off the ground.

Sheriff Anderson led him to a holding cell in the back of the station. He brusquely emptied Dax's pockets and gave him a push. The door locked shut. Footsteps retreated.

Dax sat on the cot and gripped the rough white blanket in two fists, willing himself to remain calm. He tried not to look at the bars and their stark, unnatural verticality. He had never been locked up before. Claustrophobia clawed its way up his throat.

Voices drifted down the hall.

He suffered hours with nothing to turn over in his mind but the carnival creeping slowly down the road, creeping relentlessly forward, dragging all its dead weight into town. His mind turned everything else to white noise and zeroed in on just that, as if to torment him.

Trailers filled with secrets, imbued with carnivalesque mythology— the mystery of it all.

As evening fell, a deputy he'd never seen before unlocked the door of the cell and walked in with a sandwich on a plate.

"You look hungry," she said. Her curly brown hair was pulled into a ponytail, but stray hairs had freed themselves to fall in coils around her face. She held out the plate. "Sorry if you don't like tuna. I'm a vegetarian, didn't have any cold cuts."

For a brief, wild moment he wondered if he could bulrush her and slip out the door, which stood ajar, and out into the gathering night. He could be free from this cell and its iron bars. But he would never make it far enough before something snaked out its tentacle, wrapped around his ankle, and dragged him back.

"Not much of a talker, are you?" she said.

Dax licked his chapping lips with a parched tongue and said nothing, for there was nothing to say.

She set the plate on the floor. "In case you change your mind." She left and locked the door behind her, locked him in again so that he almost called her back just to breathe through the open door, as though by some trick of abstruse physics, fresh air refused to pass through the wide openings between the bars and he breathed only the stale, rotten air of the cell. Her footsteps echoed down the hall, and the lights shut off.

One lone bulb still shone out in the hallway, washing the floor in an ugly fluorescent glow. He wished she'd turned that one off, too. Shadows crept up from the corners of the cell and threw deranged shapes on the walls. He thought he saw the outline of a coyote moving against the brick, and he looked into the hallway, half-expecting to see the creature stalking outside the cell, but there was nothing.

The bars made long, thin lines on the walls, encasing him in a dimension of dark stripes, and the light in the hall flickered and buzzed, sent shadows soaring over him. He lay on the hard cot, listening to every whisper of the wind outside, every creak of the building as it settled, and within those sounds were greater horrors, voices from beyond the thin gauze of reality.

He watched the shadows, afraid they would move in on him the moment he closed his eyes. Forever he lay in the cell—beyond time. Alone with his whirring thoughts.

At long last, morning broached the horizon. His jaw ached, and he realized he'd been clenching it. The scabs on his palms itched. His mouth felt filled with cotton. The morning light struck his prickling eyes with such rough brightness that it made him feel sick.

After a while, the sheriff appeared, holding a steaming mug of coffee. He sipped it while he stood outside the cell, staring in at Dax.

"Why were you trespassing at the old Willoughby farm yesterday?"

His sluggish mind picked through a few replies. "I thought I could help," he said and cleared his throat. The sheriff did not offer him a glass of water. "You said Zeke disappeared after the party. I thought maybe I could find some clue there, about what happened."

"So you went over there, never mind a tornado just tore through, to play detective?" The sheriff stepped closer to the bars. "I don't believe you," he said. "Try again."

Dax shook his head, mute.

"Nothing, huh?" He frowned. "That's what I thought." He reached into his pocket and pulled out a silver watch, which he dangled in front of the bars. "Recognize this?" When he spoke, his lips quivered and curled back against his teeth. "Does this watch belong to you?"

Dax shook his head. His throat seized up.

"Then why did I find it in your pocket yesterday?" He didn't wait long enough for Dax to respond. "Where did you get this?"

"I—"

"Did you purchase it? Was it a gift? Did you steal it?"

"I ... I found it."

"You found it," the sheriff snapped. "You found it where?"

"At the Willoughby farm." Dax managed to get out the words around the ball of anxiety in his throat. His eyes burned, skin itched; he wanted to curl up in the black void of deep sleep.

Still holding the watch, the sheriff curled his hand into a fist and banged the side of it against the cell.

Dax flinched.

"Do you know whose watch this is?" the sheriff said. Again, he didn't wait for Dax to respond. "This is Ezekiel's watch. I gave it to him on his eighteenth birthday. He wears it every day." The sheriff lowered his voice. "So you'd damn well better tell me why this watch was in your pocket and not around my son's wrist."

Panic made speaking a nearly insurmountable task. "I don't know," he choked out. "I found it on the ground."

"You're a goddamn liar. Zeke is my son." He slammed his fist against the bars again, sloshing coffee over the rim of the mug and onto his hand. "My *son!*" he said again, voice rising. "Where is my son?"

"Sheriff!" came a voice from down the hall, then footsteps jogging closer. The deputy appeared. "What's going on?"

"You keep the hell out of this," the sheriff growled without taking his eyes off Dax. He thrust his mug at her, and she reluctantly took it before heading back down the hall.

He pulled out a ring of keys and unlocked the cell door.

"Now I'm going to ask you one more time," he said as he stepped inside.

His presence in the small space was terrible, dominating.

Dax slid back toward the wall, but there was nowhere to go.

The sheriff bent over the cot, over Dax, and gripped him by the collar with one hand while the other found his holster and produced a sleek black .40 Smith & Wesson. The barrel of the gun rose to greet him.

"Where is my son?" he asked, his voice deadly calm.

Dax couldn't breathe.

"I don't know."

"Don't you lie to me!" The sheriff snapped. "I know your kind—lying, drunk piece of shit. Just like your daddy. Know how many times I had to drag him in here, right into this cell, and lock his raving lunatic ass in for the night? No helping your kind."

"Please ..."

The sheriff stared at him with the breathless plea floating between them. Then he let go and stepped back, looking with abject dismay at the gun, which he lowered slowly, deliberately. His voice was a low grumble when he spoke again: "I need to know what happened to my son."

"I know," Dax said, and he did—and he hated himself for not telling the truth. But how could he bring himself to implicate Sarah and Wyatt? And yet ... how could he bring himself to curse the sheriff with the same grief of uncertainty that had driven his father to such an end?

For a moment, Dax thought they shared a mutual understanding. He felt connected to the sheriff by their circumstances, and he wanted to help this man who he had never particularly liked or admired.

But then the sheriff's face went cold again. He holstered his gun and said, "You'll tell me what you did. Or I'll find out on my own. Until then ..." and his eyes moved slowly around the cell to imply that Dax had better get comfortable.

CHAPTER 12

Comfort, however, was not to be found.

Dax slept on and off, waking with aches in his neck from the stiff cot. All the world beyond the walls seemed to have vanished. When he opened his eyes again, he found the deputy standing just outside the cell looking in. She held out a sweating bottle of water through the bars.

Gratefully he stumbled over, grabbed the water, and downed half the bottle where he stood. "Thanks," he said after catching his breath.

"Slow down or it'll come back up."

Before he could reply, his stomach churned. He held the cold bottle against his forehead and exhaled slowly.

The deputy watched him. "The comedown is brutal."

"Personal experience?" he asked.

"My uncle," she said. Perhaps his face showed some measure of surprise because she added, "I'm from Bannon. You know what they say: If you're not working the chain, you're probably on crank."

The uneaten tuna sandwich she'd left him yesterday was still on the floor.

"Vegetarian from Bannon," he said. "You don't hear that too often." His stomach began to settle, so he sipped more. "So I guess you never worked the chain at the slaughterhouse?"

"Sure did. For a whole week," she said. "Why do you think I'm a vegetarian?"

They stood in silence while Dax finished the water.

At last she said, "I hope this is a wakeup call for you."

"What?" When he realized what she'd meant, he huffed the barest semblance of a laugh. "Oh, no. I've never ... that was the first time."

Exhaustion settled over him, and he gripped the bars to hold himself up. "And I'm pretty sure it'll be the last."

She fixed him with a stare that gave away nothing of what she was thinking. Premature lines grooved her young face, as if she had lost a considerable amount of weight recently or had experienced a considerable amount of stress. She held her shoulders back and squared away, the posture of someone who knows how to take care of herself.

"What happened to Deputy Harding?"

Dax recalled the elderly man who used to sit at the desk she occupied, snoring into his long white beard while all manner of small-town crime went unnoticed by his gray, myopic eyes. There had been one other deputy Dax remembered, but not the woman who stood before him.

"Passed a few years back. Guess I haven't properly introduced myself. I'm Deborah Mendoza. Sheriff's deputy."

"Dax Howard."

"Well, Dax," she said, "You might want to lie down. That comedown's not done with you yet."

She turned to walk away.

Dax leaned against the bars and said, "You know where Prairie Rose Ranch is?"

She stopped and looked back at him. "Why, what's there?"

"Not much anymore. It got destroyed by the tornado." The bars were cold against his forehead. He felt chilled, but he was sweating. "They're all dead."

Deputy Mendoza took a step toward him, her eyes gleaming fiercely.

"Say again?"

"The family. They're dead. The house looked wrecked, so—"

"Why didn't you report this yesterday?" she snapped, reaching for her radio. "You can't know they're dead. What if they're trapped under the rubble?"

She pulled her radio up to her mouth.

"The tornado didn't kill them," Dax said. "They were already dead."

"What?"

"Something else got them. I found them before the tornado even hit."

She lowered her radio and narrowed her eyes.

"What were you doing there?"

He gripped one of the bars and fought to stay upright. "I was looking for the girl who lives there. Savannah. But I didn't find her. Everyone else—but not her."

The deputy frowned. "We'll talk more when I get back."

She walked away, and he sat down heavily.

His body ached, the way a fever seems to set your bones on edge. He lay back on the cot and focused on a crack running along the ceiling, traced it from one end to the other, where it spiderwebbed off into hair-thin lines like the branching of spindly twigs on a dead tree.

Closing his eyes, he felt himself spiderwebbing off into the distance, cracking into hairline fractures and dissolving into a semiconscious daze of half-sleep, trapped somewhere in the liminal space between waking and dozing.

The shrill ring of a phone woke him.

He groaned, pressed hands to his ears to block the mechanical sound. It stopped abruptly, and he heard the murmur of a voice down the hall.

"How long has she been missing?" the voice said. "Uh huh. And where did you last see her?" A pause. "Could be she's just out with friends, lost track of time. We'll be on the lookout. If she's not home by tomorrow morning, come on by the station and we'll file an official report."

The sound of the phone hitting the receiver made an effective punctuation mark on the conversation. The phone didn't ring again.

Dax dozed in merciful silence.

Try as he might, he couldn't stop picturing Prairie Rose Ranch. He forced his mind away from the gruesome images and saw, instead, a drawing of a pink flower blooming in a barren land. He breathed slowly and envisioned his mother's drawing of the prairie rose and the story that went with it.

How did it go?

He tried to remember.

Outside, the wind whistled in through the cracks in the walls.

The wind blew in, blew him into the past.

Dax, a child of no more than five or six, sat cross-legged on the back porch. His mother sat in the rocking chair, gently swaying back and forth. The sun was setting, catching her eyes with its burnt orange glow. A Mason jar sat beside her. She had given it to him rather than filling it with ashes. Young Dax had packed dirt inside and planted two little flowers.

"My grandfather told me this story when I was about your age," she said, rocking back and forth in the wind. "Long, long ago, when the world was young, no flowers bloomed on the prairie. Only grass and shrubs. It was an ugly land. A dead land. And Earth was sad. She wanted flowers on her prairie: blue flowers like clear sky, white flowers like winter snow, yellow flowers like midday sun, pink flowers like spring dawn. Instead, the prairie was gray and brown.

"A little pink flower that lived in the heart of the Earth said she would go to the prairie and make it beautiful. But when the Wind Demon saw her, he rushed at her and blew out her life.

"Other flowers tried to go forth, one after another. Wind Demon killed them all. The prairie was his playground, where he blustered and roared and blew death into the world.

"At last, Prairie Rose offered to go. Mother Earth said she was lovely and fragrant, and surely the Wind Demon would let her stay. Prairie Rose made the long journey up from the dark cold ground, crawled up from the dirt and the roots, and sprouted onto the drab prairie. When Wind Demon saw her, he rushed forward to blow out her life, drawing his breath in great gusts. As he drew closer, he caught the fragrance of Prairie Rose.

"He thought perhaps he didn't have it in his heart to blow out the life of one so beautiful and sweet. He decided she would stay there and he would make his voice gentle so as not to frighten her away.

"Thus, Wind Demon changed. He became quiet. He sent soft breezes over the prairie grass. He whispered and hummed. He was no longer a demon. Other flowers came up from the heart of the Earth, through the dark ground, and made her prairie beautiful. Even Wind came to love the blossoms.

"Sometimes, Wind forgets to be soft and grows loud and blustery, but it doesn't last long. Even when the tornados come, eventually they dissipate back into the air because Wind remembers not to hurt the flowers, especially not Prairie Rose."

Clouds disturbed the sunset on the horizon, but their low rumblings were soft and faraway. All was calm on the Howard farm. Dax liked the story and stored it away with the other strange tales his mother passed down from her grandfather. He imagined the prairie rose alone among the cold grasses, blown by the Wind Demon until it was almost torn from the ground and thrown into the air.

The image transformed into Savannah with the tornado reaching into the barn, lifting her off her feet, but when she opened her mouth with that demonic voice, he realized the tornado wasn't blowing her: *she* was blowing the tornado. Her breath summoned it from the clouds.

To bring something down from the sky, or to pull something up from the ground?

He sucked in a breath and opened his eyes. He lay on his side on the cot, twilight growing long shadows on the floor of the cell.

The old tuna sandwich had been replaced by a new one. Flies circled around it.

He heard Deputy Mendoza talking to someone in the lobby in a soothing voice.

"We'll find them," he heard her say. "Don't worry. It's probably just kids being kids. I'm sure they'll turn up soon."

A door opened and closed.

"How many is that now?" the other deputy said.

"Four," she said. "All teenagers."

"Christ."

They stopped talking, but Dax couldn't go back to sleep. A sudden panic had overtaken him. He wondered what Savannah was doing; he wondered if the teenagers the deputy had mentioned were dead.

How many more would die?

He lay still, heart pounding, and tried to control his breathing. She was out there somewhere, killing people, and he was stuck here, useless, in this tiny cell.

Footsteps down the hall.

He cracked open his eyes; the lids slid against crust that had gathered in the corners. His head pounded so hard he felt it in his gut.

Deputy Mendoza stood outside the cell, looking pale and troubled. The downward curve of her mouth soured and aged her face. Her body managed to convey a sigh without exhaling.

"You were right," she said, her voice calmer now. "We didn't find Savannah." She impatiently batted a few loose ringlets of hair behind her ear. "You have any idea where she might be?"

Dax shook his head.

"Is it possible …" The deputy put her hands on her hips, looked down and then up again. "Is it possible she and Zeke might have run off together?"

"No."

"That was a quick answer," she said. "Why not?"

He shrugged. "I just can't see it."

She gave him a skeptical look. "You sound pretty sure of yourself."

"Shouldn't I have a lawyer before I say anything?" Dax said.

She held up her hands. "I'm just trying to figure this out. I thought you could help me. Can you?"

He shrugged.

"Everything okay back there?" the other deputy called from the front.

"Fine, Bobby," Deputy Mendoza said. "Why don't you see if the sheriff needs your help out there. I'll keep an eye on things."

Footsteps moved in the lobby, and then the front door opened and shut.

"I'm trying to help you, Dax," the deputy said. "And I thought you could help *me*, too. Now, about that watch."

Dax exhaled slowly and looked at the floor. He ached to go back in time and leave the watch at home—or better yet, chuck it in the lake. Get rid of it.

Why had I kept it?

"You said you found it—whereabouts? At the Willoughby farm, I mean?"

Dax felt the lie crawl out of his mouth like a creature separate from himself: "In the parking lot—the field."

"And did you see Savannah at the party as well?"

"Yes."

Her face seemed eager to repress something, some internal conflict.

"The sheriff wants this to be something it's not. I'll tell you that because I think you deserve to know. We never want to believe the ones we love the most will leave us. But he's too close to this."

"So you think Zeke ran away with Savannah. Then who killed her family?"

"Well, that's the question, isn't it?"

"What if it was Savannah?"

The deputy froze, giving him a look of disdain and disbelief. "What makes you think she could do something like that?"

"Because I saw those bodies. They weren't killed two days ago. They'd been dead for ... *weeks*. And she was there, all that time. Never called 9-1-1."

The deputy crossed her arms and leaned against the bars of the cell.

"Maybe she wasn't living there," she said. "Maybe she didn't know they were dead."

Dax snorted.

"Her parents have called us a few times, asking us to find their girl because she ran away. She's run away from home maybe five times in the past year. It wouldn't be a stretch to think she'd done it again."

"Well, maybe you should look for her, then."

"That would be the thing."

"Listen, just ..." How could he warn her what Savannah had become? "If you find her, be careful. In case it *was* her, after all."

"Well, aren't you a gentleman," she said, her voice dripping with sarcasm.

Deputy Mendoza had clearly taken his warning the wrong way.

"No, I know you can handle yourself, that's not—"

"I got it," she cut him off sharply. "You don't get to be a Crow County deputy without weathering a little casual sexism every now and then."

Dax caught her eye and held it seriously. "I think she's dangerous. I saw her at the party. There's something ... *wrong* with her."

Scorn slipped from the deputy's face. "Wrong how?"

"I don't know. Maybe she's on drugs or something," —another lie, piling up, but the closest he could get to the truth— "but I plan on staying the hell away from her."

Her eyebrows came together. After a moment, she reached to her belt, pulled out a ring of keys, and unlocked the door. It creaked open, and she stepped aside.

"What is this?" he said.

"You're free to go."

He stepped forward, out of the jail cell, surprised at the relief that washed over him. He looked back at her as she closed the door. She handed him his wallet, phone, and keys, and he hesitated with these useless objects in his hands.

"What, you want an explanation?" she said, sounding a little incredulous. "Look, we've got no reason to keep you here. But be clear:

just because you're free to go doesn't mean you shouldn't watch yourself. The sheriff wasn't ready to let this go. You get yourself involved in anything—*anything*—and he'll bring you right back here. You got me?"

"Yeah," Dax said. "I got you."

She walked him to the front door of the station and saw him out. Evening had spread its creeping darkness across Main Street; a cool breeze usurped the warmth of day. He looked to the church that stood at the end of the street, reaching into the clouded sky, and remembered the church in Pastor's Grove. He turned the other direction and started walking, giving a small wave to the deputy still in the doorway.

His keys were in his pocket now, but his car was still at Wyatt's house, so they would do him no good. His phone was long dead. His wallet was the only thing of any use, so he walked down past the gun shop, past a diner trapped some forty years back in time, past a bakery, butcher shop, feed store, locksmith—and finally to The Rusty Doornail.

The outside of the bar was utterly nondescript: wood and brick grown jaded and fractious with age and obsolescence, a red neon sign above the door that buzzed and flickered manically.

Dax pushed open the door and stepped inside.

It was dark and musty, and even coming in from a dim evening his eyes had to adjust to the muted light. Everything was dull, brown, wooden, but for the bottles lined up and gleaming behind the bar.

He took a seat on a wobbly stool. A few older men sat at a round table in the corner playing cards. The bartender approached Dax, looked him up and down as if deciding whether he wanted to bother carding him. Dax knew the man, as anyone knows anyone else in a small town, but couldn't remember his name. Out of habit, he reached into his wallet and pulled out his ID.

The bartender squinted at it, then looked up at him again.

"You're Roy's boy?"

Dax nodded.

The bartender turned away, opened a bottle, and slid it over.

"First one's on the house."

He wanted to ask the bartender about his father.

Had he sat here, at this very stool, stoic and quiet? Or had he joked around with the bartender? Had he played cards? Had he sat here with Zeke, swapping stories?

That thought was too much—it crawled across his skin like centipedes. The bartender walked away, and Dax asked him nothing. Instead, he nursed his beer, sinking into memories that were not his and maybe did not even exist.

Time passed, but not visibly, for there were no windows. He might have sat here all night, lost in time. He wondered if his father had felt the same way, safe from the trespasses of time in this gloomy cocoon. Maybe he should stay here. The carnival could not come into the bar. Neither could Savannah, being underage. He was safe here, with his father's ghost.

The door opened, letting in the night, and Phil Sawyer came over, paused, and took the seat beside him.

"What are you doing here, Dax?"

He kept his eyes on the bottle and said, "Drinking."

"Cut the shit," Phil said, turning to face him. "You spent the night in jail?"

"Yeah, figured I needed a drink after that."

"Right back to it, then. Isn't that why you were there to begin with?"

Thinking it was better than admitting to doing drugs, Dax shrugged. "How'd you know I was here?" he asked.

"I didn't," Phil said. He sighed and leaned forward on his elbows. "Been working on Beau Montgomery's car all day. Your friend Wyatt came in to check on it a little while ago and told me you'd had some trouble with the sheriff, sort of asked me to check on you, in his own roundabout way. Deputy Mendoza said she saw you go this way when you left."

"Is Wyatt okay? Where is he?"

"At home and in a hell of trouble. He crashed the car, but he's fine—nothing broken that wasn't already. Seemed worried about you, though. Guess I don't blame him."

"Well, good news: I'm fine."

"Like hell you are," Phil said.

The bartender looked over at them, as though he were considering asking Phil what he wanted to drink, then seemed to intuit that he'd better hang back washing glasses instead.

Dax didn't appreciate the company; he wanted to sit here by himself—with his father. Yet he had never disliked Phil's company before. He had often preferred Phil's company to his father's, in fact. They were more similar than he and Roy. Phil understood him in a way he wasn't sure his father ever had. Phil was the one who had encouraged him to go to college, not his father. He had helped him find scholarships. He had told Dax about his abandoned desire to be an engineer, and how he had never tried college because he had worried he wasn't smart enough, that he couldn't do it.

"I can't sit by and watch you do this to yourself," Phil said. "You have school—you're so close to finishing. If I'd known it would be this hard for you to be back, I wouldn't have suggested you stick around."

Dax snorted at the mention of school. The one beer was already going to his head, probably because he hadn't had anything to eat since yesterday. He rolled the bottle back and forth in his hands. He'd told so many lies recently. Truth festered inside him and he wondered if he had the voice to tell it.

"I can't go back," he said at last. "You told me I could do it, but you were wrong, after all. I've failed all my classes, and I'll lose the scholarship after this year. I won't graduate."

Phil didn't say anything for a moment, and Dax felt shame rushing through him. He didn't dare look up to see how he had let him down.

"That's it? You're giving up?" Phil said. "I didn't take you for a quitter. So things got hard, so what? It's not the end of the world. Hell, Dax, I'll help you apply for a loan. You'll go back to school. You fail once, that doesn't mean you lie down and let the world walk over you. You try again."

As Phil spoke, a heaviness began to lift from the pit of Dax's stomach, which had been there so long he thought the gnawing shame would be part of him forever. That same relief he'd felt when stepping out of jail returned, prickling through him like a rush of drunkenness.

Phil reached out and patted his shoulder. "Everything's going to be okay."

Believing him, Dax put down the almost-empty bottle and pushed it away.

"Now, come on. Let's go back to my place." Phil got up, and Dax followed, but not without wobbling slightly. The withdrawal and lack of food was finally catching up to him, and Phil put a hand on his shoulder to steady him, but thankfully didn't make any comment.

He paused to toss a few bills onto the bar and then led Dax to the door and out into the night, which had slowly been clearing itself of clouds while he sat in the bar. The moon shone fat and indolent overhead.

They got into Phil's car and drove.

An American flag hung out front of his place, limp and still until a breeze fluttered it into motion, rippling the stripes and stars. On the lawn were several bizarre sculptures made out of spare car parts—gears, grilles, and scrap metal constructed into oddly humanoid forms. Dax found them vaguely grotesque and uncanny. Phil liked to make these in his spare time and pose them up around the lawn, and Helen had either resigned herself to the peculiar décor or appreciated that Phil had a creative side.

A warm glow issued from the living room windows. They stepped onto the porch where a swinging bench creaked in the wind, its chains groaning with the slow, gentle movement. Their presence was sensed; a dog barked within. Another joined it, growling just inside. Phil opened the door and told the dogs to sit. The corgi gave a yip and then walked away disinterestedly, but the lab sniffed them eagerly, even while it sat squirming, its tail thumping the floor.

"What did I tell you?" Helen said. "I knew you'd be late, even though you promised, and now dinner is cold—oh." She stopped short as she stepped into the front hall, seeing them. "Hello, Dax." She wiped her hands on a towel, threw it over her shoulder, and came toward him with her arms outstretched. After the hug, she stepped back, still gripping his arms, her amber eyes sharp as glass. "Dinner," she said, letting go of him. "I'll warm it up, and we'll all sit down to eat." She disappeared back into the kitchen, and they followed.

Throwing decency to the wind, Dax shoveled sweet corn, mashed potatoes, and roasted chicken into his mouth, grateful beyond words for the home-cooked meal. As he ate, Helen kept clucking her tongue, quietly, but not quiet enough to keep it to herself.

"Look at you, you're rail thin," she murmured as she wiped her mouth. "Phil, why didn't you tell me he looked so poorly?"

"He's fine, Helen."

"Hungover. Hmm. Well, he should know better. Dax, you really should know to stay away from that stuff," she said, unable to keep the judgment out of her voice. "Alcoholism is genetic, you know."

"He doesn't need you lecturing him," Phil said.

She harrumphed again and started buttering her corn.

Dax chugged a glass of water, not even minding her lecture behind the comforting blanket of food.

"Anyway, I've talked to Father O'Malley," she said, "and I think we'll plan the service for this weekend. Dax, you really should be there. It would be wrong not to have you there."

Phil sighed. "Don't you think that's *his* business?"

"Some of us think Roy deserves a proper funeral, and I think it would be selfish to deny us that."

They both looked at Dax, so he said, "You can do whatever you want." He knew better than to argue with her.

One week after his mother disappeared, Helen had orchestrated a vigil at the church. She and Renée had an odd sort of friendship: a harmony of contrasts, a yin and yang.

Dax had ridden his bike to the church that night. He couldn't just now remember what his father had been doing, only that he hadn't gone, but when Dax got to the church that night, it was already full dark out, with miles of stars. He'd dumped his bike on the lawn and had walked up the steps to the double wooden doors, feeling very small.

The doors had given an almighty creak, which had resounded in the echoic chamber. The church had been dark inside. Heads bent in prayer had turned to stare at him with hooded eyes, their hunched figures like etched silhouettes against the pews, edges flickering and bleeding in the candlelight. Their familiar shapes had become monstrous and unrecognizable.

Candles, scattered like stars around the sanctuary, had thrown shifting shadows over the pews, making movement out of stillness. The interior of the church had shivered and danced.

Dax remembered starting the long walk up the main aisle.

Above the pulpit, a wooden crucifix had hung before him, robed in shadow against the candles' bewitching light. Jesus, in his crown of thorns, had appeared to scream in silent horror—reluctant sacrifice of some black mass.

"Dax," a whisper had come from behind him, and he'd flinched when Helen's hand clenched on his shoulder. She'd kissed the top of his head and had said, "It makes me so glad to see you here. If you reach out to God, He will reach back into your heart."

She'd ushered him to the front of the church, right in the wooden gaze of crucified Jesus. Averting his eyes, he'd watched wax drip down the candles in front of him. Helen had put a long match in his hand and had guided him to an unlit candle. After the wick had ignited, she'd waved out the match as the flame grew tall.

"We're all praying for your mother. Why don't you say a prayer?" she'd said, pushing him to his knees. She'd taken his hands, weaving them together for him, fingers interlocking.

He hadn't known how to pray.

All he could do was wonder: *Where had she gone?*

Dax had watched a bulb of wax slide down the candle he'd lit; he'd watched the wick turn black.

Had the wind blown her away? Had she whirled into the sky?

Helen had knelt beside him and had said in her soft, lilting voice, "Heavenly Father, please watch over Renée Howard and use these candles to guide her home to her family and friends. If she has already departed this earth, I pray she is welcomed into the Kingdom of Heaven for life eternal with the Lord. Amen."

He shivered, then and now.

That was the first time he'd thought his mother might be dead.

He hadn't understood the grief that had overcome him then. Part of him had still expected to see her burst into the church and tell him she'd just been on a wonderful journey and was sorry she hadn't called home. In his own way, even then, he'd recognized wanderlust in the tone of her voice when she told stories of places far and grand.

Weeks later, he'd clung ever more desperately to the possibility of her return. He'd refused to look at the front door, thinking she might walk through it if he wasn't looking.

Yet his slim hope had waned but had never fully disappeared. It had decayed by its half-life each day, but somehow, even now, the tiniest splinter of hope remained embedded in the depths of his heart. In the end, the hope had hurt more than grief.

He could not have known this as he sat in the church that evening, so he'd allowed himself to hope, and fiercely. He'd allowed himself to wonder if she might ever return.

He'd left the candlelit vigil shortly thereafter, but in his mind, the memory changed: crucified Jesus sloughed off his wooden skin until he was just a skeleton with black empty sockets; the church sank into its foundations, fell into the disrepair of the Pastor's Grove church; the people crumbled into bones that scattered across the floor; Helen became Savannah with animal eyes, praying to a different father in the candlelight; and he was running for his life, running from the otherworldly presence looming over him—

"Dax?"

He blinked and looked up sharply to find Helen and Phil staring at him across the table. "Sorry," he said. "I'm a little tired."

At once, he didn't think he could eat any more of the food on his plate. He stared down, the comforts of home vanishing piece by piece back into a gulf of anxiety. He wished he could go back and bask in the moment of a quiet, normal dinner, but the memory had reminded him that all was not well in Conjunction.

"Have either of you heard about the carnival that's in town?"

Helen and Phil exchanged a look. Then Helen shook her head and went back to cutting her chicken into pieces. "Just one of those amusements. They come every now and then. Don't worry yourself over it."

"More potatoes?" Phil said.

Dax looked between them. "It's the one."

"I think I've had enough," Helen said. She put down her fork and knife, stood, and took Dax's plate away along with her own. "It's late," she said while she rinsed them in the sink. "I'm going to bed. Why don't you set Dax up on the couch."

When she was gone, and it was the two of them sitting quietly across from one another at the table, Dax said, "He was right, you know. He was looking for it, and it's here."

"Dax." Phil threw his napkin on his plate. "I know you want closure. But chasing ghosts …. That's not the way to find it. Your dad's obsession with carnivals wasn't healthy. It was—"

"What?" Dax said, heat curling in his chest. "Delusional?"

Phil leaned his elbows on the table. "I'd rather not think of him like that. You don't need to go down the same path—"

"But he was right," Dax said. "He was right, and no one believed him."

Phil shook his head. "Don't be like this, Dax. Don't do what he did. You know how your father was. I don't want you to end up like him." He took a breath, steeling himself. "Don't get me wrong. Your father was a good man," he continued, and he looked pained to bring forth those words. "Whatever his flaws. He was a good man at heart. It's not that you shouldn't *be* like him, but you shouldn't do what he did. Being a good man isn't enough. It doesn't make it okay to do these things, to get caught up in this madness. I know I can't stop you, but—God, I can't go through it again with you, too. I don't want to watch you drink yourself to death, Dax. He would have drank himself to death sooner or later, and he knew it. He knew it, and he didn't care."

Dax stared at him across the table. "What do you mean, 'he would have?'" His heart started to beat faster. "That's how he died, isn't it?"

Phil was silent for a moment, head lowered, hands folded on the table in front of him. "It should have been," he said at last. "That would have made sense. We all would have seen that coming. Somehow, it's easier to think of it that way. That's why I told you ... It seemed—*fair*, somehow. Like it might hurt less."

Dax's heart skipped and redoubled its beats.

"How did he die?"

"It was completely random," Phil said and licked his lips. "An animal attack, we think. I found him, out back."

"What kind of animal?"

Phil shook his head. "I don't know. Bite marks weren't big, what I could make out. Seemed like a small animal. But it ... it wasn't pretty. It got his throat. His tongue. His eyes."

Dax felt a coldness settle in his veins.

"I'm sorry," Phil said. "I wanted you to feel certain about what happened to him. To know and to be able to move on. I don't know what got him, and I didn't want you to feel like—like you'd never have the full story... with either of them. It just didn't seem fair."

"You lied to me," Dax said.

Phil came around the table to stand beside him.

"I'm sorry, son."

Dax pushed his chair away when Phil reached out to put a hand on his shoulder. He turned and stood, moving to keep the table between them.

"Don't call me 'son,'" he said. "I'm not your son."

"I know you're mad right now. I don't blame you." Phil let his hand drop to his side. "Why don't you get some rest. I'll get some pillows and blankets for the couch."

After a moment's hesitation, Phil left the room.

Dax couldn't move. His feet were rooted to the floor, his lungs depleted. A terrible cold glided through him, clutched his frantic heart, made his skin prickle. He put his hands on the table and leaned against it for balance, closed his eyes. Against his lids, he saw his father in the dirt, his throat torn open, his eyes mere gaping sockets, and he knew who it was, he knew who had done it—for who else could it be but her?

At last the cold fully enveloped him, and the pain of betrayal melted away into rage. *She killed him,* he thought, feeling nothing but that resolution, that murderous calm.

Savannah had killed his father.

CHAPTER 13

The thought of killing a human should have horrified him—but Savannah *wasn't* human, was she? He was going to kill her.

If she's not human, though, what is she?

The question shattered his essential beliefs in nature, those uncompromising rules by which the physical world functioned. He'd studied math and physics—numbers, logic, indissoluble laws. Now the laws collapsed upon themselves. He found he had lost his old definition of reality and faced instead an infinity of awful possibility.

Dax had killed chickens before and hated it, the snap of their necks and the death-twitches that followed. It would not be so simple to snap Savannah's neck. He had no plan, only the immediacy of this violent impulse for revenge.

Eventually he went to the living room, where Phil had set up pillows and blankets, but he didn't lie down. He couldn't. Instead, he paced the room in darkness.

Moonlight unspooled from the windowpane, fell over the floor.

What can one do with such motive compromised by a kind of terror and inability to act?

He tried to sleep, but was accosted by visions of peeling back his father's eyelids at the coroner's only to find hollow craters.

After several hours of uneasy deliberation, Dax decided he could not stay here—not with Phil's deceptions and Helen's judgment. He considered leaving a note, then thought better of it.

What do I owe the Sawyers the luxury? Let them worry. Let them stew.

These unkind thoughts gave him a kind of bitter satisfaction.

He stepped out of the house into the cool blue of predawn, which offered a misty peacefulness of dew and gentle insect sounds. It was a sleeping hour, in the time before waking when the world is yet holding off a return to grinding daytime routines and burdened consciousness. A precious time to be awake, to be alive, for the simple nature of its fleeting.

As he made to cross the lawn, he paused; twisted silhouettes like those of malformed creatures brooded over the land. Phil's car-part artworks lost their definitions and became alien figures in the dark. Savannah could have been standing among them, and he wouldn't have known until he walked up to the sculptures.

Instead, he went in the opposite direction, away from the figures and off toward the road. He walked for some time, enrobed in the quiet almost-darkness; soon the sun would broach the horizon and pull from him night's cloak of anonymity.

By the time he trudged up to the Montgomery house, a sliver of sun had crested the horizon, lighting the morning sky to a pale gray-blue. There against the curb was the scratched and mud-caked Bronco. He leaned his back against it and took out his keys.

He was about to unlock the car when he heard a light tapping—soft but insistent. He looked up for the source and found a pale face looming in a second-floor window of the Montgomery house. Sarah, tapping her finger against the windowpane. When she had Dax's attention, she put up the flat of her hand as if to say *stop* or *wait.*

Then she vanished from the window.

Dax waited.

After a few minutes, two figures emerged from the house and came toward him.

"What happened?" Wyatt said as he shuffled forward. "Did you make a jailbreak?"

"Deputy let me go. I don't think the sheriff's done with me yet, though."

Wyatt shook his head. "Man, I would have come, but I've basically been on lockdown for the car, and Sarah hasn't had it much better—"

"Don't worry about it."

"Are you okay?" asked Sarah.

Dax said, "I'm fine" in a way that was perhaps so unconvincing that Sarah and Wyatt both paused to scrutinize him.

Wyatt asked if Phil had come to see him and seemed briefly put at ease when Dax confirmed, until he added—"It wasn't his liver."

"What?"

"Phil lied. It wasn't his liver. That's not how he died. My dad was attacked by something." He looked from Wyatt to Sarah, in whose eyes he sensed an awful anticipation. "Something that tore out his throat … his eyes … and his tongue."

It was Sarah's turn to say in a whispered, disbelieving voice, "*What?*"

"Shit," Wyatt murmured—then, in a tone of sudden annoyance: "Shit! Mom and Dad'll be up any minute. Let's get gone or get fucked."

They got into the Bronco and Dax started it up to find it was almost out of gas. By the time they pulled up to the Howard farm, they were running on fumes.

"So what are we going to do about Savannah?" Wyatt said as they crept up the driveway.

"We don't know for certain it was her."

"Damn it, Sarah, not this shit again."

"I mean …" But she trailed off, losing the thread to whatever she was clinging.

The car gave out halfway down the driveway, and they got out to walk. Dax looked up at his father's old Jeep parked near the house, but it had a flat and looked like it wouldn't run anyway. He wondered if Wyatt knew how to siphon but saved the question—for as he started for the house, he fought a sudden growing sensation that something wasn't right.

He slowed, and the others seemed to sense something too, for their footfalls grew arrhythmic and tentative. Dax came to the end of the drive for a better angle of the house. He stopped when he realized there wasn't much more of the house to see.

Behind the front wall lay a ruin. A pile of rubble—pieces of roof, planks of wood, broken furniture—littered the area the house had once occupied. Several walls remained like broken pillars of defiance, but they had been stripped and eaten away.

"Dax …" Wyatt started, but it went ignored.

He walked numbly to the stunted remains of a wall and stepped over, into the wreckage the tornado had left behind.

His bedroom, *gone*. His mother's armoire, *gone*. His father's ashes …

Gone.

Everything.

He bent over the rubble, dug his hands between two planks of wood, pried them up and tossed them away. He heaved up shingles and threw them aside. He dug with stiff arms he could barely feel, dug desperately for something, anything, that remained of his old life. All his father's things, the articles he'd collected over the years, anything that would lead Dax to an answer about Savannah or the carnival— *gone, gone, gone.*

"Hey, Dax," came Wyatt's voice again as he stepped around the side of the house to join him. He put a hand on Dax's shoulder, but Dax shrugged him off and kept digging, his movements growing more and more frantic.

Dad's ashes. I have to find his ashes. He can't just be gone.

As he dug, a layer of dust accumulated on his arms. Splinters burrowed into the grooves beneath his fingernails. The cuts on his palms reopened. He panted, not feeling the sting in his hands, only the heat coursing through his body, the fiery mix of rage and grief. He kept digging.

"Dax, stop," Sarah commanded, reaching for his hand.

He shoved her out of the way. He was beyond them both. They had become distant from him in some metaphysical sense. He had sunk to his knees while he dug, and now his efforts slowed. With every brick or table leg he shifted out of the way, more fragments slid in to fill the hole. Shards of glass, metal pipes, chunks of plaster, doorknobs, beheaded light bulbs, fan blades, the toilet still grounded and standing, roof fragments—everything in one great heap.

He stopped digging.

Dax leaned back on his heels and stared ahead, trying to catch his breath. Sunbeams grazed the edge of the façade and slanted over the wreckage. He had to squint against the glint of something silver reflecting the sun, and his heart leapt.

He sprang to his feet and climbed across the mound with feet that slid and hands that scrabbled for purchase until he came to the urn. When he pulled it free, the shifting debris exhaled a puff of dust, and he held the urn for a moment before realizing it was upside-down. He shook his head, *no*, but the lid was gone. He turned it over—*no, no*— but could feel how light it was. He looked inside.

The urn was empty.

He sat at the top of the heap and leaned his head between his knees, clutching the empty urn. When he finally made his way back to Wyatt and Sarah, he felt hollow. Nothing remained, now, of *either* of his parents.

No bodies to bury. Nothing.

"We should go," Sarah said.

He could say nothing. His voice was gone, like everything else.

"Where are we gonna go?" Wyatt snapped.

The sun rose steadily, turning what remained of the cornfields out back to spun gold and casting long shadows over the collapsed house. Dax clutched the urn and gazed across the field. His eyes followed the trail of dirt that marked the path of the tornado. Finally, he let the urn slip from his hands, and it landed on the ground with a dull thump.

All this time, he'd had so little regard for this house, this farm, this shed of memories—but now, knowing it was gone, that it would not be waiting for him when he finally decided to stop hating this place, he felt the loss like the death of another parent. He wondered how much more of his childhood was to be wiped away; and sickly, unreasonably, he wondered if it wasn't his own doing, if his brain hadn't conceived this very destruction from his subconscious and now taunted him with its fruition—

This is what you wanted, isn't it?

The sound of a car pulling up the drive made him turn.

The sheriff's cruiser crept up to the end of the driveway and parked. As the sheriff stepped out, he whistled, surveying the damage.

"Terrible mess," he said after a moment.

Sarah and Wyatt moved to stand slightly in front of Dax in a way he found both annoying and oddly endearing. He pushed between them, not wanting to use the Montgomeries as armor.

"What are you doing here?" he asked the sheriff.

"You left so quickly, thanks to my deputy, that I didn't get the chance to ask you any more questions." The sheriff opened the back door of the cruiser and stood there, his face drawn and lined in the glare of the morning sun, which reflected on his sunglasses. "Get in."

"Like hell," Wyatt said.

"I wasn't talking to you," the sheriff said pointedly. "Obviously, you can't stay here—" He motioned vaguely to the crumbling house. "I'll take you somewhere more comfortable, where we can sit and chat. Just a few questions, that's all."

Underlying the innocuous words, Dax sensed danger simmering beneath the surface. It was as though the sheriff were straining to maintain a level tone and a calm demeanor; his limbs were stiff, his jaw clenched. Something inside him wanted to get out.

"Questions about what?" Dax said.

"About Prairie Rose Ranch, for starters." The sheriff seemed to weigh his next words carefully. "And about your father ... seeing as they died in the same way."

"Listen, man," Wyatt said, "he'll answer any question you want to ask, but now's really not the goddamn time. As you can see," he added, gesturing to the wreckage.

The sheriff did not move, and in his stillness lay a coiled menace.

"Get in," he said, his voice stony and low.

"I don't think so," Wyatt said. He grabbed Dax by the shoulder, preparing to shove him back down the driveway to the Bronco, but the sheriff pulled out his gun. He raised it without aim, needing only to show them he had it, that in an instant he could turn its gaping devil's maw upon them, and all three of them froze.

"Get in."

Sarah and Wyatt, both pale and somber, stalked to the car and slid into the back seat, Dax just behind them, knowing all the while the sheriff could not possibly be telling them the truth. A moment later, his suspicions were confirmed; the sheriff holstered his gun, grabbed Dax's arms and wrenched them behind his back. He felt the cold snap of cuffs locking around his wrists.

From the car, Sarah and Wyatt protested:

"Hey—"

"What the hell are you—?"

"Quiet," the sheriff barked, and shoved Dax into the car.

The door slammed shut.

Dax had to lean forward as he sat with his arms pinned behind him. The tightly-cinched cuffs dug into the bones of his wrists. He twisted his hands, tested the length of the chain separating them, and let his head droop forward to stare at his shoes.

Sheriff Anderson reversed down the driveway. They drove in silence; he didn't radio either of the deputies. And when they got back onto the road, instead of heading west to Main Street, he took them north, then east on Dunes Way.

Dax tilted his head to peek out the window.

Sarah had noticed as well, for she asked, "Why aren't we going to the station?"

"Shut up."

They pulled up to the Willoughby farm, and the sheriff killed the engine. Without looking at them, he got out of the car and opened the door on Dax's side.

"Get out," he said.

At first, Dax didn't move.

"You hear me? I said get out of the car."

A glance at Wyatt and Sarah revealed the fear in their eyes. Wyatt shook his head. They shared their mute apprehension for only a moment before the sheriff grabbed Dax by the arm and hauled him out of the car, onto his knees in the grass. Then he removed the gun from his holster.

Dax could focus only on those dark sunglasses and the eye of the gun.

"All right. Now tell me. You fucking tell me. Where is my son?"

Dax swallowed. He tugged his wrists apart as far as they would go. Metal bit into flesh.

"Tell me!" the sheriff snapped, pointing the gun wildly at Dax. Immediately he reined himself in, lowered the gun, plucked off his badge and put it in his pocket. Then he took off his sunglasses; his cold blue eyes pierced the air. He took a breath and raised the gun again. "Right now I am not the sheriff. I'm just a man who wants to know what happened to his son." He took a calming breath. "A man with a gun."

The sun glared into Dax's eyes over the tops of trees in the distance, turning the sheriff into a shadow. He knelt in the dewy grass, trying not to look down the black length of the barrel. He closed his eyes and felt the warm breeze glide around him, the sun in his face, and wondered how long he could keep lying. He could almost feel Zeke's presence under the dirt, all around them, stopped forever in time as his broken watch, just out of Sheriff Anderson's reach.

Dax opened his eyes.

The sheriff's face appeared to be melting. His lips dragged into a terrible frown. His voice wavered when he spoke next.

"Is my son dead?"

Dax nodded.

At first, the sheriff only stared at him, his face blank. His frown began to quiver and transformed into a snarl. He lurched forward, clenching the gun.

Dax saw death coming for him.

Then a figure hurtled through the air above his head and collided with the sheriff. They both went tumbling across the ground, and the gun went off.

Ears ringing, Dax looked down at himself, but he was unscathed. Extricating himself from the sheriff, Wyatt hit him in the head with his cast before curling up around the broken arm in obvious pain. The sheriff stirred on the ground, reaching across the grass toward the gun that had fallen from his grip, but Wyatt stumbled to his feet, still clutching his cast, and kicked the sheriff in the side. Bending over, he grabbed the gun and hit him with the butt of it. And again. And again.

"Stop," Dax said. The ringing vanished as sound bled back into the world. "He's out."

The sheriff lay still, blood seeping from his cracked and purpled lips.

Wyatt looked at the gun in his hand and dropped it with a surprised twitch. There was blood on the handle.

Sarah leaned out of the car. "Jesus," she said.

Wyatt stood panting, looking between Sarah and Dax. "You're welcome!" he said.

"We're in such shit," Sarah said.

Dax struggled to his feet—he felt off-balance with his arms pinned behind him. "Thanks," he said to Wyatt. Then he looked down at the sheriff, still and bloodied on the ground. He pulled anxiously on the cuffs, feeling trapped.

Sarah climbed out of the car. The wind blew her hair over her face in a long blonde banner. She crossed her arms and voiced the question they were all thinking.

"What the hell do we do now?"

CHAPTER 14

"Let's get out of here," Dax murmured. "Before he comes to."

The others nodded and helped him slide his arms under his legs, bringing his cuffed hands to the front.

"We need to get your hands free, man," Wyatt said. He looked around, then waved them forward. "I got an idea. Come on," he said, and led Dax in the direction of the barn, Sarah falling farther and farther behind.

Dax looked back and saw her hesitating.

"I can't go in," she said.

"I think we can bust those cuffs with one of these blades!" Wyatt said.

Dax ducked inside the barn, where Wyatt crouched over the farming tools in the corner—relics from the Willoughbies. He found an axe and instructed Dax to spread his hands on either side of a worn and grooved chopping block. The axe didn't look sharp, but bore a hefty blade.

"No."

Wyatt raised it up by his shoulder. "Seriously, dude. Unless you want to stay cuffed."

He imagined Wyatt bringing down that axe on the few inches the cuffs afforded between his hands, and missing, instead cutting through his wrist, severing an artery, his hand separating from his body. He put his wrists against the chopping block, then immediately pulled them back.

"Don't be a pussy," Wyatt said, holding the axe with his good hand and steadying it with the fingers protruding from his dirty cast.

"Good god, Wy, you look like an axe-murdering psychopath," Sarah said from the doorway. She looked around the barn, her eyes lingering for a moment on the floor where the dirt had been overturned to cover Zeke's blood. She inhaled, exhaled slowly, and came up to Wyatt, taking the axe from him. "Let me. Unless you want to cut off his fingers with your shit aim. Or have you forgotten what you did to Dallas during that game of darts last year?"

Wyatt reached for the axe, but Sarah turned her back to him and stepped up to the chopping block.

"His head healed up fine, didn't it?" Wyatt grumbled as he slouched away.

Sarah rolled her eyes. "Ready?"

She looked cool, composed, so Dax stretched the cuffs apart.

With a huge arcing swing, Sarah brought down the blade on the chain. Metal clanged against metal. He flinched. Nothing. She tried again as Wyatt glowered peevishly to one side, then turned and disappeared into the back of the barn.

The chain had warped, one of the links bent out of shape. Each time the metal clanged, Dax's heart ricocheted, and his hands went numb in anticipation.

Sarah geared up for another swing, brought the axe down, and this time the bent link snapped free.

Dax pulled his hands apart, two short chains swinging from each of his manacles. He released a breath as adrenaline leaked away into relief.

Sarah nodded and dropped the axe, then turned back to the door.

"Thanks," he said. Dax looked around for Wyatt, who stood hunched in the far corner.

"Let's go," he called out.

Wyatt straightened up and turned around, a long metal blade glinting in his good hand.

"Jesus, put that away."

Wyatt lifted the panga machete and examined its edge. "I don't know, man. There's a crazy murderer out there—think I may want a weapon."

"That's not all that's out there," Dax said. "Did you know there's a carnival in town?"

"Heard about it, yeah. You think it's the one?"

"Yes." He left no room for doubt. "And Savannah's connected to it, somehow."

"So do we go, or do we stay the hell away? I know which one has my vote."

"She killed my dad."

"Well," Wyatt said, swinging the machete and sighing, "then I guess we'd better suit up." He put down the weapon, picked up a bundle of tools, and dumped them in the dirt. Some were bent and rusted, others missing pieces. Among the pile lay two pitchforks, a broken hoe, a cross-cut saw, a canthook, a scythe, and a thatching rake. Wyatt spread his arms over them. "Behold! A poor farmer's jackpot. Take your pick."

Sarah peeked in at them from the doorway. "What the hell are you doing?"

"Looting," Wyatt said.

With his newly-freed hands, Dax picked up the scythe, and the blade immediately loosened and fell to the ground. He dropped the wooden handle.

"Lot of good that'll do."

"What on earth for?" Sarah said.

Dax and Wyatt looked at each other.

Then Wyatt turned to his sister and said, "We're going after Savannah."

Sarah's face remained studiedly blank. "What do you mean, 'going after?'"

"You know what I mean."

She didn't say anything.

"Come on, Sarah," Wyatt snapped. "Face it. That's *not* Savannah. Not anymore." He picked up the canthook and frowned. "We seem to be the only people aware of that, and it's not like we can count on the sheriff's department to take care of this, can we? So, you're either coming with us to the carnival, or you can go home and hide out there. Your choice."

He tossed the canthook back into the pile and picked up the machete again.

"I'm coming with you," Sarah said. "But I'm not taking one of those piece of shit tools."

Wyatt glared at her. "Pick up that axe."

"Fuck you," she said, and exited the barn.

Dax eyed the cross-cut saw, but finally settled on a pitchfork, feeling a little American Gothic as he stood with it in hand, tines to the ceiling. He followed Sarah as Wyatt kicked the side of the chopping block on his way out, grumbling.

They emerged from the dark, musty interior of the barn into the day.

Sunlight blazed on the back of Dax's neck.

Sarah walked ahead of them as they picked their way through the weed-choked grass, locusts buzzing amid the dragonflies that flitted from blade to blade.

Holding the machete precariously between his thumb and forefinger, Wyatt used his free hand to itch around the edges of the cast, which had attained a grubby yellowish hue. As they walked, he grabbed a stick off the ground and shoved it deep into his cast, rubbing it up and down against his forearm.

Sarah pulled out Savannah's pocket notebook and flipped through it as they walked.

"It's funny," she said. "There's nothing in here about what she's been talking about lately. Nothing about the Watcher in the Stars."

"There wouldn't be," Wyatt said. "Savannah died at the lake."

Sarah went quiet.

Dax speared the ground with the pitchfork, using it as a walking stick. He passed an elaborate web between two tall stalks of wheat; its strands glinted in the sun while an orb weaver crawled slowly over its masterwork.

"Do you know anything else about Savannah's god?"

Sarah was silent for a moment as they walked, and then said, "He comes from beyond the stars. I guess that means heaven or something. She says he's coming back to us ... I don't know, like the Second Coming or something." Sarah frowned at the grass where she stepped. "He has many names. The Watcher in the Stars. Father Death." She paused as if in thought. "There was one more I heard her use, only once. I think it was ... Algol?"

Dax stopped walking.

Sarah was the first to notice; she faltered and turned around.

Wyatt kept going until she called to him, and then he whirled around, fifteen paces ahead of them, looking startled to find himself alone.

"What is it?" Sarah said.

"Algol ..." Dax said, his mind flitted through the ghostly remembrance of textbook pages. "The Demon Star."

"What's that?"

He turned his pitchfork over, thrust its tines into the dirt, and leaned on it. "I learned about Algol at school. It's a binary system—two stars orbiting each other. Every few days, the dimmer star passes in front of the brighter star, so it looks like it's winking." He squinted in the glare of the sun, then turned to face west, into the shadows. "In the constellation, Perseus is holding Medusa's severed head. The binary system is one of Medusa's eyes. Almost every culture in the world has attributed bad omens to it. Most call it the Evil Eye."

He remembered the numbers and letters ringing the outer edge of the iris in the drawing he'd copied from the Willoughby farm: 68.816664 hr 93 ly. He laughed with the sudden shock of recognition. "I don't believe it," he murmured. "It's some kind of chart—or map to Algol. The eye winks every 68 hours or so, and it's 93 light years away."

He pried the pitchfork out of the ground.

"Why in the hell would Savannah need a map to a goddamn star?" Wyatt called out. "She got a spaceship we don't know about?"

"Maybe Algol isn't his name," Sarah said as she and Dax caught up with him. "Maybe it's where he's from." She found a beat-up cigarette in her pocket. It held together, but the end sagged like a broken limb when she put it in her mouth. "Got a light?"

Wyatt handed her a lighter.

When she handed it back, smoke trailing from her downturned lips, she sighed and said, "I still don't know what it has to do with the carnival, though."

They walked in silence for a while.

"You even know how to use a machete?" Sarah said.

Wyatt swung the machete casually before resting it against his shoulder. "I think a big-ass blade will speak for itself when the time comes."

"Right," she murmured, her voice disappearing in a puff of smoke. She put out her cigarette against Wyatt's cast, leaving a burnt circle near his elbow. He pulled his arm away, and she dropped the butt into the dirt.

A cloud rolled over the sun. Dax felt the shadow creep over him.

The dirt road ended at Dunes Way crossing east to west through shrub and prairie grass. They could head east, away from everything, and walk nowhere, into the scattered farms and the nothingness between towns. Instead, they went west, where eventually they would hit Hells Hollow Road.

Dax would see the carnival at last, and maybe finally have the answer his father had sought all these years. His legs began to ache as the sun dipped past noon and inched its way forward, until they walked straight into its vast and blinding eye.

Ahead, Woodview Lane cut across Dunes Way at an angle, and just beyond that the forest became visible, dense and dark. Somewhere deep within those trees lay the dead husk of Pastor's Grove. And nestled among the trees, on the western edge of the forest, lay Sandpiper Lake, its outer banks shrouded by reeds.

Dax headed off the road and through the grass, toward that dark blue inversion of the sky. The others followed. He dropped the pitchfork, sat on the muddy bank, relieved his tired legs for a minute. He splashed cold water onto his face, let the sun dry it off.

The afternoon was dying.

An animal rustled the bushes off to the side, where a thicket of trees swallowed the sunlight. Wyatt startled at the sound and raised the machete. Nothing happened. At last, he lowered the weapon, still looking suspicious of everything around them.

Sarah came up beside Dax, pulled off her sneakers, and dipped her bare feet into the water, trailing ripples with her toes.

"Hey ... I don't know if I ever said thanks." Instead of looking at him while she spoke, she stared down at her feet.

"For what?"

She looked surprised at his question, and he felt suddenly like he did during those classes when everyone seemed to understand the professor while he furiously wrote notes in hopes that something would begin to make sense.

"For helping me. You were in jail, Dax. You could have—probably *should* have—told the sheriff what I did. I wouldn't have blamed you. What we did ... I don't feel right about it, but I'm wondering if it's too late now to make it right. If we've gone too far."

Dax didn't say that he agreed, although he did. She had acted in self-defense, but in hiding the body, they had acted in self-preservation; between that and beating the sheriff senseless, Dax thought there was no clean way out of this mess. Maybe they didn't deserve a clean way out, anyway.

"So basically, we're screwed," he said.

"Probably."

Dax looked around for Wyatt, and found him standing away from the lake with his back to them. Faced into the wind, Dax smelled smoke.

"Oh, you've got to be kidding me," he grumbled, gaining his feet. Before his friend could react, Dax grabbed the pipe and chucked it at the lake, where it arced through the air, caught the sun, and landed with a splash in the water.

Wyatt gaped, his face turning a darker and darker red. Finally he spat out, "What the hell, man? I need that!"

Dax's anger radiated outward from an internal fire, blind and indiscriminate.

"Then go get it."

Wyatt threw his machete to the ground and stomped toward the lake, where he hesitated on its bank, peering into the water. He sloshed in up to his knees and felt around for the sunken pipe. Water splashed up on his cast, soaked into his ratty jeans. He let out a frustrated grunt.

The commotion startled the animal creeping through the bushes from its hideout.

While Sarah yelled at her brother to stop being a baby and get out, Dax turned toward the parting shrubbery from which the emaciated form of a coyote slunk out into the daylight, mange glistening with blood, chest half-crushed. It bared yellow saliva-slicked canines, growled, and hunched its back with hackles raised. It sniffed in their direction, blindly. Two hollow sockets where eyes once had been. It took three steps forward, swaying back and forth as it sniffed.

Sarah and Wyatt continued to yell at each other.

Dax opened his mouth to shout when the creature pounced.

Sarah was closest. The coyote, smelling her, ran and leapt through the air.

Dax surged forward as the coyote launched itself at Sarah and knocked her off balance, its claws tearing her sleeve to ribbons. Her startled cry rang out over the lake.

Wyatt tried to step toward her, but was pulled into the mud.

Before the coyote could sink its teeth into Sarah's prone neck, Dax threw himself onto it, grabbing fistfuls of fur as he wrestled it onto its side, onto the grass. Its wiry body writhed; its jaws clamped fiercely on thin air. He slid and rolled with the coyote, away from Sarah, and landed on his back. The coyote's teeth closed around his wrist, but the broken handcuff caught most of the bite. He grabbed the animal's underbelly and pushed it away.

As the coyote stumbled back, it swung its head wildly to and fro, trying to catch his scent, the deep unsighted wells of its bare sockets staring around at nothing.

Beyond the struggle lay the still surface of the lake—the silence of deepest blue reflecting shimmering trees and the eternity of the sky— and here, the coyote's jaws clamped down on Dax's ankle.

A sharp pain registered, and he kicked out instinctively. Somehow the coyote clung on, and its teeth sank deeper into his flesh. He had a moment to wonder at this scavenger turned predator—and the unlikely strength of its jaws as they crushed down on his ankle— before the coyote thrashed its head.

Pain like a mad howl into the wind—his ankle bent unnaturally, twisted, and he fell back onto the grass, staring at the breathless, empty sky.

Then Sarah lunged, landing on the coyote, and speared it with the pitchfork. The tines embedded into the back of the creature's neck and sank deep into its flesh. It let go of Dax's leg and gave a wounded cry—a sound not like an animal's but something altogether unearthly, neither beast nor human. It whipped its head to dislodge the weapon protruding from its back.

Sarah grabbed the pitchfork and wrenched it free. The coyote stumbled, lurched forward to attack, but she stabbed it again, this time in its concave chest, shoving it back until it stood upright on hind legs. It toppled backward, still snapping its jaws, and as it lay thrashing, she drove the pitchfork further into its belly.

Dax propped himself up on his elbows to watch the coyote's heaving stomach. Black pockets, abandoned by its eyes, stared skyward, revealing nothing.

Sarah leaned into the pitchfork. Blood oozed up around the tines and flowed onto the grass. The stomach convulsed and heaved again, this time into an unnatural bulge that stretched its flesh to its ultimate elasticity, then finally burst.

A swarm of white insectoid creatures the size of golf balls emerged from the wound; they spilled onto the grass, clattered on multiple spidering legs toward the lake. Out poured multitudes of white parasites, more than seemed possible—more than could have fit inside the carcass.

Sarah let go of the pitchfork and stumbled back.

Dax dragged himself away on his elbows while the creatures scuttled across the ground, past his feet. When they started disappearing into the water, Wyatt screamed and splashed to the bank, fell, and clawed his way frantically across the mud.

The last white creatures vanished into the water with a metallic echo, leaving behind the deflated corpse of the coyote, seemingly robbed of all its organs, which perhaps the parasites had eaten in order to survive in its flesh.

Wyatt broke the silence: "What the *fuck* was that?"

Adrenaline leaked away and left Dax unable to ignore the sharp pain in his twisted ankle. He looked down at his torn jeans and the mangled flesh beneath. Blood soaked the fabric.

Sarah's face was a mask of shock as she bent over his leg. "Damn," she said. "It got you good." She looked at Wyatt, who stood covered in mud, trails of dirty water drying on his arms and face. "Don't just stand there," she snapped.

"The hell you want me to do, drip mud onto the wound?" he said, his voice shaking.

Sarah tore off her ripped sleeve and wrapped it around Dax's ankle. A burst of pain released a reflexive groan from the back of his throat.

"Are we not going to talk about those fucking *things* that came out of the coyote?" Wyatt said, his voice on the precipice of hysteria.

Dax cringed at the thought of insectoid legs—that looked all too much like tiny finger bones—prickling their way out of the corpse.

"I'd rather not," he said.

Sarah leaned her elbows on her knees as she crouched over him. "That thing was infected with ... something. You need to get this looked at."

He breathed through his nose and shook his head. "I'm fine." To prove his point, he pushed himself to his feet. His bad ankle cried out, twisted sharply, and wrenched his ligaments out of place, sending him ungracefully to his knees.

Wyatt laughed. "Well, that's great! That's just fucking great!" His teeth chattered. He was dripping wet, and he held the mud-gunked pipe in one hand like an afterthought. "We've got a sky god from a goddamn demon star and a white-tarantula-filled coyote whose eyes were stolen by a dead chick who makes tornados and kills people and you can't walk and all I've got is this *fucking machete!*' He whirled around to pick up the weapon and gazed at it with a kind of manic hopelessness.

"Get a grip, Wyatt," Sarah snapped.

Dax tried again to stand, and this time Sarah grabbed his arm to give him leverage. He got upright and tried gingerly to put some weight on his foot, but the pressure against his ankle sent knives through his bones. His leg wobbled, and he leaned heavily into Sarah, who did her best to hold him up.

"We have to keep going," Dax said.

"What?" Sarah looked at him. "Walk the rest of the way, like this?"

"You have a better idea?" He took a limping step forward, and she hurried to follow when his balance faltered. He didn't know how to describe his impulse to keep moving forward. All he could say was, "I have to get to the carnival."

Why, he wondered, *do I need so badly to get to the carnival? For my father? For my mother? For the teenagers in town, dead or missing, for Savannah's mutilated family? For the very same thing Sheriff Anderson is searching for—an answer, or an end?*

Dax took another limping step forward, hopping so that his other foot didn't quite touch the ground. Sarah stayed with him, and he was grateful for the shoulder she offered. If she had trouble bearing his weight, she didn't let on. He paused to look down at the dead coyote, the pitchfork protruding from it crookedly. He decided to leave the weapon there.

They turned away from the lake with its deceptive serenity, the murk and mysteries below hidden beneath its clean reflective surface. The sun glared upon it like a vast white eye.

With every step, his ankle trembled and throbbed. Sweat gathered above his brow, and he tried to keep his breathing steady as he limped along with Sarah's aid, and with Wyatt slouched beside them, an earthen figure with haunted eyes the naked color of the lake.

They walked back to the road with painstaking effort and resumed their trek. They walked along the pavement in the silence of the moribund afternoon. They walked westward, into a blinding glare that beckoned them to brewing nightfall.

Slowly, agonizingly, deliberately, they kept walking.

CHAPTER 15

A reddish twilight feathered out from the horizon as they turned down Hells Hollow Road and approached Frieda Redding's house. The pain in Dax's ankle had developed into a part of his existence that both muddled and somehow defined time. There was no longer such a thing as hours or minutes, but pulses of pain that translated both time and space. Something about it reminded him of the interior of black holes, where the radial dimension reversed from space-like to time-like; steps did not move him across the ground but through time, from one moment to the next. But there, ahead of him, solidifying his temporal place, loomed the impending sunset with its ribbons of celestial orange light spreading across the sky.

A sheen of sweat slicked his skin, cool in the breeze.

Frieda's cottage appeared before them. The old windmill spun lazily, its blades whisking through air. Chimes danced and tinkled over the wraparound porch.

Frieda stood on the side, hands on the railing as she gazed south. When they stumbled within earshot, she turned sharply to face them.

"What in the hell happened to you?"

They labored up to the porch, and Dax dropped heavily onto the front step. All his energy drained in that moment, and he had to lean back against the wooden railing to stay upright.

Frieda came over, bent down, and began unraveling Sarah's shirtsleeve from around his ankle. He hissed as the material came away, sticky with congealed blood. Frieda frowned at the ragged bite, at his ankle purpled and swollen.

"What did that?"

Dax looked over at Sarah and Wyatt. "Coyote."

Frieda made a skeptical arch with her eyebrows and a sound in the back of her throat. "Some coyote," she said, but didn't press the subject. "Wait here." Her knees cracked when she stood.

Dax looked across at the stone well, an ancient hole in the earth. The lowering sun drew long shadows on the grass behind it, and the well itself seemed to be an impenetrable darkness. He reasoned it must be an effect of the stark contrast with the sun's last bright gasps.

"There it is," he heard Sarah say behind him.

He didn't turn around. Instead, he closed his eyes and leaned against the wooden railing, smelling hickory and distracting himself from the dull ache in his ankle by tugging at the broken handcuffs until they cut into his wrists.

"Here," Frieda said to him, and he opened bleary eyes to a bottle of Jim Beam floating in front of his face. "I didn't have any aspirin."

Dax took the bottle, unscrewed the cap, and took a swig. The whiskey burned, settled hot in his stomach. He coughed. The throbbing in his ankle didn't dull, but at least he forgot about it for a few seconds.

The older woman began tightly wrapping his ankle with a sturdier cloth.

He took another swig under the rough ministrations of her wrinkled hands.

When she was finished, she nodded and stood. "That'll hold, I think, but I'm no doctor. 'Fraid I don't have anything stronger for the pain."

"I do," Wyatt said.

Sliding a flattened plastic bag out from the recesses of his cast, he produced his remaining meth, the crystals gleaming milky white against the glare of the setting sun.

"That won't help you," Frieda said.

Dax blinked at Wyatt. His ankle throbbed. His wrists ached within the cinched metal cuffs. He felt in a powerful grip of fatigue.

"It'll keep you going, if that's what you want," Wyatt said.

Dax looked behind him, around the edge of the porch. He could make out, in the distance, the dark silhouettes of tents, the great spoked circle of a Ferris wheel, and other unnatural shapes rising from the horizon. Figures moved about in the gathering dusk, mere shadows. The setting sun gleamed red over the tents.

"You don't want to go there," Frieda said. "Best just get on out of here."

"It's the same one," Dax said. "The same carnival."

Frieda's eyes shone strangely in the dying light. "Just let them be. Let them do their business and leave."

"I thought you didn't like carnivals?"

"I don't," she snapped. "But they're on my land, aren't they?"

Sarah looked startled and said, "You own all that land?"

"That can't be legal," Dax said. "They can't use your land without your permission."

"They have my permission. I signed off on it."

Dax leaned forward with his elbows on his knees. "Why?"

"The man promised me he'd get rid of it," she murmured. Twilight stretched long fingers of wine-red radiance over her rutted features. "It's calling out, now. I think it knows. I think it wants to come out. You hear it, don't you? Don't you?"

Dax heard only the gentle clink of chimes in the wind. He shook his head.

"Of course you don't believe me," she said, her voice taking on a desperate edge. "But the man—he said that if I let them use my land he would get rid of it. My whole life, no one ever ... not even Luther. No one *listened* like I listened. Don't you hear it?" She looked around at them. Her eyes widened as far as they could, and her mouth hung open. "It's a voice, but it ain't human. It ain't even *human*."

Sarah found another cigarette—they seemed to keep appearing like magic from her pockets—and put it between her lips, glancing at her brother.

Wyatt snatched it from her, put it in his own mouth, lit it, and started to smoke. "All right," he said, smoke shooting from his nostrils. "All right. Sure. We believe you. They definitely didn't just say that to get you to sign off. That's very nice of them to want to fix your problem."

Sarah held up the crushed, empty cigarette box and chucked it at Wyatt, and he batted it away with his cast.

"Not just my problem," Frieda snapped. "It's been there a long time. A *long* time. Longer than I've been alive. You've got a weak mind, boy." She fixed her glare upon Wyatt. "You can't see what's right in front of you. Like my Luther. He had a weak mind, couldn't handle what he saw, and look what happened to him."

"What couldn't he handle?" Dax said.

The setting sun turned Frieda into a hunched silhouette with a cratered moon for a face. When she spoke again, her voice was brittle. "Maybelle Willoughby."

"What happened to her?" When she looked hesitant to respond, Dax added, "Please. I believe you."

Finally, she spoke: "The carnival had just taken off. They paid my father a good sum to use the land, and they had just left. Luther and I were out enjoying the sunset when she came running. The Willoughby girl. I didn't know where she was going, why she was running, so I called out to stop her. But she ... there was something wrong with her. Her eyes. It wasn't *her*." Frieda's lips quivered into a frown. "Everyone thought some drifter came through and killed the Willoughbies, but I know better. *She* did it."

Frieda ran her fingers over a spot on her jaw, just below her ear, and Dax noticed the faint white line of an old scar grooving the skin there.

"I took her by the arms and bent down and told her to talk to me, tell me what was the matter, but she pulled out of my grip with the strength of a grown man, not a little girl, and she attacked me. She was changed—had nails like claws. Whatever she was, she meant to kill me. So I pushed her. Down the well. But ... she didn't stay down."

Frieda drew a shuddering breath.

"She *crawled back up*."

Wyatt's cigarette slipped out of his fingers and landed in the grass. Thin wisps of smoke curled up and vanished.

"There was something in her face when she surfaced. I didn't like it. Then she ran off, west, where the carnival had gone. Laughing the whole way."

The sun had sunk almost entirely to the rim of the earth now, leaving nothing but a strip of red light at the horizon as darkness descended. Stars gasped awake overhead, and Frieda's countenance suddenly changed, colored with red, then purple, then blue, then green. She flashed illusively between shades.

Dax craned his neck to peer south. In the distance, bulbs of colored light had flickered on, swirling with unnatural hues. And the wild tunes of carnival music, warped by wind and distance, carried on the filaments of the air. The lit-up Ferris wheel made a wide gyre against the sky, turning and turning. Dax thought he heard laughter, but it might have been the wind.

Spinning lights reached out to them, but the shadow of the house cast darkness over the front yard and the well. Its stone rim caught the very last of the sunlight, and within hid a darkness blacker than the void of space, more absolute than anything of this world.

Sarah walked to the well and leaned over to peer inside.

Dax wanted to shout at her to get away, but he couldn't find his voice, could hardly catch his breath. He expected something to reach up from deep within the well and drag her with it into the unknown. As she gazed down into the abyss, he imagined something gazing back, something in that churning, breathing darkness in the depths of the earth that was somehow ... *alive.*

After a moment, she stumbled back, shaking her head and turning toward the others.

He couldn't make out the look on her face. The sun had finally plummeted below the horizon and had left them in darkness.

"I've been trying to keep kids away from that thing my whole life," Frieda said. "Trying to scare them away. Whatever those folks are going to do—those folks at the carnival—you'd best just let them do it."

Dax could barely see the others around him now, the darkness was so thick. The distant lights reached across the expanse and beckoned him. "Don't you want to know what happened to Maybelle Willoughby?" he asked. "Don't you want to know why she killed her family?"

"No," Frieda said in a flat voice. "It's sleeping. That's all I need to know. It's sleeping, and God help us when it wakes."

A formless, inchoate dread roused in the trenches of his soul, and Dax stood to dispel it. Almost too late, he remembered his ankle, which buckled in pain. His hand shot out for the railing, and he lowered himself back onto the stoop, feeling paralyzed and inadequate. When he inhaled, he caught the lingering stink of ash from the expended cigarette in the grass.

He knew his father was gone, distributed across miles, perhaps, into particles so minute and fragmented as to become nothing, and he did not believe in any kind of existence beyond death—yet he felt his father's presence, within or just around him, not a comfort, but a reminder of his unrealized purpose, some last-ditch trick of Dax's mind that impelled him to finish what his father had started. If not for himself, then for Roy. Otherwise, he thought those formless particles of ash would choke the air wherever he went, and in them he might hear the remote lure of carnival music forever out of reach.

He looked up at the dark shape that was Wyatt.

"Give me the pipe."

The shadow reached into its pocket, then held out the small glass object in its extended shadow-hand. Lights flashed sporadically over the figure, transforming it in succession from black to green to blue to red. Dax felt himself sliding through the slipstream of these surreal identities. The pipe landed in his palm.

The shadow bent over his still-outstretched hand, pinched crystals into the bowl, and handed him a lighter.

Dax lifted the pipe to his lips, flicked open the flame, inhaled the burnt-acid smoke—staring through the shroud of night, all the while, at the well. He coughed and felt his chest tighten. He took another hit.

"I remember my mother telling me about the sacred pipe given by the White Buffalo Calf Woman," Dax murmured. "As you pass it around, your prayers would drift into the sky with the smoke." He breathed deeply and exhaled, watching the smoke curl away and disappear in the dark. He did not think his thoughts went anywhere—just dissipated the way smoke does in open air.

He handed the pipe back to Wyatt. "We're going to the carnival," he said, flicking the lighter to watch the rippling flame. "We have to. My parents are *dead*." His voice hung in his ears like a punctuation. "Because of that fucking carnival. Because of Savannah. I'm not just going to turn around and go home—hell, I don't *have* one anymore. It's gone. Everything's gone. I have nowhere else to go, so that's where I'm going."

Wyatt snatched the lighter from him and tucked it away.

"You're going to hurt yourself worse," Frieda said, "if you don't keep off that ankle."

Dax looked up at the beams of hazy light; in them, dust sparkled the air, and he wondered if there was a soul within that dust, something that had once been some*one*.

"No," he said. "I won't."

He pushed himself to his feet; cool wind rushed in his ears; he swayed. He had been sitting for too long. That didn't bother him, though. Nothing bothered him. He took a few steps forward, carried on momentum alone, before his ankle bent sharply and he found himself on the ground, staring up at the star-speckled sky.

"Let's try that again, huh?" Wyatt said. He grabbed him by the arm and hauled him back to his feet.

Dax stood facing the carnival. The lights reached out their tongues and licked his nose. Across the darkened field, the carnival threw a riot of color into the night. As he lurched toward that sinister bacchanalia, the stars left tracers in the sky. The stationary dots grew comet tails that swooped around him. He wondered if that was his fate: to run toward the carnival like a comet plummeting toward the sun, burning off his ice until only a cold and lifeless rock remained.

Sarah and Wyatt appeared on either side of him. Sarah carried the machete now, and it looked sharp and alien in her hand.

Dax glided along and realized only after a moment that Wyatt was bolstering his arm so he didn't have to put much weight on his bad leg. He twisted out of Wyatt's grip and limped ahead, breathing hard. He turned toward the receding figure of Frieda standing on her porch, and then they were past her and on their way across the field toward the carnival.

Ahead, the lights corkscrewed impossibly toward them with the dizzying motions of the rides. He felt already enveloped in the sounds of laughter, the creaking of the great metal structures, and that insidious melody of music, bright and brash and off-kilter.

The glowing silhouette of the carnival grew larger until it took up the entire horizon. The lit-up edges of misshapen rides and the great spinning wheel and the peaks of tents all crowded together like one massive cobbled-together creature.

At the entrance, a banner welcomed them in huge, old-fashioned letters.

"Hold on," Sarah said. They stopped in the shadow of a lone tree, far enough from the entrance that the people trickling in may not have seen them. She leaned against the trunk. "Just wait. Shouldn't we take a minute to talk about this? What exactly are we going to do once we go in there?"

Dax rounded on her impatiently. "What do you mean, 'what are we going to do?' We're going to find Savannah. That's what we're here for, isn't it? We're not here to shoot down milk bottles, are we?"

He turned to leave her behind, but she said, "Just wait a second."

"What the hell is this?" Wyatt said. "I thought you wanted to come with us."

Sarah hesitated. Her face grew odd contortions from the moon, a Picasso of light and shadow. She took a few breaths, her mouth working around the words that struggled to come out. "We look like a fucking mess," she said. "And I can't take *this* into a carnival." She held up the machete, then plunged it into the earth so that the handle protruded near the tree's roots. "Stop and think about this. Shouldn't we know what we're doing?"

"I know what I'm doing!" Dax snapped. "I'm here for *her.*"

Sarah's eyes glittered in the lights. "You're here to *kill* her, you mean."

"She killed my father."

"You don't know that."

"Go on," Dax said impatiently. "Tell me otherwise. Try to explain this. She may talk like she's some kind of prophet here to save you, but you try to convince me she isn't the cause of all of this. Try to convince me that whatever she is, she doesn't deserve to die. Go on."

Sarah's mouth was a downward crescent. "Who are we to decide who deserves to die?"

"Come on, Sarah," Wyatt said.

"Don't," she said sharply. "You know what it's like to kill someone? I can't be part of that. I can't." She gritted her teeth. "I can't."

Wyatt shook his head. "It's not like that. Christ, she isn't a *person* anymore, she's ... she's something else."

Sarah turned to her brother and snorted. "Right. Of course, you're siding with Dax." She crossed her arms. "He takes off and doesn't talk to you for four years, and you still do whatever he says. You made so many excuses for him, but he's just using you for his bullshit revenge!"

"He isn't," Wyatt said. "I want to find her, too."

"Because of your arm?" she scoffed.

"No." Wyatt's face grew stony. "Because she left you in that barn with Zeke."

Dax lost himself in the dizzying fête of lights.

The entrance seemed to mock him. His pounding heart created a dull ache in his chest. The edges of his vision crackled.

"If you don't want to come with me, I'll go alone," he said.

He limped away, not turning to see if they followed. Patches of dead grass rustled dryly around his feet. He listed to the right to keep weight off his ankle, but the effort seemed a meaningless subconscious signal now that he barely felt the sprain. Instead, he focused on the cool air and the dazzling nightmare ahead.

"Dax, wait," Wyatt said behind him.

He kept walking. He was almost there. Whether or not they followed him seemed irrelevant now in the orgiastic light and warmth of the carnival's embrace. He had the sense of things falling together in the confused and seemingly random patterns of nature. This was where he was meant to be, and he would do what he had set out to do. He would not fail again.

Alone, he stepped through the entrance and into the carnival.

CHAPTER 16

"Five tickets for the Tilt-A-Whirl! Tilt-A-Whirl, five tickets!" Voices swarmed and coalesced around the rides and tents. "Try your luck—shoot a duck, win a prize!" Carnies at booths stood in striped attire, calling out to passing patrons. "Do you dare to ride the Cosmic Eye?" Customers lined up at the ticket booths. They counted bills from their pockets and traded them for long strips of red tickets they looped around hands or folded into wallets. The smell of hot dogs and funnel cakes fried the air. At the food stands, customers walked away with greasy paper bags of popcorn and pastel bulbs of cotton candy.

Past the ticket booths stood a dozen tented game stands where teenagers threw darts, balls, and rings, and shot fake guns and streams of water, all at impossible targets outlined by stuffed animals and inflatable prizes.

Beyond, lights danced around the edges of the slowly rotating carousel, its plastic horses rising and falling in a mesmerizing glide, and on the spinning Tilt-A-Whirl, which flung its riders in crazy loops, and on the towering wheel in the back. In the dark, over the sound of the clarion music, the whoosh of a wooden coaster added a background roar to the screams, the silhouette of rickety tracks dark on the darkness of the sky.

It was a place where reality gave way to fantasy, and the normal rules of life were torn up and thrown away.

A pair of preteen girls shoveling peanuts into their laughing mouths gave Dax a wide berth and a look of disgusted unease.

He limped ahead, past the ticket booths, through strange-hued illumination swirling in impossible patterns, through the unfamiliar crowd where everyone seemed to be wearing a mask of colored light. Possibly some of these unrecognizable folks had come from nearby Bannon, and maybe they had brought the smell of burning meat with them from its slaughterhouse, for he could somehow detect it on the air.

Farewell to flesh, he thought.

It was a moment before he understood that what he mistook for burning meat was burnt popcorn and cooking hotdogs. The odor prodded his gag reflex.

Ahead, he spotted Mason Tesoro swinging a huge fake hammer down at the strongman game. Lights scurried up and back down, not quite reaching the bell at the top.

Dax froze.

If Mason turned around, he would see him, only ten feet away.

Did he share the sheriff's suspicions about Zeke? What would he do if he knew the part Dax had played?

Mason swung the hammer again, muscles flexing. This time, the lights went all the way to the top of the apparatus, and the bell dinged violently. He threw the hammer down at his feet and punched the air. A small group gathered around the game and cheered. Before Mason could turn around, Dax staggered into the curtained opening of a striped tent.

The tent enclosed a dimly-lit interior, saturated with the smoky smell of incense and sweat. A small group stood on the grass, facing a wooden stage lit from above by beaming spotlights with the silvery aspect of moonlight. A stifling warmth soaked Dax's skin and drew out beads of sweat.

Upon the stage in the strange, bleak light stood a woman drawn in dizzying colors. Designs arced across her form in unnatural shades, and when she moved, the light made her shimmer, as though the images were dancing across her skin. She wore only shorts and a tank top, and almost every inch of her shone with the alien artifice of tattoos, which ran in waves over her legs and arms. Long brown hair hung over her shoulders; she sat at an angle, her back to the audience as she painted effortlessly on a canvas, switching colors with the flick of her fingers.

Someone stood on the stage beside her, telling a story. In the story there was a train, and the woman sat painting a train in her watercolors, which seemed to be speeding across the page. Then she flipped the page over to a blank one and began a new painting, which manifested with such dexterity it was as if the painting had been there all along and she was only revealing it, piece by piece, by waving her paintbrush like a magic wand.

Dax realized the painting corresponded to the story. It took a turn for the fantastical—thieves or train robbers running through the compartments, pursued by police. Thieves appeared on the page. Then the narrator of the story stepped out and tripped one of the thieves— *no joke*, he said, *no joke, I'm not making this up! This is a true story!* The audience laughed skeptically, having heard too many stories in their lives to take each one at face value. When he tripped the thief, a ring fell out of his bag, and he reached down and picked it up. *Why not?* He put it in his pocket before the police showed up and called him a hero.

All the while, the painter kept time with the story, as if she could predict what the man was about to say.

Dax found himself lost in her tattoos. Brilliant orange bulbs like Van Gogh's flaming stars cut through blue; red and purple geometric shapes contorted into tesseracts; spiked green vines wrapped around her limbs, arced across her skin, art-ified her living body. There, a flower—*a prairie rose?* There, a buffalo. There, a symbol he had no hope of deciphering but which held a mysterious familiarity.

She sat in the dusky imitation twilight, painting rhythmically. A spider crawled across her skin, but no, it was only a tattoo.

While he stared, she captured the story impeccably on the page, her hand moving like liquid, and then she flipped to a new page as the man continued; after the train ride, he used the ring to propose to his girlfriend.

But the girlfriend recognized the ring! It had belonged to her grandmother, but was stolen before the old woman had passed away.

The coincidence made the audience gasp with delight. Audiences love coincidences in stories, for they tie up loose ends the way reality tends to neglect, and that's how Dax knew the story was bogus.

He wondered if everyone here also knew the story was fiction but made themselves believe it anyway because it was such a good tale, because it would have been a terrible story if the ring simply ended up being worthless junk, or if the train part had never happened and it was really the story of a man proposing to his girlfriend with a ring of no significance. If that were the case, the story would be meaningless, and no one liked a meaningless story because it felt too much like the arbitrariness of life.

The final canvas depicted their marriage in a happily-ever-after sort of way, and the audience applauded the painter's remarkable skill. It turned out that the man was a random person from the audience, and the painter tore off the pages she had completed from the story and handed them to him to keep before he stepped down from the stage.

Another man stepped on stage, this one clearly a member of the carnival.

"Isn't she wonderful?" he said, and the audience applauded again. "Who else has a story to tell? Share you tale and watch it come to life before your eyes!"

Instead of looking around to see who wanted to go next, Dax watched the woman. She turned slightly toward the audience, but at best he could only see her in profile. He caught a glimpse of another symbol tattooed upon her skin—impossibly familiar. It was black, but he thought it should be red. He thought it should be painted red upon a wall, and that's when he knew the symbols were the same ones Savannah had drawn in blood at Prairie Rose Ranch.

He took a step forward, thinking he might be able to squeeze through the crowd to the stage. He had to talk to the woman—

"Dax," came a voice from behind him, and he turned to see Sarah and Wyatt standing just inside the entrance to the tent.

Someone else volunteered and came to the stage to tell their story. The man on stage revealed a glass jar he opened, and told the new storyteller to blow into it for good luck.

"What's this?" Wyatt said.

Before the next story began, the tattooed woman turned briefly to the audience, and Dax found his gaze immediately drawn to the tattoo on her chest, stretching across her clavicle—the key symbol inside the leaf-shaped outline of the eye.

"Her tattoo ..." murmured Dax.

"If we're here to find Savannah," Sarah said in a hard voice, "let's find Savannah."

"Seconded," Wyatt said.

The next story began, and the tattooed woman started to paint.

Dax would have to interrupt the show to talk to her, and he did not want to draw any attention to them. Reluctantly, he nodded and followed them out of the dark, musty tent, and into the lit-up, chattering, peopled night.

A *whoosh* rushed through the air on the wings of an unnatural breeze, undercut by the rickety sound of wheels speeding across wooden tracks. Screams echoed from the roller coaster in the distance, and pulled away as the car dropped.

They started through the crowd again, edging their way around the tents and games as they scanned the sea of faces. All around them, the sound of babbling voices converged, rose, ebbed like waves. Dax couldn't seem to piece together the voices around him into any kind of intelligible words. Language had muddled into incoherence with so many people talking at once, voices lost in a sea of confusion until they were all just making meaningless noise.

When they had come around to the other side of the carnival, Dax looked up to the giant Ferris wheel looming above them, seeming, to him, implausibly large for a traveling carnival to set up and dismantle all the time. Lights flashed from the innermost circle and out along the spokes, making them appear to race outward as it spun. A blue-and-red lit-up sign stood above the entrance, giving name to the rotating goliath: The Cosmic Eye.

"Bet you can see this whole damn place from up on that thing," Wyatt said, leaning back to observe. "We should ride up. Maybe we'll spot Savannah." He pulled out a few wadded bills and handed them to his sister. "Get us some tickets."

"Why me?"

"Because I look like I took a bath in a swamp today, and Dax is on drugs and wearing broken handcuffs and can barely walk."

Sarah scowled. She looked disheveled with her torn shirt, but Wyatt was right: out of the three of them, she was the least suspicious.

She took the money and said, "This isn't enough."

"Well, it's all I got," Wyatt grunted.

Dax pulled out his wallet and added a few more dollars to her hand.

She looked at him with a kind of grudging gratefulness, then exhaled and took off through the crowd without saying anything.

Dax and Wyatt stood in the shadows behind the Ferris wheel.

"How's your ankle?"

Dax looked down and shrugged. "Fine."

"Uh-huh, my ass," Wyatt snorted. He pulled out his bag of meth, lighter, and pipe. Holding the glass in his casted hand, he filled it and stuck it in his mouth. The lighter kept going out, and he growled at the dousing breeze. "Damn it." He turned, cupped his hand around the pipe, and finally got a drag. "Don't tell Sarah," he added as he exhaled a plume of smoke. When he was done, he laughed and tucked away his tools. "Bet you didn't think this was what you'd be coming home to."

"No," Dax said.

South of the carnival lay a quiet darkness with a calm array of stars. Dax felt like he could stand there all night, counting them, one by one. He even started, but he'd barely gotten to ten when Wyatt's voice interrupted him.

"Wasn't sure you'd ever come back."

Dax pulled himself back from the stars and said, "*I* wasn't sure I'd ever come back."

They were silent for a moment. A guilty feeling corrupted Dax's high. He wanted to go back to star-counting, but he couldn't.

"You wish you hadn't?" Wyatt said.

"I don't know."

Wyatt blew smoke at the stars. "Maybe you shouldn't have."

An apology had been creeping up his throat this whole time, so finally he said, "I'm sorry I never—"

"Save it," Wyatt said, cutting him off. He let out a mirthless laugh. "I mean, I don't need your apologies. It's a little late to think that matters now. Besides, we've got bigger fish to fry."

He couldn't let it go, though. The meth focused his attention sharply on the subtle sounds of Wyatt's voice, and now he could hear beneath the brittle sarcasm—buried beneath the caustic jokes—a kind of repressed hurt. He looked down at the million blades of grass that sprang up from the dusty field.

"You never went to Iceland," Dax said. "I thought … you know."

"Iceland?" Wyatt looked amazed. "Haven't thought about that shit in years. Hell, you really thought I was going to go to Iceland?"

Dax felt suddenly foolish.

Wyatt shook his head and said, "You should know by now I don't mean half the shit I say. You really thought I was just going to be cool, cruise on out of here, have a grand old fucking time? You just left. I mean, I always knew you wanted to get out of here, but hell, did you have to leave me here? What did you think would happen when you said 'adios?' What did you really think I was going to do?" He put the pipe in his mouth and then took it out, realizing there was nothing left to smoke. "You were my best friend. My *only* friend." He shrugged. "And you just fucking left."

Dax knew if he tried again to apologize, Wyatt wouldn't hear it. The apology didn't matter, but he still needed some way to relieve the feeling of guilt that had wedged itself into his gut—or maybe he didn't.

I deserve to feel it, don't I?

"Is that why you started smoking?" Dax said, knowing the answer and knowing it would only make him feel worse and *wanting* somehow to feel worse, all at once.

Wyatt put away his pipe and looked at Dax with an ironic arch to his eyebrow.

"What do you think?"

"I think I'm some shitty friend."

"Well, you're *my* shitty friend," Wyatt said, his mouth curving into a sardonic grin.

"Guess you're stuck with me then."

"Guess I am." Dax gazed into the carnival. "Hey, she's coming back."

Sarah headed their way with a wad of red tickets. She tore off a few, handed them to Dax. Tore off another few, handed them to Wyatt. She peered up into his face with a frown.

"You dickweasel," she said. "What, am I going to be the *only* one here not high?"

"Depends," Wyatt said. "You want some?"

She shoved him. "Fuck off. All right, we've got three tickets each. That's enough for one ride on the Ferris wheel. Make it count."

"Hey, you've got four," Wyatt said.

Sarah tore off the extra ticket and stuck it in her pocket.

"I could only get them in packs of ten."

They went to the short line in front of the ticket-taker. The man was silent as he took them and stepped back to let them pass through the open gate.

Wyatt hopped up onto the wobbly carriage an elderly couple had vacated. Sarah and Dax climbed in after him. They swung the door shut, and the carriage lurched forward a few feet before stopping again to let a new group into the carriage behind them. It swung back and forth, hovering above the ground, then lurched forward again, stopped again.

"This is the worst ride I've ever been on," Wyatt said. "Hey! Can we get rolling, or what!"

"We're not here to have fun, asshole," Sarah said, "We're here to—"

"Shut up." Dax leaned forward, to the edge of the carriage. He had been scanning the carnival and now he spotted, not far away, a girl slipping through the crowd, with long dark hair and a gray dress. "I think I see her."

Sarah and Wyatt both turned their heads.

Dax tried to point her out, but she kept moving, and her face was turned away.

"There," he said, moving his finger. "There." A thrill of dreadful anticipation raced through him. "Do you see her?"

Sarah shook her head.

Wyatt said, "Nah, man, I don't see anything."

He dared not take his eyes off the moving figure, but she kept vanishing behind other people, game stands, and tents. A desperate frustration filled him, and he felt trapped within the confining carriage, although it wasn't yet too far off the ground.

"I can make it if I jump," Dax said. "I can make it."

"Are you crazy?" Sarah hissed. "You'll break your ankle this time."

He shook his head, grabbed the bar that ran around the edge of the carriage. He would have to jump soon, though, for he could sense her getting away, moving farther and farther from the Ferris wheel.

"You sure it was her?" asked Wyatt. "I didn't see."

"It's her," Dax snarled. He leaned out, and Sarah grabbed him by the shirt and yanked him back. "Let go of me—she's *there!* Don't you see her? We have to catch up before we lose her again!"

The carriage lurched, rocking them back and forth. Wyatt swore and grabbed for the railing as they started climbing. The swinging made the carnival swoop erratically below them.

Dax lost her, and tried to find her again in the crowd. He thought he spotted a flash of gray, a swish of black hair, but the people moved in different directions and swallowed her.

"No. No!" He pitched himself forward, ready to leap out of the rising carriage, but this time both Wyatt and Sarah pulled him back in. "Damn it!" he snapped. He thrust himself violently away from them and into his seat as the carriage climbed steadily higher.

"We could've had her," Dax said. He leaned his elbows on his knees and felt a twinge in his ankle. The ache surprised him. It reminded him that he wasn't invincible, and the reminder brought with it a feeling of gnawing terror. "Do you have more?" he said to Wyatt. "To smoke?"

Wyatt's eyes narrowed slightly.

"Don't take this the wrong way, but I don't think you should have any more."

"You don't believe I saw her."

They rose into the air, curving around the edge of the wheel. The smoky heat that seemed to radiate from the carnival hovered near the ground, and they glided up into the cool dark air, higher and higher, until the people became indistinguishable shapes far below.

"This was a bad idea," Sarah murmured, chewing on a fingernail.

The ride slowed, and they came to a stop at the top of the wheel. From here, Dax could see beyond the carnival: the dark shape of the water tower in the distance, gently outlined by an illusion of thrown light; in the other direction, the glowing windows of Frieda's cottage. From here, everything seemed far away and surreal.

There was a magic in it, this floating away from the ground. He had risen into the stars. Dax looked up, but the constellations appeared foreign to him, mysterious and indecipherable symbols like the ones on Savannah's walls and on the tattooed woman's body. He wondered what it all meant.

Am I never meant to know?

That was the theme of his life, after all—the constant burning disappointment of never knowing. He believed, fervently, that he had seen Savannah, but he also *didn't* know, and this sparked a cold rage— at himself, at the others, at the world.

The carriage began its descent.

He gazed into the crowd as the ground rose to greet them. Part of him did not want to see Savannah again, to let her disappear forever. The wheel drew them inward, toward the bottom.

Wyatt waved at the ticket taker, who stood beside the controls pulling a lever. They slowed, then stopped.

"You get one more go-around," the man said.

"Yeah, thanks, that's enough for us," Wyatt said.

Looking nonplussed, the man walked over to them and lowered the gate so they could step out of the carriage.

Wyatt thumped him on the shoulder as he went past and said,

"You're doing a great job, though. Keep it up, and they'll have to make you top carnie soon."

The man continued to stare at Wyatt while Dax and Sarah exited the ride.

As they walked away, Dax could hear the whir of the wheel starting up again. He didn't know which way to go. Savannah could be anywhere, and every direction seemed wrong. He picked one and started walking.

They hadn't made it five steps when it became clear they each had a different direction in mind. They all stopped and turned back to each other, pointing three different ways through the carnival. Sarah and Wyatt began to bicker, and Dax felt it was pointless to speak up.

He looked across the carnival, to the vast stretch of populated field.

Savannah could be anywhere, he thought.

Then he saw Deputy Mendoza appear ten feet in front of him, and witnessed the very moment she realized they were there—her face displaying a modicum of surprise, quickly concealed by the cool authority into which she so easily stepped.

"Hey," she said. "Hold on, you three. We need to talk."

CHAPTER 17

"Oh, what in Jesus Christ's asshole—"

"Wyatt and Sarah Montgomery?" Deputy Mendoza said as she took a few steps towards them. A measure of relief passed over her face. "Well, that makes two."

The Montgomeries looked at each other, displaying equal parts surprise and confusion.

"Uh ... what?" Wyatt said.

"Your parents called the station, reported you two missing. They're worried sick," the deputy said. "And, to be perfectly honest, you're not the only teenagers who have gone missing in the last few days—but you're the only ones I've found, so I'm going to take this as a win."

Wyatt said, "Hey, I'm not a teenager—"

"Who else is missing?" Sarah said, cutting him off.

The deputy shook her head. "Let's just get you back home. Why haven't you been in contact with your parents?"

Every moment they stood there, Dax felt Savannah slipping away, a ghost dissolving in the air like a burnt afterimage superimposed on the dark.

"Someone else you're looking for is here, too," he said. "Savannah."

"How do you know that?"

"I saw her."

The deputy eyed him carefully. "You saw her," she said slowly, cautiously; she was working something out in her mind. "You said it was the last time."

"What?"

"Your pupils are dilated." As she came closer to him, Dax backed away, and she grabbed his wrist to stop him. She caught the handcuff, the broken chain swinging against her. Deputy Mendoza looked down at the cuff, and an indecipherable frown worked its way onto her face. "Where did those come from?"

"Where do you think they came from?" Wyatt said. "Your sheriff. Didn't tell you he cornered us, did he? Not surprised, considering he drove us out to nowhere and tried to off us."

The information seemed to strike the deputy in the face. She let go of Dax's wrist.

"What?" she said, "No."

"Yes," Wyatt said. "He dragged us out to the Willoughby farm, cuffed Dax, and tried to shoot him."

The deputy shook her head. "I don't believe that."

Wyatt looked unconvinced by her protestation.

"He wouldn't—he's the *sheriff.* I know him. He's not that kind of person."

"Anyone can be that kind of person," Sarah cut in. "Under the right circumstances."

"All right," the deputy said. "All right. Let's figure this out." She pulled her radio from her lapel to her mouth and asked for the sheriff to respond.

Wyatt, Sarah, and Dax looked at one another in alarm.

The radio crackled, and the sheriff told her to go ahead in a clipped voice.

"I've got two 864's found and a 10-40 at the carnival. Request assistance."

"*Who's the 10-40?*"

"Dax Howar—"

Wyatt grabbed the radio, tore it from her uniform, and tossed it away, where it disappeared into the foot traffic. The deputy whirled on him, but Wyatt took off before she could make another move.

Sarah grabbed Dax's wrist and pulled him along until he was able to keep up. She let go when they darted into the babbling crowd, people blurring past them.

Again, Dax grew dizzy in a confusion of words and voices. With the deputy behind them, and the sheriff now aware of their location, the only thought on Dax's mind was to find someplace where they could hide or lose themselves.

A tent, a ride—

"Here," he said when he spotted a building. He veered toward it. Words lit up, flashed, lights crawling across each individual letter:

FUNHOUSE. With a burst of energy, he tore past the line, hopped the railing in front of the surprised ticket-taker, and plunged into the black orifice beneath a painting of a clown's face with flames for eyes.

Into the clown's mouth and into the cocoon of quiet dark, down a hallway lined with black curtains. Manic laughter echoed from somewhere, from some hidden dimension, and he whirled around until he was face to face with a flat alien entity that had chosen a clown as its earthly form. It began to recede back into the curtains, swallowed up, and was gone.

Dax looked around for Sarah and Wyatt, but they were gone, too. They hadn't followed him inside. His heart skipped, beat, skipped again.

Others moved in the distance, ahead of him, behind him—it was hard to tell. Green lights descended, and he was transported to an alien world. Then the light changed to blue, and he was underwater. Though he could breathe, he felt drowned in the blue light and thought he must swim to the surface of the lake, break through and then float into the sky like Savannah.

Where is she? Is she here, with me, swimming in the blue?

Gravity yanked Dax back to the earth when the lights turned red. The hallway filled with blood. A dead body hung from the ceiling, black and rotten, a twisted skeleton. He thought of the priest from Pastor's Grove.

Did the Savannah-thing crucify him, or did the Savannah-thing become *him?*

Blood poured from the ceiling and ran down Dax's skin. Blood ran across the walls in strange shapes, and there was the eye, the Cosmic Eye, but not the Ferris wheel, the other eye, the one whose pupil was a constellation and whose iris contained a key to locked and long-silenced mysteries.

The light changed again, and Dax moved forward. He reached the end of the hallway and stepped through a black curtain, lost, momentarily, in the limbo of outer space.

When he emerged, he was staring at himself—a version of himself, at least. This Dax looked pale and sick, with dark hollows beneath bloodshot eyes and matted hair, and he stood hunched and tilted to one side, chest heaving, his clothing dirty and ripped. Dark spots of blood stained the bottom of his jeans where the coyote's bite had torn through skin. Broken chains swung from the metal around his wrists.

This Dax looked deranged. This Dax looked nothing like the Dax he thought he was. This was some imposter.

He reached forward, and the other Dax did the same. Their fingers touched. The fingertips were cold, smooth, hard. Inhuman. He knocked against the other Dax's knuckles. He pressed his palm against the other Dax's palm. This other Dax, he realized, was not some other Dax, but him. He stared into the mirror and did not recognize himself, but knew he and this mirror-Dax were the same. As he turned away, he spotted dozens of duplicate Daxes all around, staring at him, each with those bright drugged eyes.

Is this what I've become? A flat facsimile?

He waded out among the sea of Daxes, bumping into himself wherever he went, unable to tell the difference between the way ahead and the thousand glassy faces of the mirrors.

Then he thought he saw another. Not a Dax this time, but a girl— dark-haired and wearing a gray dress—staring out from one of the mirrors with sickly yellow eyes. He darted forward, reached out for her, but she moved and was gone. He spun around, searching the surfaces, the endless portals into identical dimensions, and saw her again. She stood, facing him, but as soon as he moved to catch her, she disappeared again, no more than a reflection.

"God damn you!" he shouted as he lurched forward through the maze.

Where's the real Savannah?

He could see her moving through the mirrors, slipping in and out of sight. She couldn't exist solely as a myriad of reflections; there *had* to be an original to create the reproductions he saw. Reflections could not exist on their own any more than shadows could roam without someone to cast them.

Unless that's all she was: an illusion, a shadow thrown against the surface of the world.

Dax stopped and shook his head. He refused to entertain the idea that she wasn't actually here at all, that he had imagined her. He knew he had seen her below the Ferris wheel. No matter what Wyatt and Sarah thought, she was here. She *had* to be here.

His breathing echoed in his ears, uneven and labored.

Each time he turned in a new direction, he hit another mirror, another Dax frowning at him, shaking his head, telling him he was going the wrong way.

Savannah flitted in and out of the mirrors, never fully there. He chased the ephemeral illusions like his father had chased his mother's ghost through old newspaper pages. Then he stumbled through a narrow passage between two mirrors, a dark doorway. Relief filled him as he pushed through the curtain and emerged into the darkness on the other side—and found himself before a swirling vortex. On the edge of a precipice, it seemed, but rather at the mouth of a rotating tunnel. He felt dizzy. He gazed across the eternity between here and the other side of the spinning black hole, and there, standing at the opposite end, was Savannah.

She stood perfectly still, which seemed impossible against the churning movement of the portal. Blue lightning streaked across the spinning circles, drawing him forward.

He didn't know what would happen when he stepped through the wormhole: which new and horrible dimension he might find himself in, which Dax he would be when he came out the other side. Or maybe, like a black hole, the passage would crush him to the size of an atom, to virtual nonexistence.

Savannah gazed at him. It was as if she had summoned this vortex the way she had summoned the tornado, and now she stood in the eye, as she *always* stood in the eye: in the center of the destruction but impervious to it, pulling it around her faster and faster until she broke the fabric of reality.

Dax stepped forward. The spiraling lines engulfed him, and he nearly toppled over. An unseen and perhaps imaginary force pushed him to the side until he found himself hopelessly off-balance. He did not stand upon solid ground; he tilted on an axis, away from gravity until gravity no longer made sense.

He forced himself to train his eyes, unblinking, on Savannah at the end of the tunnel. He couldn't lose her again. His eyes stung and blurred with tears, but still he did not blink. It had become impossible to move. The world had turned upside-down and he could only cling to the floor and crawl forward while everything spun and spun as he lost himself in the dizzying whirl.

"What do you want?" he asked her unmoving form. "Why are you here?"

She did not respond.

He could barely keep his eyes on her anymore. His vision swirled.

"Why did you kill him?"

She stared down at him with cold yellow eyes.

At last, she spoke: "For the same reason I was going to kill you." Her voice came to him like a dream, a voice that held almost nothing of humanity.

Panting and gritting his teeth, Dax put his head down and closed his eyes. In blind darkness, he crawled forward, but when he reached the end of the tunnel and opened his eyes, Savannah was gone.

He looked back at the spinning vortex, feeling as though he had transitioned to some other plane of reality, but knowing, simultaneously, that it was just a carnival attraction.

A glowing exit sign hovered in the air before him. He followed it, and out, and entered the night behind the funhouse.

"There you are!"

Sarah and Wyatt appeared beside him and pulled him into a shadowy overhang and around the side of the building. They looked out beyond the edge of the carnival, onto the vast dark field. A low wind blew the long, dead grass.

"I thought I saw you go in there," Sarah said.

"I saw her in there." Dax's said, his voice hoarse in his ears. "I saw her, but she got away."

"Well, she didn't come out the back," Wyatt said.

"Maybe she's still in there," Sarah said.

Dax shook his head. "She's gone."

A young couple exited the funhouse, laughing and teasing each other, before vanishing back into the carnival.

"What do we do now?" Sarah said.

"We keep looking," he said. "If she really was in there, she can't have gotten far." He took a limping step toward the front of the funhouse.

"Hold on," Sarah said. "After you went in the funhouse, we hid behind some garbage cans and heard Deputy Mendoza talking to someone who works here. She told them to start shutting down the carnival."

"What?"

"She said they had to shut everything down and get everyone out— except for the four people she's looking for."

"Four?"

"Us," Wyatt said, "and Savannah."

Dax looked out at the field and felt the night tugging him away from the carnival. Reluctantly, he turned back to the others.

"Well, we'd better find Savannah before she does."

They crept around the funhouse and peered back into the crowd. The deputy must not have begun the evacuation yet because people continued to mill about leisurely.

"Where do we go?" Dax said.

"Let's just start zigzagging," Sarah said. "We'll try to cover the whole carnival, but we need to be careful if the deputy's still around. Stick to the shadows if you can."

Dax and Wyatt nodded, and they headed through the crowd.

"I gotta say," Wyatt murmured, "This is the craziest shit I've ever done, and I once smoked a teener, stole a bunch of chickens from the Fergusons' coop, and threw them off the water tower to see if they'd fly."

Sarah looked at him. "You're an idiot."

A multilayered canvas of sound painted the night with laughter and shrieks, bells and music, rickety wheels and undertones of cranking machinery.

Dax felt, more than heard, the grass crunching under his shoes. Memory flickered around him: he was eight, he was twenty-two; he was with his parents; his parents were dead. Past and present peeled away the palimpsest of time.

They approached the other side where there were fewer rides. Poor lighting turned the edge of the carnival into a black chasm—the end of the world.

Dax thought they could crouch in the darkness for a moment, look around for Savannah or the deputy, and keep going. He had nearly made it to the rim of the light when someone grabbed his hand.

He whirled to find an elderly woman clutching him in her leathery grip. She stared just past him with eyes filmed by milky white cataracts. Dreadlocks unspooled over jutting shoulders and in the lights appeared to writhe, snakelike. Her lips cracked into the distant cousin of a grin.

"I know who you are," she said in a voice so low it seemed more a vibration in her throat.

Dax tried to pull his hand away, but she held it tight in her warm, dry grip.

He was eight; he was a child searching for his mother; the woman cocked her head at him, seeing without seeing, and said, *What's the matter, child? Have you lost something?* He shook his head; he was twenty-two, and the woman was older now but timeless.

"I will tell your fortune for one ticket," she said.

"Back off, lady. We're not interested," Wyatt said. He walked past her dismissively.

"Come on, Dax," Sarah said. "Let's go."

"But you've come so far," the woman said, leaning closer, speaking even lower. "Don't you want to know the truth?"

"What truth?" Dax said. He tried again to slide his hand free, but she crushed his fingers together. "What do you know?"

The woman smiled. "I know what you lost fourteen years ago ..."

His heart seemed to freeze in his chest; he stopped trying to pull away.

"... and I know where you can find her."

She tilted her head, and the two pale moons of her eyes locked him in their eerie, sightless gaze.

This time, when he tried to disentangle his hand from hers, she let go. Without looking at Sarah, he held out his hand.

"Give me the ticket."

"What?" Sarah's voice came out a whisper. "Are you serious?"

"This old bitch is playing you, man," Wyatt cut in. "Now let's *go*. I thought we were here to find Savannah."

He felt the woman's lingering touch tingle on his hand, the way he'd felt the ghost of his mother still holding him even after she'd disappeared. Now his hand shook, and he could feel every one of his heartbeats. He had to look away from her, felt he could not breathe unless he looked up into the clear darkness of the sky. He wanted the truth so badly it hurt; yet paradoxically, the need was so old and intense he wasn't sure he could bring himself to act on it.

Why does the truth have to be so wonderful and terrible while remaining unknown?

"I've been looking for you," the fortune teller said.

Wyatt barked out a laugh. "*Looking!*"

Her head swiveled to the right, then left again. "I see more than you'll ever dream." Her lips curled into a distant, pensive frown. "You can either follow me and learn the truth, or you can turn away and finish your business. The choice is yours."

Dax lowered his head and pinched the bridge of his nose. He had only a moment to make up his mind, but the moment seemed interminable. Before Sarah could protest, he reached into her pocket and fished out the last ticket, then pressed it into the fortune teller's palm.

The woman closed her fingers over the paper and sealed his fate.

"Come with me."

He started to follow, but Sarah grabbed his arm and said, "How can you be sure she's telling the truth?"

"I can't," Dax said and pulled away.

"Then why?"

He glanced at Wyatt, who stood half in the shadows, his mouth open in a mixture of shock and outrage.

"Because I have to," Dax said.

Without waiting to hear their protests, he followed the fortune teller as she wove through the crowd, a self-assurance in her step that belied her blindness. Tassels from her woven shawl swung to and fro as she walked, swishing across her back like pendulums.

They came to the southwestern edge of the carnival—the other side of the Ferris wheel, past the whooshing wooden coaster. It grew quieter and darker the farther they tread. As they distanced themselves from the crowd, Dax looked back, but he didn't see Wyatt or Sarah. He dared not wonder if he had made the wrong decision.

At last they came upon a graveyard of trucks and trailers staggered across the field, where a small tent had been erected, too far from the carnival for it to be an attraction. The incongruous placement imparted the tent with a surreal and ominous quality. In the darkness, its red stripes appeared black. The fortune teller led him to a part between the stripes, seamless and almost invisible in the side of the tent.

"What is this?"

"You'll see." She pulled back the flap to reveal a snatch of darkness, and when he hesitated to move, she said, "Inside." Moonlight glinted on her gold teeth.

Taking a breath to steady himself, Dax ducked beneath the flap. Inside he found darkness punctuated by a low flame encased within a bulb of dusty glass. A paltry yellow glow suffused the space immediately around the gas lantern. A figure sat beside it, half-cast in shadow.

When he stepped inside, the figure looked up, and a pair of green eyes met his.

CHAPTER 18

She stood slowly, a taut woman with a painted canvas of skin. He recognized her as the painter from earlier, but also recognized her as someone else now that he could see her face, one whose features had been lost to all but memory and photographs: the ghost of his childhood. There was the woman he'd seen turning stories into pictures, the carnival act, and there, behind the tapestry of tattoos, was his mother.

"Dax?"

She stepped forward and lifted the lantern so its glow reached out to him.

Now he could see her face more clearly.

Winter afternoons came to him, building animals out of the snow, and autumn evening bonfires, sparks crackling up to the sky while Renée pointed out constellations, here, the Dried Willow, and here, the Hand, and mornings of burnt pancakes and milk she had taught him to squeeze from the udder. And then it was gone, like a wisp of paper in the wind, an empty house, her face turned corpse-gray on newspaper.

An unearthly glow radiated from the lantern, from the voice of she who was not dead. He stared in wonder at the tattoos, which crawled over her skin as though alive, creeping with every flicker of the lantern. His tongue could not select which question to voice—from the thousand raging through his mind. Instead, he said, "You're alive." Then, "Let's get out of here."

The apparition drew hesitantly closer, one hand uplifted with fingers that sought to touch him but could not seem to cross the separating space. The fingers curled back into her palm, and when she spoke, she sounded weary and uncertain.

"And go where?"

"Anywhere," he said. "Anywhere! The only one outside this tent is some old fortune teller. We can go."

She shook her head, more for herself, it seemed, than for him. "The fortune teller is my friend—maybe the only one I trust. I asked her to find you if she could. She's helping me ... and I thought maybe you could help me, too."

"Help you do what? Escape?"

"No," she said. "No, this is my home."

She wasn't talking about Conjunction.

"The carnival is your home," he said slowly.

Dax took a step back and looked away, his head buzzing. The sound of her voice kept pulling him back into the past, into a long-abandoned nostalgia that hurt his chest. He wanted to sink into it, to sink, with her, back to his childhood, but it was wrong. This was all wrong.

"When I left—"

"When you *disappeared*," he cut in. "What happened?"

"Listen, Dax. I was never cut out for the life your father wanted for us. He knew it, too. I tried—I ... I was just never cut out to be a mother." Her eyes were vast green wells fraught with secrets. "You try to explain yourself, and nobody listens. Your voice means nothing. I did the only thing I could. I ran away."

Dax shook his head. "But I thought ... they *took* you."

"I didn't mean to get separated from you. That was an accident." She took a breath. "Leaving with them was my choice."

Dax's center of gravity tilted. His teeth chattered together, and something dark and leaden settled in his gut.

"Why?"

Renée placed the gas lamp onto a worktable beside a knife and turned it up so the flame burst into a new vivacity, blazing on the tent's interior. It seemed to be a supply area. Cabinets and boxes filled the space, drawers half-opened and spilling over with toys from the game booths, a cache of swords, a chest of costumes. There were shelves lined with glass jars—and those jars were filled with disembodied eyes and tongues floating in some preservative liquid.

"What the hell is this?" he said and took a step back.

"How much do you know about this carnival?"

"No," he snapped. He looked away, anywhere but at her, his heart pounding. "No, you don't get to ask *me* questions. You ... you chose to stay. You chose the carnival over us."

"It's not that simple."

"No." He clutched his head with both hands as if it would burst, and roughly dragged his palms down over his face to wake himself from this dream. "It is that simple."

"Dax—"

"Shut up!" He was on fire, his hands flexed into fists. "You left us." He staggered back and forth at a frantic pace, unable to contain the swell of overlapping emotions. "Why didn't you take me with you? I would have gone with you anywhere. I tried to leave, too. I tried. I went to college. I hated it here. You were gone, and Dad ... I would have gone *anywhere.*" His voice broke. He swallowed. "Did you know? Dad's dead. That's the only reason I'm back here. Your people killed him. You did this. He's dead because of *you.*"

Renée looked stricken into silence—a stranger, his mother—and despite the alien green eyes and the mosaic of tattoos, he recognized himself in her.

Unbalanced, he leaned and felt his mistake in the pain that stabbed his ankle. He stumbled at the shock, but the pain snapped him from his uncontrollable rage. He bent forward and put his hands on his knees.

"I'm sorry," she murmured in the sudden quiet. "You're right. It is my fault. She killed him to get to me—because she knows I'm trying to stop her."

Dax felt lightheaded, faint. The ground crawled under his feet. The tent around him and all its bizarre artifacts, previously stationary, now seemed incapable of remaining still; the world moved and breathed around him. The eyes swam in their jars, staring.

"Stop her from what?"

She didn't answer at first.

Dax watched the light creep over her tattoos. An eagle flew over churning sea waves, its feathers etched in pencil-like detail. A serpent coiled around her arm, each of its scales rendered in slick gray-green, flicking its tongue against her elbow. A red figure drawn in pointillism, composed of a thousand beads of blood, crouched over a rabbit. He recognized in these tattoos his mother's own drawings of Lakota myths. They came alive across her skin, and Dax had to blink and remind himself they were not really moving. He traced his eyes over the interlocking images, up to her exposed clavicle, and there was the image of the eye, the key, the constellation.

He straightened and pointed to her chest.

"What is that?"

She stared at his outstretched hand for a moment, at the chain swinging from his broken handcuff. "His symbol," she said, and ran her fingers over the key inside the eye. "I believe it unlocks a doorway to where he comes from."

"The star system, Algol," he said. "That's where, right? And ... what *is* he?"

"He goes by many names." The lantern shifted shadows over the tattoo, and the eye winked in the flickers of darkness. "I call him Baykok."

Dax recognized the name from somewhere, some long-ago myth. "Death," he murmured. "Father Death."

"Can I tell you a story?"

He closed his eyes and imagined himself sitting on the floor in front of his mother while she smoked and sketched, and the drawings animated and detached from the page. Still, with closed eyes, he nodded, not yet ready to return to the present. He floated in the limbo between times while she spoke, and her voice lulled him into a false calm.

"Almost a thousand years ago, Baykok descended from the heavens. For years, he roamed the Great Plains, bringing death like a plague. He colonized the earth, consumed entire tribes, appropriated their beliefs into whatever nourishment sustains him. He feasted on the energy of life until at last a shaman cast him deep into the bowels of the earth and trapped him there. But it was too late. The once-strong tribes were decimated, weakened by the monster, and could not defend themselves the next time someone came to colonize their land.

"Then came the Prophet, and the Prophet called him Father Death, for the Prophet was his child. Yet the Prophet did not know where Baykok had been imprisoned, or how to free him, and for hundreds of years searched the country. No ritual could locate or raise him from his unmapped prison. The Prophet traveled with a familiar—a coyote— and learned how to take different forms as a disguise, a kind of camouflage. Eventually, the Prophet gathered followers to aid in the search. They were taught to believe in the transcendent power of death, the existence of untold wonders awaiting only true followers beyond the end.

"Those followers came to travel as a carnival, again as a kind of camouflage, but also as a way to gather what they needed as offerings to their god. Our lives are told through stories, and Father Death consumes life. So I became the Storyteller, collecting the stories of our visitors. We take their perspective of the world, their experience of life—what they see."

Dax saw the jars with the floating orbs of sightless eyes.

"We take their voices," she said.

The jars with severed tongues.

"And we offer these to Father Death."

Savannah's family of corpses, eyes and tongues ripped out.

His father—

Dax opened his eyes.

"The Prophet?" he said warily.

"The one who has worn many faces. The one I call Iktomi. You may know her as a girl named Savannah."

"And you're one of her followers?"

"I was." Her mouth wavered between a smile and a frown, like the ripple on a lake. "I thought I was doing something meaningful. Hell, I helped her find her counter-ritual—the one that would raise him."

"But you changed your mind?"

She pressed a hand against her mouth, then removed it. "I should have changed it sooner." Her eyes were sharp and bright. "Our stories—the stories of our people—were never about death. They were about life. And now every story has been taken over and perverted by the pale monster, been made about death. All animals, all plants, all living creatures—we're connected. We're all made of the same stuff. But not these beings. They're not of this world. They don't belong here; they corrupt life, take what is sacred and bastardize it. They've managed to insinuate themselves so cleverly into the world, coming to us in the guise of our gods so that we believe in them, but I don't believe that anymore. Do you know what I believe now?" Her eyes flashed dangerously. "All gods are merely devils in disguise."

Dax wondered if there was anything left of the woman he'd once known. Then he wondered if that woman had been an illusion all along, if this was her true self.

"But it's too late to stop her. We're already here." She picked up the knife from the worktable and clenched the handle in her fist, making the tattoos on her arm pop with veins. "Baykok has been in Conjunction all along."

Dax found it hard to breathe, the air stifling.

While his mother had been telling her story, he imagined this ritual as some obscure and far-off thing, something to be performed in a remote, unpeopled location—a cave, maybe, in a mountainside, or the middle of a vast forest—but it was upon them now. It was here.

Savannah meant to do it here, and now.

Renée put down the knife and stepped forward.

Dax backed away, out of her reach, thinking if that tattooed hand touched him he would be touched by the dead, and the thought made his flesh crawl.

"The Prophet suspects I'm no longer on her side. She wants to cut me off from any possible help. That's why she killed your father. That's why ..." Her eyes glistened. "I had to find you. To keep you safe."

"Keep me safe?" He snorted. "That's a fucking laugh. You disappear for fourteen years and *now* you want to keep me safe?"

"I also thought you might help me," she said. "I may have found a way to fix this—a way to send him back to where he came from. But first she needs to raise him."

Perhaps that was the real reason she had brought him here, not to keep him safe, but to use him.

"Are you out of your mind?" he said. "You're going to *let* her summon this ... this monster?"

Dax wished he had ignored the fortune teller and had never come to this tent. His mother had chosen the carnival over him, and now she was trying to convert him somehow, to get him to help raise their demonic god. It was all a trick. She was no longer his mother. She was a stranger who wore the very tenets of the carnival on her skin.

For a moment, he was glad his father was not alive to know what she had done.

The burn of betrayal outweighed the pain in his ankle, and he grabbed the worktable and shoved it over, spilling the contents to the floor. The knife slid away, its blade clattering. The lantern remained intact, despite the fall; he snatched it up and thrust it toward her, the light burning into her face, which had pulled back in fear or wonder. "I'm not helping you," he snarled. "She'll never get the chance to do her goddamn ritual. I'm going to kill her first."

She took him by the arms then, and he let her.

"Listen to me, Dax. It's the only way. I need to make sure it all goes off without a hitch, and if she decides to stop me ... I have to make sure. He has to burn."

Dax shook his head. "Let go of me."

"You're making a mistake."

With great effort, he yanked himself free of her. The light swung wildly around him as the lantern swayed from its handle.

"You're the one who made a mistake," he said and stepped back.

"Dax—" She stepped forward, reaching out to him, but he turned away from her and made for the opening.

"I wanted you to be dead. You should have been dead."

He threw back the veil and stepped outside. The tent flap closed behind him, rippling in the breeze. The night air was cool, making him realize how hot he'd been in the tent; sweat had collected on his brow and under his arms. With the light of the moon and the dazzling colored bulbs that decorated the carnival, he hardly needed the lantern, but held onto it.

The fortune teller was nowhere in sight.

When he took a step forward, his leg collapsed beneath him, and he found himself suddenly on his side in the grass. A rust-colored circle had seeped through the dirtied bandage that enwrapped his ankle beneath the torn jeans. He struggled to rise, but couldn't.

Dax rolled onto his back and stared up, the carnival gone, the lights gone, nothing in his vision but the clear black star-spattered sky and death. He felt strangely hollow.

He lay there on his back in the dark and thought maybe he hadn't seen his mother in that tent after all. Maybe it was a vacant tent, and the fortune teller or his mind had created the illusion. The lantern lay beside him on the ground, though, cracked but still burning.

She could have been a figment of the meth staring back at him from the mirrors like the dozen Daxes trapped in a limbo of surfaces. He felt comforted by the possibility that she hadn't been real, even though he knew it wasn't true.

The carnival had become unexpectedly quiet. No screams, no whooshing coaster, no music. He closed his eyes against the spinning world and imagined he wasn't here at all.

After several long minutes, he struggled to his feet, his ankle buckling slightly. It didn't give, so he bent to pick up the lantern and took a few steps, then a few more.

The crowd had vanished.

Dax searched the game booths and rides, but found them all abandoned. Even the carnival workers had disappeared into the night. He wondered if he had stepped out of that tent into another dimension, an empty ghost-land of dormant machinery and the desolate waste of human decadence. He wondered about the time. He wondered if time existed here.

He limped past darkening shut-down rides, crunched over broken bottles, with the staggered lights on the edges of the carnival blinking out like fireflies.

The carnival, this last bit of reality, blinked out piece by piece.

Farewell to the carnival-goers, it seemed to say in its empty and ever-darkening patch of night. *Farewell to flesh.*

He limped on, feeling more and more like the last man on earth, the sole survivor of some quiet, inexplicable apocalypse. The sensation troubled him until a voice hissed, "Dax!"

A thin figure crouched beside a trashcan, shadowed to a silhouette. He stopped and lifted the lantern. Yellow light washed over Sarah.

She stood, grabbed him, and pulled him back with her into the shadows.

"We've been looking for you," she said.

"Did you find Savannah?"

She shook her head. "The deputy managed to clear out the carnival, so we hid, but we didn't know where that fortune teller took you. We split up to find you quicker. The deputy's patrolling the grounds now. We've got to get out of here."

"Where'd all the workers go?"

"I don't know," she said, the lantern casting sharp contours against her cheeks. "What about ... your mom?"

It took him a moment to work out how to use his voice.

"She's one of them."

From below, the lantern made black pockets of her eyes. When she tilted her head, the light found her pupils and reflected in the dark pools.

"Let's find Wyatt," she said.

They walked out into the midnight barrenness over dead grass and cigarette butts. A wad of cotton candy rolled like a tumbleweed.

Dax spotted two red tickets stomped into the dirt.

A tap—the sound of a footstep—drifted from the carousel with its sleeping horses, and Dax stopped. He imagined, for a horrible moment, the white spiders that had escaped from the coyote now scurrying over the carnival rides. Their tiny clacking legs crawled over the ground, around the carousel, and into his mind until he felt his skin itch with the phantom sensation of them. He stared at the darkened ride. There were no spiders.

Sarah pointed to the Tilt-a-Whirl, indicating without words that she'd seen something there. She hurried ahead.

Dax opened his mouth to call her back, but he heard another footstep from the carousel and turned instead, lifting the lantern, which threw vicious shadows over the ride.

Someone was in there.

He stepped forward, hesitantly, and peered around the poles.

"Wyatt?"

A figure sprang out from behind a horse and into the light.

"Oh thank Christ, it's you," Wyatt said, his eyes huge and unblinking. "This place is giving me the fucking creeps."

Relief at Wyatt's presence gave way to a twist in Dax's gut. He turned in the direction Sarah had gone. "She thought she saw you over there—"

A distant shout cut him off.

They traded a quick glance before taking off across the field. As they zigzagged around the obstacle course of rides and stands, he lost sight of Wyatt. Dax stumbled as he ran, limping heavily because of his bad leg.

Ahead, the Tilt-a-Whirl stood bathed in darkness, and he held aloft the lantern, its glow swinging frantically. When Dax was close enough, the lantern light revealed Sheriff Anderson holding Sarah by the upper arm with one hand, a gun with the other. They stood on the raised platform of the ride, giant apples facing in various directions around them.

The sheriff's eyes glinted with fury; puffy bruising distorted his face where Wyatt had hit him earlier. Sarah tried to pull herself free, but he gripped her tighter, swollen purple lips retracting from his teeth. "Let go of my sister, you pile of pigshit!" Wyatt snarled. He lurched forward, about to climb onto the platform, but the sheriff turned the barrel of his gun to Sarah.

Wyatt stopped, looking mutinous.

"Step back," the sheriff said, looking at Dax. "I let you get away twice. You won't get lucky a third time." The moon washed over his deranged face and bloodshot eyes. "Now, you tell me *exactly* what you did to my son, or I'll pull this trigger."

Dax put down the lantern and raised both his hands over his head.

"Fine," he said, "But let her go."

The sheriff didn't move. "Where is he?"

"At the Willoughby farm," Dax said, "where I buried him."

The gun trembled as the sheriff's face twisted into a hideous frown. "You killed him," he whispered, his face twitching and contorting in a mad fury of grief. "You killed him. You killed my son. You ... you ..." The gun shook wildly against Sarah's head.

She stared ahead of her, wide-eyed and still but for her heaving chest.

"I thought your daddy was bad, but *you...*" the sheriff said, shaking his head. "You, Dax. *You.* You never should have come back here."

Suddenly he pulled the gun away from Sarah and trained it on Dax.

As soon as the sheriff moved, so did Sarah.

She slammed her foot against his shin so that he cried out and fell to his knees.

The ride lit up then, burst to life in a riot of color and sound. The platform started rotating, and the apples swung wildly with the movement. Wyatt stood at the controls.

Sarah scrambled across the spinning platform, then stopped and turned back to the sheriff. He struggled to his feet atop the whirling ride, and so she dove at him and reached for his gun while the platform pulled them around and around, faster and faster.

The sheriff fought her off, but Wyatt had jumped onto the ride and was darting around the apples to get to him. He used his cast like a battering ram and knocked the gun out of his hand. It went skittering across the platform, where it danced and spun like a live thing. Sarah dove for it, but the sheriff grabbed her ankle and yanked her down.

She landed hard on her stomach and rolled across the moving track.

Dax limped forward, but his leg shook dangerously; he leaned heavily on his good leg as he staggered to the controls. He threw down the lever, and the ride wound down, went dark.

Sarah tumbled off the edge of the platform into the grass.

Wyatt lunged, but the sheriff retrieved his gun and smashed it up into Wyatt's face. His nose, still swollen from when Dax had punched him—what felt like ages ago—burst into a red firework, and he stumbled away. The sheriff pushed Wyatt's shoulder until he fell, then kicked him in the stomach when he was down. Wyatt curled up around himself, moaning.

"Now *that's* justice, isn't it?" the sheriff snarled. He turned back to Dax and raised the gun. An ugly rage suffused his face.

"Sheriff!" Deputy Mendoza called, standing not twenty yards away, gun drawn.

Dax felt, for a moment, two guns trained on him and could only think that within one of them was the bullet that would end his life. He couldn't run anymore. His ankle hurt so badly, now, that he could barely put any weight on it.

Deputy Mendoza slowly approached, but her gun was aimed at the sheriff.

"Is this an arrest, she said, "or an execution?"

The sheriff did not lower his gun.

"He killed my son."

"If that's true, then arrest him," she said. "Now, holster your weapon."

A low, rumbling laugh escaped the sheriff's throat, filled with bitter irony. "That how it's going to be? After all I've done for you, after I helped you with your uncle—you'd betray me like this?"

Deputy Mendoza raised her other hand to hold her gun steady.

"You want to protect this lying, drug-addled murderer?" the sheriff said.

"Holster your weapon," she said. "Now."

The sheriff swung his gun in her direction.

Dax felt the weight of the barrel leave him, and he struggled to remain on his feet despite the growing tremor in his legs.

"I am the sheriff, you useless bitch, and you remember that. You do what *I* say. Dax Howard murdered my son, and he is going to pay. Now *drop your gun!*"

The deputy did not waver. Her hands clutched the gun, one finger poised delicately above the trigger. Her eyes gleamed in the moonlight, but her face remained stony.

Without looking away from the deputy, Sheriff Anderson took aim again at Dax.

"You put down your gun, or I'll shoot him," he said.

Unable to maintain his balance, Dax slipped to his knees. Sarah crouched not far from him, at the edge of the raised platform. For a moment their eyes met, and Dax knew she must be thinking the same thing he was: even if the deputy lowered her gun, the sheriff would shoot him anyway.

The deputy held her ground.

Sheriff Anderson made eye contact with Dax, a steely glare of pure hatred, one with total commitment to crossing this moral line, as well as the deep, almost subconscious knowledge that even the fruition of this revenge would not satisfy him. It would not bring back Zeke, but that would not stop him from pulling the trigger. Nothing would stop him.

Dax held his gaze. Then, unable to watch death come for him from Sheriff Anderson's gun, he closed his eyes.

A gunshot cracked through the air.

Dax felt nothing. He wondered if death had come too quickly for the pain to register. Then he noticed his ankle still throbbed, that he could still feel the wind in his face and the cold ground biting against his knees, and he opened his eyes.

Shock colored the sheriff's face as a circle of red spread across the front of his uniform. The gun slipped from his fingers and clattered to the floor of the platform. The corners of his mouth sagged. He clutched his gut and lurched, one bloodied hand outstretched, toward Dax, still seeking to enact his revenge, one way or another.

Deputy Mendoza shot him again, in the chest, and he stumbled back against the edge of the ride. His chest shuddered as he slid to the ground. He opened his mouth, but all that came out was a gurgle of blood. Still sitting, his body sagged to the side, and he fell still.

Dax couldn't move.

The deputy stood with her gun still raised, face frozen with horrified shock.

Wyatt crawled off the edge of the platform and into the grass beside Sarah, and they quickly moved away from the sheriff's body, toward Dax.

The deputy didn't seem able to take her eyes off the sheriff. Her throat convulsed. Slowly, she lowered the gun and covered her face with one hand.

"Let's go," Wyatt whispered, but Dax went to the deputy instead.

"Deputy Mendoza," he said.

She lowered her hand and looked at him with eyes that seemed unable to close, her face dangerously pale. "What have I done?" she whispered.

"You saved my life."

She holstered her gun, put her hands on her hips, and bowed her head, looking ill.

"Did you ever find Savannah?" he asked.

She swallowed. "No."

"We need to find her. She's going to do something … horrible. It's been *her* all along. The missing kids, her family."

The deputy shook her head and said, "I can't deal with that right now. I need to take care of this." She exhaled slowly and straightened up. "I should detain you."

"If we don't find Savannah, it won't matter because we'll all be *dead*," he snapped. "You saw them at Prairie Rose Ranch. *She* did that, and she's not done. Question us afterwards, but let me find her first."

She hesitated and then said, "I need to do the right thing here."

"You know what the right thing is."

The deputy brought one hand up to her mouth and held it there. She shook her head. When she looked at him again, her eyes were filled with conflict and misgiving. Then she said, "All right." She looked back at the sheriff, and her mouth twisted. "All right."

"Thank you," Dax said.

She walked toward the Tilt-a-Whirl and pulled out her cell phone, then stared at it as though she had forgotten how to use it.

Wyatt and Sarah hurried over to him.

"Okay," Dax said. "We've got to find where everyone went."

"I saw the carnies take off," Wyatt said. "They're heading north."

"What's there for them?" Sarah said.

Aside from the forest, north led only to Frieda's house. Dax didn't think there was anything left for them at Pastor's Grove; that place was long forgotten, dead.

What would they be looking for at Frieda's?

Abruptly, a shock of recognition hit him.

"The well," he said.

They both looked at him.

"My mother said they found the Watcher in the Stars deep underground." He looked up, toward the front of the carnival, the way they'd come only hours before. "They're going to Frieda's. It's in the well."

CHAPTER 19

They found the tree where Sarah had left the machete. Wyatt yanked it from the ground, scattering dirt. The shadow of the deputy and the sheriff's body had disappeared behind them, and Dax was glad for that. After the desolation of the carnival, he found a measure of relief in taking off again into the night. They walked across the darkened field, under bloated moonlight; rather, Sarah and Wyatt walked while Dax limped. He had brought the gas lantern, their only beacon against the darkness, until Frieda's cottage glimmered up ahead.

"Wait," Sarah whispered.

Wind ruffled dry grass. Cicadas buzzed in remote trees.

"What?" Wyatt said.

Through dimness and distance, Dax discerned the outline of the house, and beside it, smaller shapes or figures ranged across the yard, unmoving—but there was something wrong with their silhouettes. They were not those of people, but rather tall and thin figures. Whatever they were, the shapes were not moving.

"Let's just keep going," Dax murmured, and he limped forward, the lantern bobbing at his side. The others followed hesitantly.

Thirty feet away.

Twenty.

"Let's go around the back of the house," Sarah said. "They won't see us coming."

Dax wasn't sure what they would find. All he could make out were those strange inhuman shapes, like statue-still monuments of death. He turned down the lantern so the flame became a quiet thumbnail of orange light.

Soon they crouched in the shadow the moon had created of the house, then crept to the side. Dax pressed a hand against the cold, cobbled stone for balance. He reached the edge first, in the enclave south of the porch, and peered around the corner.

A cloud passed over the moon, and for a moment the blind world left whatever horrors lay ahead in obscurity, and he caught only the gray pixilation his eyes afforded him. Then the cloud disentangled its wispy shape, and pale light washed over the unmoving shapes.

He thought first of scarecrows—of the Willoughby family—but that wasn't quite right.

They imitated scarecrows, but the inverted figures' feet instead pointed skyward, while their outstretched arms hung only a foot or so above the ground. Neither were they the roughly-stitched ersatz human forms farmers erected in their fields—no, these upside-down scarecrows were human beings. Thick rope bound their ankles to the inverted wooden crosses, and their bodies sagged in death.

Dax craned his neck farther and saw more of them extending around to the front of the house beyond; they had been erected in a large circle with the well at its center.

Within this circle of the upside-down dead stood living figures.

"What do you see?" Sarah whispered.

When he didn't respond, she crawled around to his side, and then her face froze, profile illuminated from above. When at last she pulled back, her expression vanished in darkness with her head bowed low.

Wyatt crept around, then swore and retreated.

"I know who they are," Sarah said.

Dax steeled himself to look again.

The inverted scarecrows were all young, teenagers. Their faces were too far in shadow, but he thought he recognized some of the kids from the party at the Willoughby farm—from Savannah's congregation.

A voice spoke.

"It's her," he whispered.

Savannah's voice came to him as from another dimension, speaking words with no meaning, sounds harsh and ominous in their incomprehensibility.

Dax crept forward—despite Wyatt's whispered protest—around the corner to the side of the house. He kept the lantern between himself and the wall, the small light shielded, and he saw some of the people standing within the circle—a dark mass of figures.

Someone grabbed his shirt from behind, and in a panic Dax whirled around to find Wyatt yanking him back to where he and Sarah hid.

"Don't give us away," Wyatt said. "We need the element of surprise."

"What are we going to do?"

Wyatt motioned to the machete he'd set on the ground.

"What, you're just going to ...? She's surrounded by people."

"So I'll cut them down, too."

Sarah remained silent through the exchange, her face hidden in the darkness.

"Just—let me take another look," Dax said, feeling a sense of foreboding.

They had arrived at a crossroads, their opportunity for an action he realized they had not quite planned.

What are we doing here? What can *we do? Am I prepared to kill someone for revenge, even if that someone is not exactly human?*

He crept forward again, mesmerized by the dark figures standing around the well, around Savannah, who continued speaking in tongues. In the moonlight, the followers were more clearly and recognizably the carnival workers.

Dax continued farther along the edge of the house and made it to the front corner of the porch, crouching in shadow, but with a full view of the circle.

Looking between the figures was like trying to see through the trees of a forest, but then one of them shifted, and he saw her.

Savannah stood beside the well, her gray face bathed in moonlight. Her skin was discolored and patchy, while her teeth had gone rotten and dark, and yellow eyes gleamed from recessed sockets. She held something in her hand over the well, which had been painted with red-black sigils in what was unmistakably blood. When she spoke, her throat clicked, the language sounding more insectile than human.

These followers could not have possibly understood the strange sounds she was making, but they stood reverently and listened all the same. Her voice held a certain power, regardless of the words, and it captivated them as it had captivated Dax back at the Willoughby farm.

She abruptly switched to English.

"Soon we will all transcend," she said. "These deficient bodies. These tired pumping organs. This yielding flesh. You have been hurt. You have been sick. Father Death will cure what ails you. All you need are these."

She held a hand over the well and dropped something into the darkness.

"Eyes with which to see." She picked up something else and repeated the move: held it over the well and let it go. "Tongue with which to speak."

Dax's stomach turned.

Savannah picked up another object, dutifully reverent, as if presenting the host at church. She held the white orb aloft before dropping it into the gaping maw of the well.

He counted long seconds before it hit the waters below, and wondered how deep the hole traveled into the earth. He listened, attuned to every sound, his flesh crawling with too-sharp sensations. A bead of sweat curled a winding trail around his vertebrae, leaving a cold tickle like the tinkling of bells in his bones. He felt the starlight prickle at his skin; he felt the velvet cloak of the dark.

Dax wondered whose eyes she'd fed to the hungry well.

Those of her own murdered family? Zeke Anderson's, dug up from his makeshift grave? My father's?

He could hardly bear the thought and yet as soon as it was in his mind, he couldn't stop—his father's eyes and tongue disappearing into the dark water below. They stood no chance against her: she had killed Savannah's family; she had killed his father; it stood to reason she would kill them, too.

This realization gave him the urge to retreat, but in his haste he stumbled, hit his head on the porch, and gasped in pain and surprise.

The crowd turned their moonlit faces onto him.

Savannah stepped forward, fixing him with her yellow gaze, and her cracked lips curled into a smile.

"Dax Howard," she said.

Now with no chance to retreat, he stood to face her, still clutching the lantern. A kind of terror froze him, and he realized his cowardice. If he were a different person—a Zeke Anderson, perhaps—he might step boldly forward to confront her; he might accuse her of killing his father; he might even attack her. Instead, he stood frozen and cowed, heart in his throat, and he might have kept standing there dumbly had Wyatt not rushed by him from behind, shouting madly.

Wyatt stormed into the crowd, swinging the machete from side to side and making some kind of wordless animal cry as he cut a path toward Savannah.

Followers jumped out of the way of the frantic blade, which sliced and battered a couple of them in their retreat, and Wyatt had almost made it to Savannah when a group of three muscular men leapt onto him and wrestled him to the ground. They knocked the machete from his hand, and it landed in the grass. Wyatt lay on his back, struggling ferociously and spitting in their faces, but they had him well-pinned.

Desperate to do something, Dax started forward, limping heavily; before he made it too far into the circle of scarecrows, however, someone grabbed his wrist and held him there—not just someone, but his mother.

She gave him a look of warning while she held him in her iron grip. She wore a long jacket now, covering most of her tattoos, but some snuck out from the collar and the sleeves. She pulled him closer, her eyes piercing him, and whispered, "Remember what I told you."

He tried to yank his arm free, but her grip was too strong.

Savannah approached him now, her eyes ancient yellow and glittering.

Dax trembled from misplaced, drug-induced adrenaline and wished his mother—no, she was not his mother, for she had renounced that title—would let him go.

"What are you doing here?" Savannah said.

Dax breathed hard, but he withheld his voice.

"What are you doing here?" she repeated.

Finally, he said, "I think you know."

She looked at Renée, then slowly turned back to Dax. She was close enough now that he could smell the rot eroding her skin, the ripe stench of a slaughterhouse in July.

"How much will you scream when I take your eyes?" she wondered aloud. "As much as your father?"

Dax's heart gave an erratic thump.

"He did not go quietly. But he was too drunk to put up much of a fight."

The confirmation of what she had done spurred him to action; however, as soon as he began throwing himself at her with blind rage—wherein one loses real control, not fully aware what each limb is doing—he felt himself held back by arms wrapped around his torso. Against these arms, he struggled, but they held firmly, tightly, almost lovingly; brightly tattooed flesh, arms snaked with images.

She did not care what had happened to her husband. She did not care. His father had worn his wedding ring until the day he died, but these hands were bare, and she did not, could not, possibly care that her leader—her prophet—had murdered him.

Despite his desperation to escape those embracing arms, and to throw himself at Savannah and push her down the well into the darkness below, his energy was waning.

Renée had managed to restrain him.

In the struggle, the lantern ended up on the ground, uselessly emitting its light.

Dax fought back, thinking of his father's pale form in the morgue and his ashes scattered in the angry wind, thinking of the rubble that had once been his home, and of Zeke's body disappearing under the dirt, and of the moldering remains of Savannah's family, and of the bones scattered across the floor of the church in Pastor's Grove, and of the drugs in his veins, and of Algol's winking eye. He fought back against Renée, and she wrestled to keep him steady.

At last, his arm broke free and in the process he elbowed her in the face, cutting open her lower lip. Freed completely, he should have turned toward Savannah, but found himself hesitating, just as his mother hesitated, the shock of the moment pinning both of them in place.

Blood dripped from her split lip to her chin. Before he could act, Renée grabbed him and threw him to the ground.

As he went down, his ankle rolled severely and sent through him a high-pitched note of something beyond pain that electrified his marrow, the very filaments of his skin, the backs of his eyes. The grassy earth cradled him as he lay there, incapacitated by the pain, his head very near the lantern with its tiny flame still glowing within the dusty glass. With his cheek pressed into the dry grass, he breathed heavily, reeling. He lay beside a scarecrow dimly lit by the lantern, and he could not help but look upon the face that dangled there, with its empty holes that once housed eyes, and its bloodied mouth, and he would have shuffled away from that ghastly face were it not for Renée gently pinning him in place. He could do nothing. And he could feel nothing but the agony in his ankle and the bitter sting of betrayal.

Then Savannah appeared, bent down before him. Her fingernails were yellowed and curled, and he remembered what Frieda had said about Maybelle Willoughby. She tore off the cloth protecting his ankle and drove two fingers straight into the wound, her long nails scraping past bruised skin and swollen tissue into the muscle beneath.

His body vibrated like a plucked string, and the world disappeared and left him floating somewhere in a white space. He thought he heard the ghost of a shout from far away: *Stop!*

When his vision returned, Savannah stood above him.

Sarah had also emerged. She stood facing Savannah, an indecipherable look on her half-shadowed face, and she held in her hand a sleek black gun—the sheriff's Smith &Wesson.

Savannah turned to her, slowly, and her expression changed. Her eyebrows tilted upward while her face became a parody of sadness and sympathy.

"Sarah, it's me."

Sarah's hand clenched around the sheriff's gun. She drew a bead on Savannah.

"Why do you want to hurt me, Sarah? Don't you care about me anymore?" The yellow coyote eyes within her human face belied Savannah's entreating tone. "Don't you remember ... that night? On the water tower?"

"No," Sarah whispered, steadying the gun. "It's not *you.*"

"We dangled our feet over the side, and I took your hand?"

"*No.*"

"And we kissed?"

"Shut up!" Sarah shook the gun, her face contorted so that her downturned mouth hung open and her eyes took on a wild expression. "Shut the fuck up! You're not Savannah. Savannah's dead. She's *dead!* You're not her!"

"We laughed all the way down that rickety ladder. Until you fell, near the bottom, and twisted your ankle. Remember how I put your arm around me to help you walk?"

She took a step toward Sarah, whose hand shook wildly as she let out an awful sound, a kind of frustrated sob.

"Remember how I said we should just run away together? Leave our families behind and take off? We can still do that. We can be together forever. Savannah won't rot ... too much ... as long as I'm here." Her voice changed subtly, gaining a guttural undertone that sounded not altogether human. She took another step closer to Sarah and said, "You still want her, dead or alive. After all, death is just a freedom from this substance. You can join her in the darkness between stars."

Sarah pulled the trigger.

The bullet whizzed past Savannah's head and into the darkness. Sarah dropped the gun, let out a strangled cry. Savannah appeared at her side, moving too quickly. She took hold of Sarah, gripped her with fingers terminating in talons, and pulled her to the well. Sarah tried to fight back, but Savannah drove her head into the edge of the stone structure.

Her forehead split open; blood wept from the gash.

Wyatt shouted and struggled, but the man holding him jerked his broken arm behind his back, and his shouts turned into a yelp. A slew of incoherent curses streamed from his mouth. "You fucking—I'll rip your goddamn—you even *touch* her—you lying fuckbucket—zombie alien hole of an *ass*—"

Sarah fell slack as Savannah propped her against the well and tilted her head back.

Wyatt kicked a clod of dirt at Savannah and said, "Hey, over here! You want to come shut me up or what?"

She ignored him.

Renée let go of Dax and took a step forward, as if to stop her, but Savannah sensed her movement and turned to the painted woman.

"Stop. Or your son will be next."

Renée opened her mouth; her eyes appeared to sharpen, and something in her demeanor changed. She moved with dreamy slowness as she reached into one of the deep pockets of her knee-length jacket and removed a small dagger, sharp enough to pierce the night. She lifted it, looking down at the blade while her teeth clenched and her eyes widened. Then the calm darkness that had once filled her leaked away. She returned the knife to her pocket and took a step back. With hollow eyes, she turned her back on the well.

"Coward!" Dax shouted.

She did not turn to face him, but her back stiffened and her shoulders hunched.

Dax made an effort to rise, but another carnival worker pushed him back down with his foot, effectively stymieing his weak attempt to fight back.

Savannah seemed indifferent to Renée's actions; perhaps she had known all along that she hadn't been in any danger. Her attention rested on Sarah, and now she spoke again, her voice changed, minutely but horrifically.

"You will see Baykok. You will see all."

Her voice transformed into that deep, garbled sound Dax remembered from the stable. The words grew disjointed, the glottal voice pausing in strange places that stuttered and confused the grammar of each sentence. She reached down and pressed her fingers around the edges of Sarah's left eye.

"And then you will. See. All that He sees. You will become. Part of Death. And you will. See. The other stars."

She dug her fingers in deeper.

Sarah cried out, her head pressed back against the edge of the well. She struggled madly, but Savannah held her down with impossible strength. Blood trickled down Sarah's cheek from the corner of her eye. She screamed.

"In Death. You. Transcend to Algol. And you will. See. Without being."

Sarah thrashed, grabbing Savannah's arm with both hands, her fingers scrabbling and tearing off ribbons of rotted skin. Blood gushed freely down her cheek and into her mouth.

When Savannah finally pulled back her hand, she held in her bloody fingers an eyeball trailing strands of nerves back to Sarah's socket.

Dax's stomach twisted. He tried to get up, but his leg was a heavy slab of dead meat. The man above him needed only to hold him by his injured ankle to keep him down, and he felt in that moment utterly useless. Here he was, a dozen feet from Sarah, so close that if he only staggered to his feet he could get to her.

Savannah tore the eye free of its nerves and placed it the on the lip of the well, where it stared out blindly into nothing.

Wyatt continued shouting, throwing himself unsuccessfully against the man who held him from behind. "Sarah!" he called over and over. "Sarah! Sarah!"

He was only across the circle, but his voice seemed to come from across a great distance. Dax wasn't even sure Sarah could hear him; she gasped in shallow, shuddering breaths, wheezing with pain, but at least it was over—

Savannah reached down again.

This time Dax closed his eyes. He couldn't watch. He couldn't.

"And in the darkness." The voice, now utterly foreign, had become the low-throated rumble of an otherworldly tongue. "You will. See."

There came a wail, which rose to an earsplitting pitch, and then fell away into hacking gasps.

The darkness was unbearable.

Dax opened his eyes.

Sarah lay slumped against the well, chest convulsing in great heaves. Blood ran down her face from the reddish mess of her ruined sockets. She sat facing him, shaking and gasping, but she could not see him.

Savannah held the eyes over the well and let go.

Releasing a feral scream, Wyatt somehow leveraged himself against the man holding him from behind to deliver a kick to the person in front of him; his foot connected with the man's chest, and when the momentum carried him forward again, he rolled the other man over his head and onto the ground. The third, standing nearby, he battered out of the way with his cast.

The rest of the carnival workers stood around them, perhaps not knowing what to do, perhaps too surprised to react.

Still screaming, Wyatt snatched the machete from the ground and charged at Savannah. As she turned to face him, her features seemed to distort, as though something were bubbling to the surface.

The blade sliced halfway through her neck and lodged against the spine.

Savannah's face shifted; something oddly-shaped moved around just beneath her skin; her yellow eyes bulged and her mouth contorted. She gurgled around the blade in her neck.

Wyatt yanked back the machete with a spurt of dark blood, then swung again. On the third swing, he severed her head from the spine. It came off in his hand, and he held it for a moment, the hair tangled around his fingers, before he grunted in disgust and flung it away. The head fell to the grass, rolled, and landed beside Dax, staring at him with blank yellow eyes.

Wyatt stood, panting, the bloody machete at his side, like a triumphant Perseus.

Turning away from the head that lay beside him, Dax tasted bile in the back of his throat. The world throbbed around him in time with his pounding leg.

At that moment, Frieda emerged from her house with a rifle and shot into the crowd.

Who's she shooting at?

Dax could only think that if she had been in there all this time, she must have known what was going on outside her house. She had sanctioned this perverse ceremony, but now Wyatt had ruined it, had stopped the dark carnival from exorcising her haunted well and freeing her, at last, from her own madness.

Is she shooting at them—at me, at Wyatt?

There was very little Dax could do about it. He remained pinned to the ground, facing, for the second time that night, the possibility of death by gunshot.

The carnival workers scattered, some running for cover from the gunfire, some zigzagging in confusion around the well. Abruptly, the man holding Dax let go and charged at Frieda, leaving him unattended in the grass.

He hardly cared what happened next. They had stopped the ritual, Savannah was dead—but it didn't feel like a victory.

Frieda shot the man, but did not turn the rifle onto Dax. Instead, she pursued the rest of the carnival workers, firing deftly into the night.

Dax managed to prop himself on his elbow.

Savannah's headless body stood before the well, swaying; blood gushed from the stump of a neck. He thought it might fall over, held up only by the surprise of the sudden decapitation, but it did not fall.

Instead, two spindly limbs emerged from the neck, like pointed tentacles made of bone, and probed the air outside the body. The appendages unfurled, bent at angles as with elbows, and then two more appeared, impossibly, from within the space where Savannah's own skeleton and organs should have been. Shedding the human-suit, the skeletal creature pulled itself free until Savannah's hollow shell crumpled limply on the ground.

Wyatt knelt before Sarah, holding her face in both hands. She was either unconscious or in shock. "It's going to be okay," he said. "You're going to be okay, goddamnit. You hear me?"

He could not see the creature standing behind him: a spider-shaped skeleton draped in a thin layer of white skin that revealed all the knobs and contours of the bones beneath. Eight pointed legs jutted from the body, which looked like a human ribcage crowned by an impossibly-faceted skull with eight deep black sockets, within which yellow pinpricks stared out like distant suns.

"Wyatt—" Dax tried to call out, but his voice was too hoarse to penetrate the commotion around them.

Frieda fired again into the advancing crowd.

Those who remained knelt and prostrated themselves before the creature. They lowered their heads, not daring to look upon the unfathomable countenance of the daughter of Death.

Then the creature turned to Wyatt, its legs twitching.

Dax crawled forward. He dug his fingers into the dirt and pulled himself up slowly, excruciatingly, until he stood on his good leg, dragging the bad one behind him.

The creature jabbed one of its long front legs at Wyatt and speared him in the shoulder. He cried out, spun around, and finally gazed upon the thing that had emerged.

Dax reached forward and called out to him, but the creature jabbed him again with its leg and let out a terrible sound.

Wyatt threw his arms in front of his face, shielding himself with the cast, but the creature's pointed leg stabbed at it, cracked the plaster, and threw him off balance. He teetered on the edge of the well, his back bent dangerously over the lip—and then he went over, scrabbling wildly at the smooth stone. He caught the edge and hung there miraculously until Dax staggered to him and grabbed the fingers protruding from his cast.

Unable to get a good grip, Dax reached down to grab the cast, too, but Wyatt's hand slipped off the edge of the well, and he descended a foot, swinging heavily as Dax caught him.

Dax's arms strained, stretched taut, bearing all of Wyatt's weight.

Wyatt made desperate, unintelligible sounds in his throat. The darkness sucked up his dangling legs.

Dax said, "I got you, I got you."

His sweaty fingers began to slip.

"No," Dax said, trying to get a better grip. "No, I got you."

Wyatt gave him a panicked look, his eyes as wide as they would go, and then his fingers slid out of Dax's grasp, and he ricocheted back into the shadowed depths. He slammed sickeningly against the side of the well as he fell, and in seconds the darkness had devoured him.

A deafening, interminable silence followed until a crunching splash echoed up from far below, and then nothing.

CHAPTER 20

Dax called Wyatt's name.

No response.

He called again, but all he heard from the bottom of the well was a low grinding sound, like the earth shifting. Again and again he called Wyatt's name into the darkness. His own voice echoed emptily back to him.

"Wyatt!"

He listened to the last echo dissolve and knew there would be no response.

Dax whirled around. His body burned with a kind of dizzying static. With the effortless momentum of fury, he grabbed the machete from the ground and lunged at the creature that had been inside Savannah. He slashed the blade across one of its legs, severing it at the joint. The creature let out a many-pitched wail, an unearthly echo, and Dax hacked off another leg, and another, as it tried to jab out with its pointed front limbs. He ducked around it, dove, hacked again, hardly aware of his own movements.

The sharp point of a leg stabbed him from behind, low, by his kidney, and he felt it pierce the skin. Crying out, he spun free, swung the machete, and hacked off another leg.

Around him, a breeze picked up until the windmill whirred rapidly, and the chimes on Frieda's roof danced and clanked.

On its remaining three legs, the creature continued to attack. Dax thrust the blade forward, into its face, and broke the thin layer of skin. The bloodless flesh flapped away like paper, and the creature shrieked as it collapsed. Dax stood over it while gunshots rang around him. He brought down the machete again and again, until the creature broke into smaller and smaller pieces. The screeching faded to a hiss; the bones clattered away; the yellow pinpricks within its black sockets sparked and went out.

Even after it stopped moving, after it was surely dead, Dax continued to bring down the machete. He grunted with every swing as he chopped up the legs and torso and grotesque misshapen skull.

The chimes rattled violently, and the wind tugged at him.

One of the bones cracked unevenly beneath the blade and sent Dax off balance. He stumbled back, away from the broken remains of the creature, and looked up, caught in the wind. Bodies were strewn across the grass as carnival workers retreated, running back toward the carnival or simply away from here.

Frieda had returned to her porch, rifle aimed and ready.

Beside the well, his mother stood looking at him with a hideous and unwanted apology in her eyes. For a moment, in his rage, he wanted to swing the machete at her.

Green eyes bore intently into his. "It's happening."

From each of her deep pockets she pulled out a bottle of vodka. She uncapped the first and poured clear liquid around the lip of the well, then splashed it onto the inner walls. Liquor streamed into the darkness and to the water far below. The liquid burbled out of the bottle until it was gone, and once she had emptied the second one, she tossed them both into the well.

Dax didn't hear the bottles land.

The roar of the wind took on a new timbre, like a freight train. It deepened, swelled, and vibrated in his heart until he dropped the machete and pressed both hands to his ears to block the noise. He fell to his knees, stared at the well, and realized the sound was emanating from there.

Wind gusted up from the depths of the well, rose in a spiraling inverted tornado, shivered the grass and the wind chimes.

It's Wyatt.

The realization clawed at his heart.

Savannah had been dropping eyes and tongues into the well as some kind of sacrifice, some part of the ritual, and Wyatt's body had offered the final piece of the puzzle.

Dax looked down the well, but the wind made his eyes water. Something was coming. There it had been trapped, at the bottom of the earth, for centuries, and now he could feel the stale air billowing up from the opened tomb of the sleeping beast. He could feel it coming up and could do nothing to stop it. The creature called Death would rise again.

Wind whirled upward, and within its twisting gale, something emerged.

It pulled itself out of that well—like the spider from Savannah's neck, like the creature folded unfeasibly into human skin—rising and unfurling.

Dax could not look away, but neither could he fully comprehend what he was seeing as the immense thing stretched up from the well.

Here it was, at last, breaking across the boundary of reality.

Baykok.

It sprouted from the well like a terrible blooming flower. Dozens of bent legs materialized, the length of train cars, skeletal and draped in paper-thin translucent skin. The legs towered over Dax as it freed itself from the well, with the relative semblance of the creature inside Savannah, but with so many more legs, so many more angles, so many more unfathomable dimensions beyond the limitations of human sight. At its center, high above, the legs germinated from a jutting ribcage ten times the size of a human's. A warped insectile skull opened its hungry black hole mouth, and above that gaping pit some uncountable amount of deep sockets each containing a glowing red point—older stars, dying stars—almost too dim to see.

Between the elongated skull and the ribcage, a ring of human eyes encircled what must have been its neck—dozens, lidless, seeing.

Dax felt his mind stutter and go blank.

Whose eyes were they?

He could almost recognize Savannah's, dark. Sarah's, blue. Staring, unblinking, eternal. The eyes gazed out while he gazed in.

Dax could not close his eyes; he saw, he saw, he could not un-see.

When he managed at last to tear his gaze from the beast, he spotted Frieda with her rifle, so small and insignificant in comparison while she gazed up and up at the creature.

"It's you," she said.

Wind twisted around them, spun the windmill, jangled the chimes.

The creature moved from the well, risen now to its full height; its long, thin legs spidered back to the ground, which they stabbed with their pointed ends.

Its jaws peeled back and made a sound that rent the air—a high, shrill note almost beyond hearing. The wind paused, and half a dozen limp bodies rose to sitting, then standing, heads lolling and limbs dangling. The dead rose into the air like marionettes, their arms stretched out to either side while their legs hung straight, not alive but floating.

While the corpses hovered, while Baykok sounded its battle cry, while the world trembled, Dax closed his eyes.

Time snapped around him like a rubber band. His fried brain tried to take in the fractured images, but couldn't; it rejected them, rejected this reality.

The sound stopped, and then all he could hear was the popping and creaking of massive bones. Then six thumps in quick succession, like a drumbeat. Like his frantic heart pedaling away in his chest, trying to ride away from all this.

He opened his eyes and realized he was on his knees with his hands over his ears.

Time twitched.

The bodies lay on the ground again, fallen akimbo, their throats torn open, their eyes gouged out; blood trailed across the ground.

Renée approached the well and struck a match, but wind doused the flame immediately, and she tried another. It, too, died as soon as it sparked to life. Her hands trembled, but she kept trying. *It has to burn*, she'd said.

He thought of the lighter in Wyatt's pocket, somewhere at the bottom of the well, and he doubled over with the sudden weight of remembrance. He could not allow himself to think of Wyatt, not now, not with the world falling apart around him.

An immense leg pierced the ground beside him, and he choked on a breathless scream. Pale flesh, like a sheer white curtain, stretched over the colossal humanoid bones turned arachnid. Dax felt his brain rattle at the proximity, dimensions shifting around him.

He reached out a hand—the leg so close, two feet away—and touched it. A subzero cold invaded him, burned his fingers, and he was gone from this world, racing across the cosmos, among the stars, soaring along the Trail of Souls, the outstretched speckled arm of the Milky Way, out into the darkness where the constellations lost their shapes and reorganized as distant stars, Perseus coming up fast now, holding Medusa's head, her eyes boring down on him, bright yellow eyes, and one of them flashing, winking, two stars orbiting each other in an endless dance, and there, within the binary, more eyes, more legs, more shapes and surfaces than existed on earth or anywhere in the human mind, and he screamed as physics shattered and everything he'd ever learned no longer made sense and meaning turned into meaninglessness. He saw the warped worlds of Algol, and he screamed—but as he screamed, he felt his voice torn from his throat, his language sucked from him, a language he never knew he had. There were voices all around him, thousands whirling up from the well, the voices of the dead.

He let go of the leg and shot back into his own consciousness; he reeled, tried to reconcile the formlessness he had been with the form he was now.

The creature was hungry. It turned to the east, toward town, and Dax knew it wanted only to consume until there was nothing left. It understood nothing of humanity; it cared nothing for rudimentary mortal life.

Dax had never cared what had happened to Conjunction. He'd never wanted to see it again when he'd left. But what about Phil and Helen? What about the rest of the Montgomeries: Dallas, Adelaide, and Noah? What about the young deputy named Bobby? What about Eli the coroner? What, even, about Meson Tesoro, a bully but still undeserving of so gruesome an end, of an early death with no chance for redemption? What about this town, with its little brick school, its rickety white church, its dark and cozy neighborhood tavern, its peaceful farms, its happy and unhappy families?

Would this story be told if the great white beast took over the land?

Dax was momentarily beset by a sense of futility, a sense of the smallness and unimportance of humanity, never to be heard because the sound waves of their voices would never carry past the atmosphere, doomed to eternal silence.

He ran toward the creature as it moved away, and he tripped over a body sprawled on the grass. His ankle splintered into a white-hot pain, and a delirious howl escaped him. He dug his fingers into the ground and tried to drag himself forward, after the creature, which had moved farther away and was somehow even more difficult to look at straight-on without losing track of reality. Dax pulled himself forward with agonizing slowness. His face was wet with either tears or sweat, and he put it down onto the ground, into the dirt.

He reached forward again, and it landed on something warm and smooth.

With great effort, he lifted his head and saw the lantern on its side in the grass. Its miniature flame burned on.

He pushed himself to his knees and reached out for the handle, then staggered to his feet. The night air sparkled with a dizzy gray fog when he stood, and he leaned heavily, breathing hard and clutching the lantern in his fist.

Sarah sat against the well, and Renée stood on the other side, her hair blown wild around her face. She held an empty book of matches.

Dax turned up the lantern until the flame burst into a dazzling brightness, and forced himself forward. When he approached the well, his mother's green eyes gleamed in the light.

"Burn it, right?" Dax said, and smashed the lantern against the lip of the well.

Shattered glass rained into the darkness while the cobbled stone erupted in a ring of orange light. The remains of the lantern landed at the bottom, and the walls of the well lit up. Brilliant flames raced over the edges and leapt out onto the dry, shivering grass where the creature had left a dripping trail. Tongues of flame shot across the ground and scurried toward the beast. Fire caught on one of the scarecrows until it transformed into a burning effigy.

Dax turned to Renée and squinted at her through the flames. She began speaking—loudly, defiantly, but in a language he couldn't understand, some personal language the creature could not take. She pulled out the dagger, held it above her chest, and sliced diagonally through the eye tattooed across her clavicle. Blood welled in the slash that severed the constellation and the key.

Dax had to step away from the well as smoke obscured the air between them. His lungs burned when he inhaled, and he coughed so hard he stumbled and fell to his knees.

The spreading fire wavered the night and exhaled smoke into the air.

He could hardly see anything through the warbling liquidity of his vision. He bit his tongue and felt a warm, coppery taste flood his mouth just as the flames reached Baykok.

The creature's thin white flesh erupted in a seething conflagration; it bubbled and turned black. A vortex of smoke wrapped around and obscured the being from the stars while it shrieked and writhed. The whirlwind carried it up and up, high into the atmosphere, and then spat the creature into the sky, where it streaked away as a shooting star, and then it was gone.

Dax fell back, panting, and stared up into the blackened night. He lay there, too exhausted to move, and listened to the whirr of the windmill and the distant chatter of chimes as the wind began to die.

CHAPTER 21

Consciousness came and went in flashes.

The burning scarecrows crackled. Flames smoldered to an ember-glow. Dax closed his eyes and welcomed the darkness. Hands dragged him across the grass, away from the smoke and heat that saturated the air around the well. The stink of burnt flesh wafted into his mouth when he opened it to protest, and he gagged. They stopped moving, and he looked up at the underside of his mother's face.

He tried to get up, but his ankle would not bear weight. Renée grabbed him again to keep him standing, and she turned him around to face Frieda's pickup truck parked on the overgrown end of Hells Hollow Road.

"Come on," she said and helped him up into the bed of the truck, where he settled on a nest of scratchy woolen blankets.

A moment later, Frieda appeared with a limp form in her arms. She carefully deposited Sarah beside him, then paused with her hands on her knees.

Dax closed his eyes.

When he opened them again, Renée and Frieda were staring at one another in silence. Frieda grunted, went around to the front of the truck, and started the engine. Renée stood there with the moon's pallor blackening the clotted slash across her chest; she receded into the night and disappeared as the truck pulled away down the road.

Sarah sat propped up beside him, and the sight of her empty, bloodied sockets made him turn away, stomach clenching.

Tires bumped over the uneven and unpaved stretch of Hells Hollow Road, away from Frieda's cottage and the carnival. The comforting rumble of the engine and the tires lulled Dax, who felt soft and fuzzy. He was cold, like outer space. He felt very little. He watched the stars.

Dax reached out—it was about all he could do, as he hadn't the energy to sit up. His hand found Sarah's, and he squeezed. Her flesh was cold. He squeezed again, frantically.

She's dead, she must be dead.

He fumbled with her wrist, gripping the veins and tendons, until he found the weak but steady dull throb of a pulse.

"Sarah," he croaked.

Slowly, she turned her head in his direction, listening. Her face was blank, and the hollows of her sockets bore into him.

"Sarah," he said again.

Her fingernails dug into his skin.

"I see," she whispered.

"What?"

Her sockets gazed emptily past him into the night.

"I see." Her voice dissipated on the wind. "I see. Algol. I see. The other stars." She screwed up her mouth as if she might cry, but she had no eyes with which to weep. "I see. I see. What He sees." She shook her head back and forth. "She was right. I see! Oh god, I can't—*I can't close my eyes!*"

Dax tried to comfort her from where he lay, but found he had no comfort to give. Only a cold hand to offer, sweat-slicked flesh draped over a structure of bones.

He held her hand for the rest of the long ride.

The dark of night enclosed them but for the scattered lights of stars, the quiet absolute but for the hum of tires on gravel and dirt, then on pavement, as they drove away from Conjunction, east, to the county line, to the next town, and finally to the bright fluorescent lights of a hospital—

The same hospital Wyatt had his cast put on, where he would have returned to have it cut off when healed—

No, no, he could not think of that. But he had nothing else to distract him, so he thought of Wyatt. His body seemed to sink. He let himself think of Wyatt, and he closed his eyes as he was taken away by the medical staff and put onto a stretcher to be saved, healed. He thought of Wyatt. He was alive. He would live. He thought of Wyatt ...

Dax lay on a white bed surrounded by beeping machines and clear tubes, his bandaged leg propped up while fluid flushed his system. He could not tell how long he had slept, but he felt groggy and dull, as though he weren't really awake.

A nurse came in to check his IV, and he asked her about Sarah. She told him he had a severe sprain, and it would take at least a week to rehabilitate his ankle. She told him he was dehydrated and malnourished. He asked about Sarah. She told him he should focus on his own recovery, for sprains of this severity were not to be taken lightly, and he had only exacerbated it by walking on it for so long. But there was good news: the animal bite wasn't infected, and he didn't have rabies.

He had pulled off the bed sheets and sat examining the livid black and blue creeping out from the bandage around his swollen ankle when he had his first visitors.

Phil and Helen brought him a cheeseburger and a rosary, respectively. They sat beside his bed and tried to appear cheerful through the troubled undercurrent of their shared glances. Phil told him there was a lot of talk in town. People claimed to have seen something extraordinary, something they couldn't explain. No one was sure what had happened last night.

"Seems like it had something to do with that carnival," Phil said. "They can't find any of the people who worked it, though. Not one. They must have made a run for it. But the damned thing's still there."

"The carnival?"

"All the rides, stands—everything. Just sitting there, empty. Someone'll have to dismantle it sooner or later."

Dax swallowed dryly. "It was the one. The carnival. My dad's carnival."

Phil was silent for a moment.

Helen gazed out the window, fingering her gold crucifix.

Dax leaned against the pillows, exhausted, while Phil changed the subject. He said they had pulled Wyatt's body from the well this morning. Dax closed his eyes and waited for the Sawyers to go away.

"We ran into your doctor in the hall," Phil said. "They want to keep you another night, but then you'll come stay with us. We'll fix up the guest bedroom."

Dax shook his head.

"Don't be silly," Helen snapped. "You'll come stay with us for a while, and you can go back to school when you're ready." She stood and looked down at him with an expression so brittle he thought her face would crack if he said no.

They left a little while later, and Dax slept.

He chewed his tasteless dinner in a daze, then dozed again.

He awoke groggy and disoriented in semi-darkness to the sight of a person standing in the doorway of his room. When he blinked, he saw it was his mother. She wore long pants and sleeves, which hid most of her tattoos but for the few curls of color stretching up over the collar of her shirt. Her hair was ragged; dark bags ringed her eyes.

"Hi," she said.

He thought maybe things would be okay, that he could have his mother back, but the idea fled quickly. His father was dust blown away, and his mother had stood by and done nothing while Wyatt—

"The carnival's done," he said. "What will you do now?"

"I don't know yet. There's always somewhere else to go." She gazed at him with longing, but didn't come any closer. "You're welcome to come with me."

"I don't think so," he said.

She nodded. "I want you to know—I've taken care of the hospital bill. I donated the carnival's profits for your treatment. For the girl's, too."

"Her name is Sarah."

"I'm sorry," she said, and placed a hand against her chest where the blade had bisected the tattoo, its magic and hallowed significance gone forever. "I'm so sorry."

Dax dredged up the words as from a pit of tar: "I don't forgive you."

She pressed her lips together and looked down.

At last, she said, "Do you think you ever will?"

He thought about it for a long moment, about all the newspapers his father had collected over the years, the beers he'd emptied into his empty heart, all in the name of a woman who had abandoned him. He thought of her back turned away while Savannah ripped out Sarah's eyes. He thought of Wyatt—

"No," he said.

She blinked rapidly; the green of her eyes gleamed.

"If you ever change your mind," she said, "I hope you come find me."

She stepped forward, then, rolled up her sleeve to reveal her wrist, and turned it toward him. In the dim artificial light of the hospital room, he saw three ornate letters tattooed in black—his name. Then she pulled her sleeve back down to her palm and stepped away.

"I just wanted you to know," she said. "I never forgot about you."

He did not say it aloud, but hoped one day he would forget about her.

Instead he said, "Goodbye."

———

The next morning, he had one more visitor before he was released.

Deputy Mendoza walked into his room just as the nurse was leaving. She crossed her arms and narrowed her eyes. A familiar badge adorned the front of her uniform.

"So, are you the new sheriff?" Dax said.

"Acting sheriff," she said. "Temporarily. Think they're going to bring in someone new, maybe from out of state."

He nodded.

"While I'm in charge, though," she said. "I'm closing Zeke's case."

Dax closed his eyes. He heard a jingling and wondered if she were taking out her handcuffs to place him under arrest. Then he felt something land on his lap, and he opened his eyes to find a small silver key.

"Unless you really like your new jewelry," she said.

He held up his wrists, startled to realize he still wore the broken handcuffs, and even more startled that he had forgotten they were there. He unlocked one, then the other, freeing his wrists for the first time in days. Red lines ringed the tender skin there.

"Ezekiel Anderson's body was found dug up at the Willoughby farm," she said. "He was missing the same thing those kids were missing, the ones at Frieda Redding's place. I found blood under Savannah's fingernails that I think will show a match, that it was all her. Just waiting on forensics."

"You saw Savannah's body?"

Her face blanked. "What was left of it." She hooked a thumb into her belt loop and shifted her stance. "Anyway. Just wanted you to know you're officially off the hook." She anxiously shifted again and shook her head. "You seemed to know what was really going on, all along. You know, I came here to ask you, straight up—but the more I think about it, the more I don't want to know." She sucked in a breath, slowly exhaled. "I just want to put this whole mess behind me. I don't even know where to begin with the paperwork. Plus there's the inquiry."

"Inquiry?"

Her head lowered, and she said quietly, "I killed the sheriff."

"You did the right thing," he said. "You saved my life."

She didn't look convinced.

"It seems unfair that to save one life, you have to take another," she said with a sigh. "I know I made the better choice, but that doesn't make it any easier. The world isn't divided up into right things and wrong things. It's just difficult choices with solutions you have to be sure you can live with." She gazed out the window; clouded light slanted in upon her. Then she turned back to him and held out her hand. "Good luck to you, Dax."

He leaned forward and shook it.

"You too."

Wyatt was interred at the county cemetery two days later.

Dax could not concentrate during the funeral. He stared instead at leaves dripping the morning's rain, and at the neat rectangular hole carved in the earth, and at the simple wooden casket where Wyatt would lie for the rest of eternity.

He did not approach the Montgomeries, but Sarah was with them. She sat in a wheelchair with a bandage wrapped around her face like a blindfold. When the service ended, Beau Montgomery wheeled her across the grass, lifted her into the car, and closed the door.

It was all over now. Dax could leave and never look back.

He waited around in the cemetery, by the new grave, until he convinced himself to drive to the Montgomeries'. He pulled up, wondering if he had the nerve to knock on the door, but then he saw Sarah on the porch, by herself. She wasn't in the wheelchair; she sat on the edge of the porch with her feet on the lower step, smoking a cigarette.

He went up to the house and sat beside her.

"Hey," he said to announce his presence.

She held out a fresh pack of cigarettes. Dax shook his head before remembering she couldn't see him; when he realized this, he changed his mind and pulled one out for himself.

"What did you see?" he asked.

She inhaled, then released a cloud of smoke, which enveloped her.

"I don't know if I can describe it," she said.

"Do you still see it?"

She took another drag and said, "Sometimes. I can block it out if I try. I can bring myself back so that there's only darkness." She exhaled slowly. "I'm just not sure which is worse."

The pungent smell of smoke surrounded them. Dax breathed in the bitter fumes.

"Have you told anyone?" he asked.

She shook her head. "They'd think I've gone insane." She thought about it, and then added, "Maybe I have."

For a moment, they smoked in silence.

Then, when Dax could no longer bear it, he said, "I'm sorry."

"What for?"

"Wyatt."

Her lips trembled, and she sucked in long and deep from her cigarette.

"I almost had him. I could have saved him. He ... slipped. I just missed him."

"It's not your fault," she said. "He was really happy when you came back, you know. Happier than he'd been in a long time." She dropped her cigarette and felt around for it.

Dax got her a new one and lit it for her, but she couldn't seem to hold it steady between her lips; she yanked it out and held it in her hand, clenching her teeth.

"I can't even cry for my brother," she said. "He's dead, and I can't even fucking cry."

They sat in silence together with smoke curling around them.

It was a long, long while before Sarah spoke again. She looked a bit dazed, and there was awe in her voice.

"The stars are beautiful," she said.

He returned to Phil and Helen's to get his things. Then he got back into the beat-up Bronco, dirtied and scratched from the trees outside

Pastor's Grove. He sat in the driver's seat, and he thought about where he would go.

He wondered about Lailani Castillo. She might understand, somehow. When he thought of seeing her again, he no longer felt that painful dread deep in his gut. Instead, he wanted to find her, talk to her. He wanted to tell her this story—had to tell it as a way to keep living.

There is a kind of death in silence.

He pulled away and glanced in the rearview mirror at the Sawyers' house, where Phil and Helen stood outside, for the last time. Nebraskan countryside glided past out the windows.

He passed the sign that read HELL IS REAL in bold white letters and drove out into the nothing of the country, along the empty road, past rippling fields of wheat and the occasional animal slinking through the grass.

All was quiet.

So maybe Hell was real. But what could any of them do about it, anyway? All anyone could do was look for ways to escape it, to keep going.

Dax thought of his father, of the empty bottles of beer collected throughout the house, sticky and attracting flies. And his mother—the joints she'd hid, her Mason jar full of ash, the pungent smoke she blew heavenward while reading fantastical stories on the back porch. He thought of Wyatt, grinning and gaunt, with his cloudy white pipe, and even Helen Sawyer, clinging to her crucifix, praying for children, for *something*.

He didn't know yet what would keep him going, but hoped he would find it. He'd keep going until he did. He might be okay, and the more he thought about it, the more he believed.

He would be okay, eventually, but today he remained wrapped in black thoughts, and tonight he would dream again of all that haunted him: his mother's hand pulled from his, Wyatt sucked back into the darkness, his father's ashes dispersed on the wind, everything and everyone receding from him—but wasn't that the way of the universe? Everything spreading apart, faster and faster, through the mysterious power of dark energy, scattered deeper and wider into the black, into the nothing, until there was nothing left ...

That was how all things would go, in the end.

ABOUT THE AUTHOR

JOANNA PARYPINSKI is a writer of dark speculative fiction whose work has appeared in Black Static, Nightmare Magazine, Chizine, *Haunted Nights* edited by Ellen Datlow and Lisa Morton, *New Scary Stories to Tell in the Dark* edited by Jonathan Maberry, *The Beauty of Death Vol. 2* edited by Alessandro Manzetti and Jodi Renee Lester, *Tales from the Lake Vol. 5* edited by Kenneth W. Cain, Nightscript, Vastarien, and more. She holds an MFA from Chapman University and is a member of the Horror Writers Association. She currently lives in the L.A. area and teaches English at Glendale Community College.
Website: **www.joannaparypinski.com**

JOANNA PARYPINSKI

DARK CARNIVAL

LATEST RELEASE

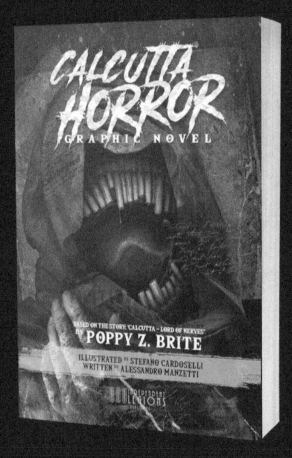

CALCUTTA HORROR
GRAPHIC NOVEL

**COYOTE RAGE
BY OWL GOINGBACK**

LATEST RELEASE

FEARFUL SYMMETRIES
BY TOM MONTELEONE

LATEST RELEASE

NARAKA
BY ALESSANDRO MANZETTI

LATEST RELEASE

"DI ORAZIO PROVES HIMSELF AGAIN A MASTER OF SPLATTERPUNK IN THIS ELECTRO SHOCK OF A NOVEL." — LUCY TAYLOR, BRAM STOKER AWARD-WINNING AUTHOR

I'M LESBIAN
I'M A DEEJAY
I'M A CANNIBAL
I'M UNDEAD

DARK MARY
PAOLO DI ORAZIO

DARK MARY
BY PAOLO DI ORAZIO

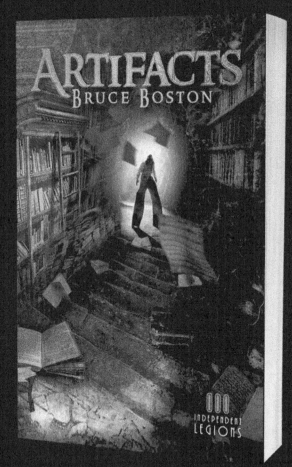

LATEST RELEASE

**ARTIFACTS
BY BRUCE BOSTON**

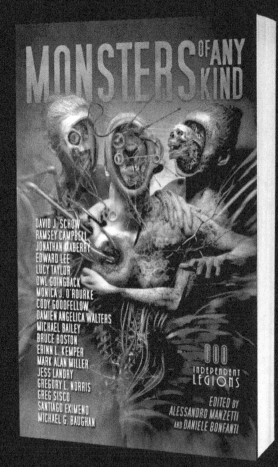

LATEST RELEASE

MONSTERS OF ANY KIND
EDITED BY A. MANZETTI & D. BONFANTI

AVAILABLE BOOKS

Our publications are available at Amazon and major online booksellers. Visit our Website: **www.independentlegions.com**

BOTH PAPERBACK & DIGITAL PUBLICATIONS

HORROR CALCUTTA (GRAPHIC NOVEL)
by Alessandro Manzetti & Stefano Cardoselli

COYOTE RAGE
by Owl Goingback

FEARFUL SYMMETRIES
by Thomas F. Monteleone

DARK MARY
by Paolo Di Orazio

TRIBAL SCREAMS
by Owl Goingback

MONSTERS OF ANY KIND
Edited by Alessandro Manzetti & Daniele Bonfanti

KNOWING WHEN TO DIE
by Mort Castle

ARTIFACTS
by Bruce Boston
NARAKA THE ULTIMATE HUMAN BREEDING

by Alessandro Manzetti

A WINTER SLEEP
by Greg F. Gifune

SPREE AND OTHER STORIES
by Lucy Taylor

THE BEAUTY OF DEATH 2 – DEATH BY WATER
edited by Alessandro Manzetti & Jodi Renee Lester

THE LIVING AND THE DEAD
by Greg F. Gifune

THE CARP-FACED BOY AND OTHER TALES
by Thersa Matsuura

THE WISH MECHANICS
by Daniel Braum

CHILDREN OF NO ONE
by Nicole Cushing

THE ONE THAT COMES BEFORE
by Livia Llewellyn

ALL AMERICAN HORROR OF THE 21ST CENTURY: THE FIRST DECADE
Edited by Mort Castle

BENEATH THE NIGHT
by Greg Gifune

SELECTED STORIES
by Nate Southard

DIGITAL PUBLICATIONS

TALKING IN THE DARK
by Dennis Etchison

THE BEAUTY OF DEATH VOL. 1
Edited by Alessandro Manzetti

THE HORROR SHOW
by Poppy Z. Brite

DOCTOR BRITE
by Poppy Z. Brite

USED STORIES
by Poppy Z. Brite

THE CRYSTAL EMPIRE
by Poppy Z. Brite

SELECTED STORIES
by Poppy Z. Brite

THE USHERS
by Edward Lee

SELECTED STORIES
by Edward Lee

APARTMENT SEVEN
by Greg F. Gifune

DREAMS THE RAGMAN
by Greg F. Gifune

THE RAIN DANCERS
by Greg Gifune

WHAT WE FOUND IN THE WOODS
 by Shane McKenzie

THE HITCHHIKING EFFECT
by Gene O'Neill

SONGS FOR THE LOST
by Alexander Zelenyj

INDEPENDENT LEGIONS PUBLISHING
Via Virgilio, 10 – TRIESTE (ITALY)
+39 040 9776602

WWW.INDEPENDENTLEGIONS.COM
WWW.FACEBOOK.COM/INDEPENDENTLEGIONS
INDEPENDENT.LEGIONS@AOL.COM

ASSOCIATION
SPECIALTY PRESS AWARD RECIPIENT

Made in the USA
Las Vegas, NV
25 March 2021